CELG

SUPPING WITH THE DEVIL

Monika Paniatowski's boss is trying to destroy her career, but the dead end case he assigns her turns out to be something else entirely...

DCI Monika Paniatowski recognises her latest assignment as advisor to the Earl of Ridley's rock festival for what it really is – an attempt by the chief constable to sabotage her career. Matters are not as simple as they first appear, but it is not until the body of a tabloid journalist is discovered that things really start to hot up...

SUPPING WITH THE DEVIL

A DCI Paniatowski Mystery

Sally Spencer

Severn House Large Print
London & New York

This first large print edition published 2015
in Great Britain and the USA by
SEVERN HOUSE PUBLISHERS LTD of
19 Cedar Road, Sutton, Surrey, England, SM2 5DA.
First world regular print edition published 2014 by
Severn House Publishers Ltd., London and New York.

British Library Cataloguing in Publication Data

Spencer, Sally author.
  Supping with the devil. -- (The Monika Paniatowski
  mysteries)
  1. Paniatowski, Monika (Fictitious character)--Fiction.
  2. Rock music festivals--Fiction. 3. Murder--
  Investigation--Fiction. 4. Aristocracy (Social class)--
  Fiction. 5. Motorcycle gangs--Fiction. 6. Police--
  England--Fiction. 7. Detective and mystery stories.
  8. Large type books.
  I. Title II. Series
  823.9'2-dc23

ISBN-13: 9780727897879

For Mike and Chris Hackney

Author's Note

'We Can Be Together' is a track from *Volunteers* by Jefferson Airplane; 'Rock 'n' Roll Suicide' is a track from *The Rise and Fall of Ziggy Stardust and the Spiders from Mars* by David Bowie; *Aftermath* is the title of the Rolling Stones' fourth album.

He who sups with the devil
should have a long spoon.

Monday, 9th August, 1976

The weathermen said it was going to be the hottest summer for fifty years, and on all the available evidence so far, they were right.

As their leaves began to wilt, months ahead of nature's intended schedule, the trees were already acquiring a crumpled early-autumn look. The grass verges and immaculately maintained lawns had been hit by the recently imposed hose-pipe ban, and were turning yellow and spiky. And even the air in Whitebridge – air which was famous for its dampness, and had been a key element in the town's rise as a centre of cotton weaving – was beginning to dry out.

It wasn't natural, men said to each other, as they mopped at their sweaty brows with the big, white handkerchiefs that their wives had carefully ironed the night before.

It was just like living in middle of the Moroccan desert, said women who had never gone beyond the county boundaries themselves.

The heat didn't bother Dr Shastri, as she drove towards her work that early Monday morning. She had been brought up in a part of India which got so hot that if – for whatever peculiar reasons of your own – you wished to cook an egg on the pavement, you would have no difficulty in doing so.

But though it had no effect on her, she knew that many of the old people in the area found it almost intolerable, and fully accepted that if the temperature got much higher, she would have to give serious consideration to hiring some temporary staff to cope with the sudden rush of new business.

She turned a corner in the road, and saw her workplace – her own little kingdom – just ahead of her. It was, she recognized, an ugly place by any standards – square and utilitarian, supported by concrete pillars which would have greyed with age had they not first been blackened by pollution – but over the years, she had found herself growing rather fond of it. And even if the exterior of the building *was* a little oppressive, she always ensured that the interior was clean and efficient, and – within the parameters that its function allowed – that it was respectful of the people who passed through it.

As she pulled in to the car park, Shastri noticed a solitary figure standing under the portico. From a distance, it looked like her old friend, DCI Monika Paniatowski, but Monika – much to her own regret – was not involved in the latest murder investigation, and so she had no reason to put in an appearance at the mortuary so early on a Monday morning. Besides, the Paniatowski that Shastri knew would never stand as this woman was standing – tight up against the pillar, as if she hoped it would somehow manage to absorb her.

No, it couldn't be Monika.

But as she crossed the car park and got closer

to the woman, the doctor had to admit that it was.

Paniatowski waited until Shastri was almost at the portico, then took a couple of unsteady steps towards her.

'I need your help,' she said, in a strained and croaking voice which was quite unlike her own.

'Has there been an accident, Monika?' Shastri asked, alarmed. 'Has something happened to Louisa?'

Because she could not imagine anything – other than harm coming to Paniatowski's beloved adopted daughter – which would have reduced her friend to this pathetic state.

'Louisa's fine,' Paniatowski said. 'I'm the one with the problem. I want you to examine me.'

'I am not your doctor,' Shastri pointed out. 'I do not have your case history to refer to.'

'That doesn't matter,' Paniatowski said miserably.

'No,' Shastri agreed, looking at her grey, tortured face – and knowing that whatever was wrong, it had to be dealt with then and there. 'No, I don't suppose it does.'

Paniatowski lay on her back on the examination table, her body still covered with a white sheet, her eyes staring fixedly at the ceiling.

'There is considerable bruising to the vagina, but you are probably aware of that already,' Shastri said, trying to sound crisp and efficient – as if Monika was just any other patient.

'Is there any permanent damage?' Paniatowski asked.

'On the face of it, I would guess not – but it is

11

impossible to say for certain without running further tests,' Shastri told her. 'Am I correct in assuming that you have been raped?'

'Well, of course I've been bloody well raped!' Paniatowski snapped. 'You don't think I *wanted* them to do this to me, do you?'

'When did it happen?'

'Last night.'

Shastri glanced at her watch. It was a quarter past eight, which meant that the rape had occurred at least nine hours earlier, and probably longer than that.

'You should have come to see me – or gone to some other doctor – straight away,' she said.

'I know.'

'You said *them*,' Dr Shastri said, reflecting on Paniatowski's earlier comment.

'What?'

'You asked me if I thought you wanted *them* to do it to you. How many of them were there?'

'Does it matter?' Paniatowski asked angrily.

'Yes – in a clinical examination, every piece of additional information is important,' Shastri replied.

Paniatowski closed her eyes. 'If you must know, there were three of them,' she said.

'*Where* did this happen?'

'How can *that* bloody matter?'

'Everything matters, Monika. Rape very rarely occurs in a sterile environment...'

'You don't say!'

'...and we need to know what kinds of possible infections to be on the lookout for.'

Paniatowski sighed heavily. 'It happened in the

woods.'

'What woods?'

'Now that really *is* none of your business.'

'I don't see why you won't tell me,' Shastri said, puzzled. 'Surely, when you report it, you will have to give those details – and many more besides.'

'Ah, but that's just it, you see, Doc – I won't be reporting it,' Paniatowski told her.

'What did you just say?' Shastri gasped.

'You heard me well enough. *I won't be reporting it.*'

PART ONE

'We Can Be Together'

4th–5th August

ONE

Wednesday, 4th August

While the butler went through the established ritual of serving the coffee, Gervaise de Court-ney, 13th Earl of Ridley, looked quickly around the rosewood table which Thomas Chippendale, the master craftsman, had personally designed for the Great Library in 1758.

To the earl's right was his wife, Katerina, the Countess of Ridley. He had married her in his early thirties – which was considered very old for the heir to the earldom to enter his first marriage – but he daily thanked God that he had waited, because she had brought a light into his life which had made him want to continue living it.

To his left sat Edward Bell, his estate manager, a solidly built man wearing a rough tweed jacket which seemed to be such a part of him that he would shed it in only the hottest weather. Bell had worked at Stamford Hall all his life, as had his father, and his father's father, right back to George Bell, who had been appointed the Hall's first steward in 1705.

They were loyal to him – both of them – the earl thought, and he needed that loyalty, because

17

sitting opposite him was his mother, Sarah, the Dowager Countess, and if there was one person in the world who really hated him, then – he suspected – that person was her.

The mother spoke. 'I wish to make it known, in the strongest possible terms, that I disapprove of the coming madness, and intend to confine myself to my apartments for the entire period it is being perpetrated,' she said.

The earl sighed. 'Couldn't you at least have waited until Barton had finished serving the coffee, Mother?' he asked.

His mother looked up at the butler, who was expertly pouring coffee from a large silver jug into small, delicate china cups.

'Does it distract you if I talk while you are serving, Barton?' she asked. 'Or do you believe, as I do, that a good servant will allow nothing to distract him from doing his duty?'

'I am not distracted, my lady,' the butler replied, in a voice totally devoid of any expression.

It really wasn't fair of his mother to put Barton in such a difficult position, the earl thought. And it wasn't fair of her to show such lack of respect for him in the presence of a servant.

But the problem was, the dowager countess didn't think that she was either making the butler's life difficult or embarrassing her son, because as far as she was concerned, the feelings and opinions of servants – if, indeed, they had any – counted for nothing. From her perspective, the servants' only function in life was to serve her, and when they were not doing that, they didn't really exist.

The butler finished his task, took an almost imperceptible step backwards, asked if there was anything else that the assembled company required, and withdrew when he was told there wasn't.

'It's not a good idea for you to stay inside all the time, Mother,' the earl said, continuing the earlier conversation. 'You know the doctor told you that you should get some fresh air at least once a day.'

'But the problem is that the air will *not* be fresh, will it?' his mother countered. 'It will have been horribly polluted by the rabble you will have allowed to invade the Hall.'

'No one will be invading the Hall,' said the earl, laying a plan of the grounds on the table, and smoothing it out with his right hand. 'The music stage will be here, close to the west wall. The main camp site, however, will be *beyond* the walls, close to the west gate.' He paused. 'The portable toilet cabins will be here in plenty of time, won't they, Mr Bell?'

'They will, sir,' the estate manager confirmed.

'And we must ensure that there is an ample supply of fresh water. In this heat, there's a real danger of dehydration.'

'That's already been taken care of.'

'Our guests will be here, in a large semicircle around the stage,' the earl said to his mother and his wife. 'When the last band of the night...'

'Band!' his mother snorted.

'...when the last band of the night has completed its set, all the fans will leave the grounds, and the gates will be locked.'

'And in the daytime?' his mother asked. 'Will the vile hooligans be free to rampage through the rose garden and the greenhouses? Will you just stand by and watch them kill the ducks and swans in the north lake, and row their sweaty bodies up and down the south lake?'

'As I have explained at least half a dozen times before, Mother, the concert area has been cordoned off from the rest of the grounds by a wire-netting fence,' the earl said.

'And what will happen when the riff-raff decide they will break down the fence?'

It was amazing how this woman – who really had a *very* limited imagination – could find so many different words to describe people she disapproved of, the earl thought.

'They will not break down the fence, Mother,' he said. 'They will listen to the music and do their best to become at one with the universe. And even if there are a few people who decide, for some inexplicable reason, to make trouble, the marshals I have appointed will soon deal with them.'

'The marshals!' the dowager countess repeated. 'Is that what you call them? I call them motorcycle thugs. Vandals! They will probably do more damage than the rest of the scum put together!'

'Since you have no interest in hearing what I have to say, I suggest you withdraw, Mother,' the earl said, his patience finally wearing thin.

'Are you *ordering* me to go?' the old woman asked.

'No, Mother, of course not.'

'Because you *could* order me to go, you know,' the dowager countess said, in a tone designed to make him feel both guilty and cowardly. 'You are, after all, the earl, whereas I am nothing.'

'Mother, this really isn't necessary,' the earl said.

'I don't see why you have to do it,' the dowager countess persisted. 'We don't need the money. You are rich.'

'The *estate* is rich,' the earl corrected her, 'but even so, running the Hall is a costly business, and if we do nothing to augment our income, the money will melt away soon enough.'

'Then do something with a little dignity to it,' the old woman argued. 'Open the house to guided tours for the respectable middle class – if you can find any! Build a safari park, if you consider it absolutely necessary.'

'That's already been done by others,' the earl pointed out. 'Besides, I believe in the Rock-Stately Festival, Mother.'

'The RockStately Festival! What does that even mean?'

'It's a play on words,' the earl said, wondering why he was even bothering to explain, since he knew his mother was not interested in the answer. 'It's a combination of "rocksteady", which is a kind of music, and "stately home", which is what...'

'Is my son charging enough?' the dowager countess asked, turning to Edward Bell.

'I'm sorry, my lady,' Bell replied, stalling.

'You're the man whose supposed to know about figures, Bell – God knows, the family paid enough to have you educated in them – so I would have thought it was a simple enough question. However, since you seem to have failed to grasp the concept the first time, I will repeat it – is my son charging the sweaty proletariat enough to make a profit?'

The estate manager shifted uncomfortably in his seat. 'If all goes as planned, we should certainly not make a loss.'

'I thought as much,' the dowager countess said triumphantly. 'This whole disaster is not to raise revenue at all – it is to indulge the decadent tastes that you, Gervaise, have developed since your breakdown.'

'Mother...' the earl pleaded.

'Your father would never have done anything like this, but then your father was a *real* man. Do you know, there are times when I wish that it had been your brother who inherited the title?'

'Do you really think Sebastian would have made a better earl than I have?' her son asked.

The dowager countess hesitated for a moment, as if she were tempted to say 'yes', but then, realizing how ridiculous that would sound – even to her – she said, 'At least your brother has never been locked up in a lunatic asylum.' She turned to face her daughter-in-law. 'I blame you for this.'

'That's not fair!' the earl protested. 'It's nothing to do with Katerina. It was all my idea.'

'Well, of course it was all your idea,' the dowager countess said with contempt. 'I may not have the highest opinion of your wife, but I know she would never have come up with such an insane scheme herself.' She stood, using his arms to jack herself into an upright position. 'The reason I blame you, Katerina, is because you did not talk him out of it – which is what any true countess would have done in your situation.' She shrugged. 'But then, I suppose that since you are not only from the lower orders but also a foreigner, I should not expect much from you.'

She reached for her stick and hobbled away.

'I am so, so sorry, my dear,' the earl said to his wife.

'It's all right,' Katerina said. 'She is old, and she is in pain, and it does not really bother me.'

But it did – the earl could see that it did.

He turned to his estate manager. 'And I must apologize to you, also, Mr Bell. You should not have had to hear that.'

Bell smiled. 'You should know by now, sir, that members of my family *never* hear what the earl does not want them to hear,' he said.

The rot had started to set in the day they had found Jo Baxter's body out there on the cold, bleak moors, Monika Paniatowski thought, as she stood in the chief constable's outer office and waited to be summoned to the inner sanctum.

The coroner had ruled that Jo's death had been an accident – that having inadvertently drunk more than she should have done, she had miscalculated a bend and come off the road. Yet few of the people who had observed the Baxters' crumbling marriage – and suspected they knew *why* it was crumbling – had ever taken that particular verdict seriously.

Before Jo's death, Baxter and Paniatowski had been able, more or less, to put the past behind them – to ignore the fact that, long ago and in a different county across the Pennines, they had once been lovers – and deal with each on a professional basis. But just as overturning her car had killed Jo, so it had overturned the sometimes uneasy relationship which Paniatowski and Baxter had built up between them, and now – from Baxter's viewpoint, at least – they were almost at war.

The green light on the office doorpost came on, and Paniatowski knocked and entered.

Baxter was sitting at his desk, bent over a sheaf of papers, and for at least half a minute he ignored her.

Finally, he looked up.

'Good morning, Chief Inspector,' he said, in a voice which told her nothing at all. 'What do you know about the events which are about to take place at Stamford Hall?'

'Only what I've read in the general memo you sent round,' Paniatowski replied.

'And could you tell me what the memo said?'

Is this some sort of test? Paniatowski asked herself. Have we sunk to *such* a low level of pettiness?

'There's going to be a big rock concert held in the grounds of Stamford Hall,' she said aloud.

'It's a rock *festival*,' Baxter said, as if he'd scored a point by correcting her. 'Carry on.'

'Based on advance ticket sales, they're expecting a hundred thousand people to turn up, though there may be more.'

24

'Exactly. A hundred thousand people. That's more or less equal to the population of Whitebridge. Just controlling the traffic flow will be a major exercise in logistics.'

Why is he telling me all this, she wondered. Since it's nothing to do with me – and since he can barely stand to be in the same room as me these days – why are we even having this conversation?

'DCS Holmes will be in overall charge of the traffic flow, and will also be responsible for policing at the camp site and the catering and toilet facilities. But those are all outside the grounds, and unfortunately, he will not be allowed to police the actual estate itself.'

'What's stopping him?' Paniatowski asked.

'The earl,' Baxter replied.

'I know the Hall is private property, but if we suspect a crime is being committed, or may be about to be committed, then we have the legal right to enter the property.'

'You'd think that would be the case, wouldn't you?' Baxter agreed. 'But according to a royal charter which was granted to the 3rd earl, nobody – and I mean *nobody* – has the right to enter the grounds without the explicit permission of the earl himself.'

'But surely that charter is hundreds of years old, and must be out of date by now.'

Baxter shook his head.

'Well, if it isn't out of date, couldn't we simply have it repealed?' Paniatowski asked.

'We could certainly try, but the whole process would take at least two years, and require a specific act of parliament which would have to be passed by both the lower house and upper house.'

She still couldn't see why she was there, what she was expected to say, or how she was expected to contribute.

'The earl has agreed, in the interest of not appearing unreasonable, to allow one officer from this force inside the walls,' Baxter continued. 'That officer will give the estate manager, Edward Bell, whatever help or advice he requests, and may act as an observer.'

'But why I am here?' a voice nagged at the back of Paniatowski's mind. 'Why am *I* here?'

'I'm sure DCS Holmes has a number of officers who would fill that role very well,' she said.

'I'm sure he has,' Baxter agreed, 'but I've decided to use someone from your team.'

That seemed a little odd, Paniatowski thought, but her team was not, at that moment, involved in any major investigations, and if it was what Baxter wanted...

'I could spare you DC Crane,' she said. 'He's well-educated and very diplomatic, and I'm sure he'll find the experience interesting. But if there's a murder, I'll need him back right away.'

Baxter smiled. It was a grim, joyless smile, and she realized that for the previous ten minutes he had been playing with her like a particularly merciless cat might play with a very helpless mouse.

'Perhaps I didn't make myself clear,' he said. 'When I told you I wanted a member of your team, what I meant was, I want *you*.'

She should have seen it coming, but she hadn't – and it felt like a slap in the face.

'It's not really my area of expertise, sir,' she said. 'I've been in the CID for most of my career. I would have thought someone from the uniformed branch would be better equipped to handle it.'

'Would you, Chief Inspector?' Baxter asked. 'Well, you're certainly entitled to think whatever you wish to think, but I'm telling you that I've decided, as chief constable, that I'd like *you* to do it.'

Giving her a menial task well below her proven abilities was meant to humiliate her. But it could be worse, she consoled herself. It would only be four or five days work, and since the job at the Hall seemed to be, in fact, a non-job, she could run her team almost as well as if she was at headquarters.

'You start this afternoon,' Baxter said.

'But the concert's not for a couple more days,' Paniatowski said, 'and it seems as if I'll have very little to do, anyway.'

'If the wheels come off on this thing – and they well might – I don't want anyone saying that it only happened because I sent my officer in too late,' Baxter told her.

There was nothing for it but to bow to the inevitable.

'Very well, if you insist,' she said.

'While you're away, your team will be temporarily reassigned to DCI Wellbeloved,' Baxter told her.

'Who the hell is DCI Wellbeloved?' Paniatowski demanded.

'He's just been transferred to the patch from
Honnerton. He's an impressive young man, by
all accounts, and working with DI Beresford for
a while will be an excellent way to acclimatize
him to the job.'

'But I'll be away for less than a week,' Paniatowski pointed out. 'That won't be anything like
long enough for DCI Wellbeloved to come to
grips with how we work in Mid Lancs. It would
make a lot more sense to give him a permanent
team of his own.'

'You'll be away for less than a week, will
you?' asked Baxter, with a hint of mock surprise
in his voice. 'Who said anything about less than
a week?'

'That's how long I'll need to be up at Stamford
Hall. You're not suggesting I stay there longer
than that, are you?'

'No, that would be a waste of valuable police
time.'

'Well, then...'

'But the RockStately Festival isn't the only
event that will be taking place this August. Even
just off the top of my head, I can think of half a
dozen more. There's the Bryston Medieval
Fayre, the Conglebury International Folk Gath-
ering...'

'You're surely not saying...'

'The experience you gain at Stamford Hall will
be invaluable when you're working on these
other gatherings, and by the end of the summer,
you will have become a real expert in the field of

outdoor events.'

Baxter didn't just want to punish her, she realized. He wasn't merely taking malicious glee in making her life uncomfortable. He was trying to destroy her.

'I wish to register the strongest possible protest at being given an assignment of this nature, sir,' she said.

'Your protest is noted, and will be duly recorded,' the chief constable told her. 'You may go now, Chief Inspector.'

TWO

Spike, sitting with his back resting against an ancient oak tree and his legs stretched out in front of him, was watching the centre of the forest clearing with the same look of anticipation on his face as that of a small, excited child seeing the circus for the first time.

The focus of his attention was Badger, who had driven a thick wooden post into the ground a couple of minutes earlier, and was now standing aggressively in front of it.

To Badger, the post was no longer a post at all, Spike thought – it was a Red Dragon or a Black Mountain Banshee or a member of any of the other ten or twelve rival motorcycle gangs with whom the Devil's Disciples were almost permanently at war.

Badger reached into his pocket, and pulled out the bicycle chain which he had modified by welding short pieces of pointed metal into some of the links. For perhaps half a minute, he swung the chain, almost lackadaisically, from side to side. Then the serious business began, and he started to arc it through the air, tracing out elaborate and highly controlled patterns as he did so.

Spike risked taking his eyes off the spectacle

for the few seconds it took him to light a cigarette.

He had been a member of the Devil's Disciples Motorcycle Gang for over two years. During that time he had been in a dozen pitched battles with rival gangs. He had taken part in perhaps fifty gang-bangs involving girls who were no great beauties, but were (usually) more or less willing participants. He had sold a little marijuana, acted as a heavy for debt collectors, and – when money had been particularly short, or one of the gang members needed expensive work doing on his machine – had even indulged in a few burglaries.

He loved being a Devil's Disciple. It could be hard in winter, living in squats with broken windows and no electricity – but in some ways that merely reaffirmed the outlaw status.

He liked the other Devil's Disciples, too. Some of them were barely literate and totally ignorant of the world beyond their own narrow sphere. Their conversation was limited, their intellectual curiosity non-existent. But they didn't bully him, as the well-educated, over-privileged boys had done at school. No, to them he was a brother-in-arms – and they would take a beating for him as readily as he would take a beating for any one of them.

But the best thing about the gang was Badger. He was the leader not because he was the oldest member of the Devil's Disciples – though he probably was. Nor was he the toughest member – he was hard enough, but straight off the top of his head, Spike could think of at least half a dozen Devil's Disciples who were harder. No, he

31

was the leader simply because he had a natural talent for leading.

He had become almost a father-figure to the younger man, and though he could sometimes treat Spike unfairly, and even vindictively, Spike knew that, deep down, Badger cared about him – and how many men could say that of their real fathers?

As if he was suddenly tired of the game, Badger let the chain fall slack against his leg, turned his back on the wooden post, and took two steps towards the edge of the clearing.

He really looked like he was leaving, thought Spike – but the truth was, he wasn't going anywhere.

When Badger did make his move, it came so fast that it was almost a blur. One moment he had his back to the post and was at least three paces from it, the next he was in a crouch, now closer to the post and facing it again, but a little to the side. As he straightened up, he swung the chain, and the cruel metal barbs embedded themselves in the wood at head height.

Badger took a step back to admire his work, and then – gently and almost lovingly – eased the chain free of the post.

On one level, the practice had been just what it appeared to be, Spike thought – a warrior honing his skills. But on another level, it had been a performance, designed to impress the bald, fat man who was standing at the opposite edge of the clearing.

The bald man puzzled Spike, because the Devil's Disciples normally had nothing to do with civilians, yet this was the second time this particular one had put in an appearance.

The first time is at a transport café on the A49. The Disciples have been there for around ten minutes. When they first arrived, there were plenty of other civilians around, but the sight of forty-three members of a motorcycle gang descending on the place is enough to make them all run for cover.

It is always like that. The café owners do not want to serve them, but they are afraid of what the Disciples will do if they refuse, so they try to look as if they are delighted to see their new customers, all the while praying that they won't stay too long or do too much damage.

The bald man in a scruffy suit arrives just after the Disciples. He does not seem the least put off by their presence. In fact, he walks straight over to the table where Badger is eating his eggs and chips, and says, as bold as brass, 'I'd like a word with you.'

'Is that right?' Badger replies. 'And why would you like it with me, rather than any of the other lads?'

'Because you're the boss,' the bald man says flatly.

Badger looks down quizzically at the right-hand lapel of his battered leather jacket.

'Of course I'm the boss,' he agrees. 'That's what it says on my badge. Except there is no badge, is there?'

'I know that you're the boss because I've been watching you,' the bald man says.

Badger's eyes narrow. 'Been watching us?' he says. 'How long has this been going on?'

The bald man sighs. 'Does it really matter how long I've been doing it?' he asks. 'Look, I can walk away, if that's what you want me to do, but if I was you, I'd be curious as to why somebody who obviously isn't a copper would spend so much time studying me.'

Badger thinks about it for a second, then stands up. 'We'll talk outside,' he says.

The two of them go out on to the forecourt, and are deep in conversation for about five minutes, then the bald man gets into his car and drives off.

Badger comes back into the café and complains to the manager that his eggs and chips are cold. The manager could point out that the only reason they've gone cold is because he's left them for so long, but he realizes that wouldn't exactly be the smartest move he's ever made in his life, and he tells the cook to make up another plate on the house.

None of the other Devil's Disciples ask Badger what the bald man wanted – you don't question the leader – and Badger himself says nothing at all about the encounter.

Badger slipped his lethal bicycle chain back in his pocket, and walked back across the clearing to rejoin the bald man. They talked for over half an hour. Each of them, at some point in their discussion, waved his arms in the air in an extravagant – and possibly frustrated – gesture. Several times, they turned to look in the general direction of Spike's tent. Then, finally, they shook hands – Badger had shaken hands with a civilian! Spike thought, shocked – and the bald man disappeared into the woods, heading for the road.

Badger crossed the camp again, passing Devil's Disciples tinkering with their machines and Devil's Disciples playing cards or drinking, and came to a halt in front of Spike's tent.

Spike looked up at him. The leader's long black hair had become dishevelled during his practice with the bike chain, but now he had combed it carefully back into place, so the streak of white hair ran directly across the centre of his head.

'How are you doing today, young Spike?' Badger asked. 'Are you fighting fit?'

'I've never been better, Badger,' Spike replied.

And it was true. He felt on top of the world – and bursting with pride – because Badger, instead of stopping to chat to any of the dozen Disciples he had passed, had chosen to come directly to him.

Badger nodded. 'Never better, eh? Good lad! We'll be moving on soon. We're going to a rock festival.'

Spike grinned. 'We going to cause a bit of mayhem, are we?'

Hearing his own words, he was suddenly horrified, because maybe Badger didn't know what 'mayhem' meant.

'I mean, are we going to have a rumble?' he corrected himself, hastily.

If Badger had noticed either the slip or the

35

correction, he gave absolutely no sign of it.

'No, we're not looking for trouble on this trip,' he said. 'We're going to run the festival's security.'

'I didn't know we did that kind of thing,' Spike said.

'We don't, normally,' Badger agreed. 'But we stand to make a hell of a lot of money – enough to see us through the whole winter.'

'Through the whole winter – Jesus, they must be paying good wages!' Spike said.

'I didn't say that, did I?' Badger asked, and there was a barbed-wire edge to his voice.

'Didn't say what?'

'Didn't say they paid good wages – all I *did* say was that we stand to make a hell of a lot of money.'

'I'm sorry,' Spike said, not quite sure what he was apologizing for, but sensing that an apology was necessary. 'I didn't mean to...'

'Course you didn't,' Badger interrupted. 'I know that. Anyway, this place that we're going to is called Stam-something-or-other Hall, and it's in Lancashire, just off the M6.'

'Stamford Hall?' Spike asked worriedly.

'Yeah, that's it,' Badger agreed.

Spike suddenly found himself fighting for breath.

'I'm ... I'm from around there,' he gasped.

And then he realized his mistake. It was one of the cardinal rules that Devil's Disciples didn't come from *anywhere*. They had no homes and no families, because the Devil's Disciples *were* their home and their family, and before they had joined, they hadn't really existed.

'I'm sorry,' he said again.

'Doesn't matter,' Badger told him, *almost* like a kindly uncle – but still with just a hint of the barbed wire to his tone. 'We all make mistakes.'

Don't make me go, Badger, a voice inside Spike moaned. Please don't make me go.

But he knew that if that was what the leader wanted, that was what would happen.

'Anyway, I thought you'd like to know,' Badger said, turning and ambling back towards his own tent.

Spike lit up another cigarette, and noticed that his hands were shaking. He wondered why Badger had chosen him – a relatively low-ranking member of the gang – to be first to hear the latest plan.

It was almost, he thought, as if the leader knew his secret.

Paniatowski broke the news to her team over a lunchtime drink at their usual table in the Drum and Monkey.

'I don't want any of you kicking up a fuss about what's just happened, because it won't do *me* any good – and it certainly wouldn't do *you* any,' she said. 'Is that understood?'

None of them spoke.

'Is that understood?' she repeated, looking directly at DI Colin Beresford, who had worked with her since she was a mere sergeant and he was a fresh-faced constable.

'Understood,' Beresford grumbled, fixing his eyes on the table.

'How about you, Kate?' Paniatowski asked her elfin-like sergeant and bagman.

'You're the boss,' Kate Meadows replied.

'And you, Jack?' Paniatowski said, turning to DC Crane, the Oxford graduate who was destined for great things.

'I'm way down at the bottom of the food chain, boss,' he said. 'Nothing I could do or say would make much of a difference.'

'Clever,' Paniatowski said.

'Sorry, boss?' he replied, attempting to look puzzled – and failing. 'What's clever?'

'I asked you to say nothing, and you said that whatever you said would make no difference – which is not quite the same, is it?'

Crane grinned, guiltily. 'No, boss, it isn't.'

'So I want you to promise me, here and now, that you'll keep your mouth firmly shut.'

Crane sighed. 'If that's what you want, boss.'

'It is what I want,' Paniatowski told him. She took a plastic bag full of ten pence pieces out of her handbag. 'Now, if you'll excuse me, I have to make my weekly call to Mr Woodend.'

The rest of the team nodded. Woodend had been Paniatowski's mentor, and both Beresford and Crane had worked with him. He had retired to Spain three years earlier.

Paniatowski stood up and headed for the corridor, where the payphone was situated.

'Why does she do that every Wednesday?' asked Beresford, when his boss was out of earshot. 'She didn't used to.'

'My guess would be that Wednesday is either the day immediately before his treatment or the day immediately after it,' Meadows said.

'What treatment?'

'I don't know, because I don't know what he's suffering from – but he's obviously seriously ill.'

'Is he?' Beresford asked. 'Did Monika tell *you* that Mr Woodend was seriously ill?'

'Of course she didn't tell me,' Meadows replied, noting the hint of jealousy in the inspector's voice. 'You're her best mate, and if she'd told anyone, she'd have told you.'

'So if *she* didn't tell you, then who did?'

Meadows snorted. 'With the greatest respect, sir, I'm sometimes amazed – not very often, but *sometimes* – that you ever managed to rise to the dizzy heights of detective inspector.'

'So I've missed something, have I?' Beresford asked, stung.

'Yes, sir, you have,' Meadows agreed.

'And are you going to tell me what it is?'

'When people change their phoning habits, it's almost always because the person they're phoning is seriously ill.'

'In other words, you're just guessing,' Beresford said.

'Not really,' Meadows replied. 'It's not just that she's phoning him regularly, it's *where* she's phoning him from.'

'All right, I'll buy it,' Beresford said. 'Why does the fact that she's phoning him from the pub tell you he's ill?'

'Where else could she have phoned from?' Meadows asked, answering the question with one of her own.

'Police headquarters,' Beresford suggested.

'Ah, but if Mr Woodend doesn't want it generally known that he's ill – and from what you've told me about him, he's not the sort of feller to welcome pity from *anyone* – then the worst thing the boss could do would be to ring him regularly from headquarters, because the news would spread and people would soon start drawing their own conclusions.'

'She could always ring him from home,' Beresford said.

'And who handles the bills at home?' Meadows asked.

'Monika does,' Beresford said automatically.

And then he began to wonder if that was true. Monika was very sloppy over any details of her life which did not actually involve police work, but her adopted daughter, Louisa, was just the opposite, so it was more than likely that Louisa, exasperated with her mother's inefficiency, had taken over the job herself, and merely gave Monika the cheques to sign.

'It could be Louisa who handles the bills,' he admitted.

'Louisa would be very likely to start asking the same questions I have, wouldn't she?' Meadows asked. 'And we all know just how fond she is of her Uncle Charlie.'

'All right, if all that's true – and, I will admit, you've made a good case for it being true – why does she ring from the pub, where we can all see her doing it?' Beresford asked exasperatedly.

'There are two reasons for that,' Meadows replied, with infuriating self-assurance. 'The first is that one of the things she'll talk to Mr

Woodend about is work – and it will give him that extra little thrill to know that she's talking from the pub where he spent so much of his working life.'

The annoying thing about Meadows, Beresford thought, was that when she challenged his judgement – and she did that much more regularly than any other sergeant would have dared – she was usually right. And in this case, she was *definitely* right. Charlie Woodend had done some of his finest detecting from the corner table in the public bar of the Drum and Monkey, and he would get a kick out of the fact that Monika was calling him from there.

'You said there were two reasons,' he pointed out.

'Yes,' Meadows said. 'The other reason is that if there's bad news, she needs people she can trust to be there to give her support.'

And she was right about that, as well, Beresford thought gloomily.

The bald man's name was Harry Elton. On the frosted glass panel in the door of his office back in Manchester, it said he was a private investigator, and while that was true, it was not the whole story. His real job description, if engraved on that same door, would either have been in almost unreadable tiny letters or would have required a much bigger pane of glass, since he was also a wheeler-dealer, a fixer, a purveyor of difficult-to-obtain – and often illegal – products, a bender of rules and a skirter of regulations, a con man and a corrupter.

As he drove away from the Devil's Disciples' camp, Elton was feeling very pleased with himself.

'All this started from just one job,' he told the St Christopher medallion which hung from his rear-view mirror, and which he regarded – with some justification – as his only real friend. 'Just one simple little job that I could have wrapped up in a couple of days. And for most men, it would have stayed at just that – but then I'm *not* most men, am I, Chris?'

The medallion swung from side to side, as if it were nodding its head in agreement, though the truth was – more prosaically – that it was just reacting to a change in the camber of the road.

'So how many extra angles did I manage to squeeze out of that one job, Chris?' Elton asked, as he pulled off the country lane and on to the motorway feeder road. 'One, you think? Maybe two? No, you're quite wrong – it was three! And here's how it was done. Firstly, I talk the original client – the original poncey idiot – into paying me to do a second job he hadn't even thought of himself. Now it's important that he agrees to that other job, because if he doesn't, I can't ring Big George in Liverpool, and make him my second client.'

A tractor and trailer were slowly chugging along the road in front of him, and since the bend just ahead made overtaking impossible, Elton was forced to slow down.

'Bloody bastard yokels – why don't you stay on the bloody farm,' he snarled, reaching into the glove compartment for the bar of chunky chocolate which he liked to think of as his emergency supplies.

The tractor successfully negotiated the bend, and the driver stuck out his arm and signalled that it was now safe to pass. Elton pulled out and accelerated. He had broken off quite a large part of the chocolate bar, but he somehow managed to cram it all in his mouth as he drew level with the tractor, leaving his hand free to give the tractor driver a V sign.

'But here's the icing on the cake, Chris!' he said, resuming his previous conversation with the patron saint of travellers. 'Here's the stroke of genius! Having got Big George on board, I call my old mate, Terry – who isn't really a mate at all, and in his way is just as big an idiot as the first client – and suggest there might be something in it for him.'

A large blue sign ahead announced that he was approaching the motorway, which meant that he was less than an hour from home.

'I can tell you're impressed, Chris,' Elton said to the medallion, 'and what you're probably thinking now is that things could turn out quite hairy in Whitebridge in a few days time. Well, you're not wrong about that. But if and when they *do* turn hairy, you and me will be at least fifty miles away, establishing an alibi that even the Spanish Inquisition couldn't break.'

'How's the chemotherapy going, Charlie?' Paniatowski said into the mouthpiece of the Drum's public telephone.

'Straight to the point, eh?' former-DCI Charlie

43

Woodend asked. 'Still, you never were much of a one for small talk, were you?'

Paniatowski, refusing to rise to the distracting bait that Woodend was attempting to dangle in front of her, kept silent.

'It's changed me, somewhat,' Woodend conceded, when it became plain his gambit had failed. 'I used to be just a grumpy old fart, but now I'm a *bald*, grumpy old fart.'

'Is it working?' Paniatowski pleaded.

'It's too soon to say yet, but the doctor's looking a bit more hopeful than he did a couple of months ago,' Woodend said, choosing his words carefully, 'so while I'm not promising anything, I think there's a chance, if the wind's blowing in the right direction, that I might just pull through.'

'Thank God!' Paniatowski gasped.

'I thought you didn't believe in God any more.'

'I don't.'

And she didn't. She had lost her faith soon after her stepfather had first slipped his cold body into her warm bed, and nothing that had happened to her since that terrible night had persuaded her she should try to find it again.

'But enough of talking about me – how are things in the Mid-Lancs CID?' Charlie Woodend asked.

George Baxter's trying to get rid of me, Paniatowski thought. He won't rest until I've gone.

'Things are rather quiet at the moment,' she said aloud. 'It's often like that in summer.'

'Aye, somehow people are less likely to turn to

thoughts of murder when the sun's shining.'

'I'd better get back to the team,' Paniatowski said.

'Give them my best,' Woodend told her.

He was clearly thinking about saying more, and Paniatowski gave him the space to do so.

'I really *do* think I might beat this thing inside me,' Woodend continued, after a few seconds had passed. 'But if I don't – if it really is the end of Cloggin'-it Charlie – then I've absolutely no complaints. I've had a good marriage, and though I don't love Joan in quite the same *way* as when I married her, the love's still as strong as it ever was. I'm as proud as punch of my wonderful daughter – she's a hospital ward sister now, you know.'

'That's great. She deserves it.'

'And looking back on my career in the force, I've not done all that badly, have I?'

'You've done brilliantly, Charlie.'

'And then there's you,' Woodend said.

Oh God, please, no, Paniatowski thought.

But she couldn't find it in her to silence a man who – for all his new apparent optimism – might be dying.

'If you don't mind me saying so, you were a bit of a mess when you first started working for me, Monika,' Woodend continued.

'I was a *complete* bloody mess,' Paniatowski told him. 'I was a robot. I thought it was the only way to survive.'

'But look at you now. You've got a daughter who adores you, and friends and colleagues who'd do anything for you. You've only been a

45

chief inspector for a little over two years, and you're already practically a legend.'

'I'm not ... it isn't...' Paniatowski mumbled.

'Given time, you'll be a better DCI than I ever was, Monika, and years after they've forgotten all about me, they'll still be talking about you.' Woodend paused, but only for a second. 'Most of that's down to you,' he continued. 'You've got a fine brain, and enough courage for a regiment ... but you wouldn't mind if I took a little credit for where you are now, would you?'

'I owe everything to you, Charlie,' Paniatowski told him.

'Now then, lass, there's no point in going to extremes,' Woodend said awkwardly. 'I mean, I appreciate a pat on the head as much as the next man, but I don't want you hanging a bloody halo over it.'

Paniatowski laughed, though she had to force it.

'I'll call you next Wednesday,' she said.

'That's right,' Woodend agreed. 'And in the meantime, keep locking the bad buggers up.'

'We should let the chief constable know just how we feel about him reassigning the boss,' Beresford said firmly.

'It wouldn't do any good,' Meadows told him. 'Mr Baxter already *knows* how we feel, and he simply doesn't care.'

'He's always struck me as a man who knows how to lead a team,' Beresford said, 'a man who takes his officers' feelings into account, because he understands that's the way to get the best out of them.'

Meadows looked at Crane for support. 'Will you tell him, or shall I?' she asked.

'It's not about the force, sir, it's about the boss,' Crane said. 'Mr Baxter blames her for his wife's death, and he wants her out.'

'But that's preposterous!' Beresford exploded.

'Yes, it is,' Meadows agreed. 'It's totally preposterous – but that doesn't make it any less true.'

As she put down the phone, there was a part of Paniatowski – she recognized it as the less worthy, weaker part – which was wondering if she should have discussed with Charlie Woodend what had happened that morning.

No! the other part – the stronger, better part of her – answered quickly. You've no right to burden Charlie with this problem, especially since it's partly a problem of your own making.

It's *not* of my own making, the weaker part argued defensively. I never gave Jo Baxter cause to be jealous. Any jealousy she might have felt came from the way her husband looked at me, not the way I looked at him.

Ah, said the stronger part, if you're examining the facts at the scene of the crime, what you say is entirely true. But if you follow the chain of evidence right back to the beginning, you'll get a completely different story.

Detective Sergeant Paniatowski – almost destroyed by her recent break-up with DI Bob Rutter – is in Yorkshire, tying up the loose ends of a case which has its origins in Whitebridge, and

Chief Inspector Baxter has been assigned to ride shotgun for her. Baxter has a shock of red hair, and reminds her of nothing so much as a big, ginger teddy bear. She is relaxed in his company, and when he makes a pass at her, she does not resist. She expects it to be no more than a one-night stand, but Baxter seems to want to go beyond that, and since she finds it both a comfortable and comforting relationship, she does not resist that, either.

She should have realized, back then, that Baxter was falling in love with her and pulled away before too much damage was done.

But she hadn't even guessed.

So it was only when Baxter realized it himself – and realized, a little later, that whatever he did, and however much she tried to make herself, she would never grow to love him – that the relationship came to a sticky end.

And the problem was that, despite his marriage, he had never quite fallen *out* of love with her. It was when Jo had begun to understand this that she'd started drinking heavily, and that, in turn had led to her lonely death amid the wreckage of her car, on the bleak moors.

If I'd broken up with George Baxter earlier – or never gone to bed with him in the first place – Jo Baxter would still be alive, Paniatowski told herself, not for the first time.

She knew it was irrational – that Baxter and Jo were responsible for their own fates, just as she was responsible for hers – but there were moments when she could not help feeling a little to blame.

George Baxter suffered from no such ambiguity of feeling. He never wavered from blaming both of them for Jo's death – there was absolutely no doubt about that. And perhaps he really did think that she had done something to engender Jo's jealousy, though it was more likely that as the guilt festered away inside him, he had felt the need – for his own survival – to shovel some of it on to someone else.

Whatever the case, his love had turned to hatred, and he wanted her off the force. But he couldn't sack her. All he could do was make life unpleasant for her, and hope that she eventually resigned.

But she would *not* resign. She had worked too hard and too long to give up now.

And besides, she couldn't do it to Charlie Woodend. While he was battling with the cancer, she couldn't pull the rug from under what he considered one of his greatest achievements.

She lit up a cigarette, and went back into the bar. Her team saw her approaching and fell awkwardly silent. It looked as if they had been talking about her – and, of course, they had.

'Drink up, you lot,' she said, 'it's about time we were getting back to headquarters.'

Beresford glanced up at the large clock on the wall – the clock that all the customers had learned to loath as they watched its big hand moving ever closer to the time at which last orders would be called.

'What's the hurry?' he asked.

'The hurry is that your new boss is reporting

for duty this afternoon, and, first impressions being very important, I'd prefer him to find you in the office rather than at the boozer.'

'Our new boss!' Crane said.

'You mean our *temporary* new boss, don't you?' Beresford asked.

Paniatowski sighed. She had already made it as plain as she possibly could what the situation was, yet Crane and Beresford still seemed to be in denial.

'Think of him as temporary if it will make it easier for you in the short term,' she said wearily.

'No, I'll think of him as temporary, because that's what he's going to be,' Meadows said.

So even the Machiavelli of the team was refusing to come to terms with reality.

'You have to make this work,' Paniatowski pleaded. 'For the sake of your own careers, you *need* to make it work.'

THREE

The grounds of Stamford Hall formed an almost-perfect rectangle, and could be entered through one of the four gates – the North Gate, the South Gate, the East Gate and the West Gate – all of them set in the high stone walls which surrounded the estate. The sign on the minor road skirting the Hall, however, made it clear that though there were, in theory, four possible choices, visitors and tradesmen should report to the North Gate, and – supposing that she was probably both those things – it was to the North Gate that Monika Paniatowski drove her little red MGA that early afternoon.

A large notice, conspicuously displayed on the ornamental gates, announced that this was private property – as if anyone would have bothered building such a high wall around something that *wasn't* private! – and that visitors should hoot to summon the gatekeeper.

Paniatowski hit the horn. While she was waiting for some response, she reached into the glove compartment for her cigarettes, but when her palm wrapped around the packet, the celluloid felt so clammy and sticky that she released her grip immediately.

It was too hot a day to smoke, she told herself,

and anyway, she had promised Louisa that she would cut down.

The door in the small lodge by the side of the gate opened, and a man stepped out. He was middle-aged, and dressed in a grey suit that was not quite a uniform, but was not quite civilian dress either.

The man walked over to the gate. He had a security badge hanging from the buttonhole of his left lapel, and carried a clipboard in his hand.

He looked down at the clipboard.

'Detective Chief Inspector Panya ... Pania...?' he asked.

'That's right,' Paniatowski agreed.

The man nodded, took a plastic card out of his pocket, and slid it into a slot in a metal strip in the wall.

The iron gates swung slowly and majestically open, and Paniatowski edged the MGA forward.

'Follow the avenue up to the Hall,' the man said. 'Mr Bell, the estate manager, will be waiting for you in front of the main fountain.'

'Is this gate always kept manned?' Paniatowski asked, with a professional curiosity which almost surprised her.

'Not round the clock, no,' the gatekeeper said. 'I'm here from eight in the morning until five in the afternoon.'

'What if anyone wants to enter outside those hours?'

'The family and staff have their own cards to open the gates.'

'And if you don't happen to be family or staff?'

'Then you ring up the Hall in advance, and, if Mr Bell decides there's a legitimate reason for you to enter the grounds, one of the servants will be waiting here to let you in.'

'And if Mr Bell decides there isn't a legitimate reason?'

'Then you don't get in.'

'Whoever you are?' Paniatowski asked.

'Whoever you are,' the gateman confirmed.

'Well, thanks for your help,' Paniatowski said.

And as she was pulling away, she was thinking, welcome to the eighteenth century, Monika.

The trees which flanked the avenue seemed almost like a funnel designed to focus the eyes on the Hall. But a funnel wasn't really necessary, Paniatowski thought, as she drove along, because the building had enough grandeur to command the watchers attention without resorting to artificial aids.

It was, strictly speaking, two stories high, though, judging by the apparent size of the windows, each one of those stories was as tall as both floors of her own little house. And it was capped by a huge majestic dome which should have looked unnecessarily ostentatious, but somehow didn't.

As she got closer, she realized that the funnel of trees had only allowed her to see part of the structure, and that beyond the central block on which the dome rested, the house continued – now single storied, but in both directions – for another fifteen or twenty rooms.

'Jesus!' she said to herself, 'so this is how the

rich live.'

She reached the end of the avenue, and found herself in an open courtyard large enough to accommodate the dozens of carriages which must once, in times gone by, have stood there for hours on end, while their aristocratic owners enjoyed themselves at formal balls thrown by the de Courtney family.

There was a big, elaborate fountain in the middle of the courtyard – a Queen Anne version of a traffic island, Paniatowski supposed – and rising up from the centre of it was a ten-foot high, bronze statue of a naked man with a leer on his lips which probably identified him as a Greek or Roman god.

Just beyond the fountain, a Land Rover was parked, and standing next to it was a solidly built man of around forty, who, while he could not compete with the ancient god, was nonetheless rather impressive.

That would be the formidable Mr Bell, Paniatowski thought – the holder of the magic keys to the sacred fiefdom.

The estate manager signalled that she should pull up next to his vehicle, and the moment she had come to a halt, he stepped forward and opened the door of the MGA for her.

'I'm Edward Bell, the estate manager,' he said, holding out his right hand to her. 'Welcome to Stamford Hall, DCI Paniatowski.' He took a step back, and opened the passenger door of the Land Rover. 'The earl has agreed to see you later in the afternoon, but before that meeting, he thought it might be useful to you to get some idea of the layout of the estate.'

'How big are the grounds?' Paniatowski asked, as they pulled away.

'All together, a little under twelve hundred acres,' Bell said. 'That includes the outhouses, the stables, the greenhouses, the ornamental gardens, the two lakes – one for boating and fishing, the other a sort of nature reserve – the deer park, half a dozen follies – some of them perched on top of artificial hills – and Backend Wood. The estate is surrounded by a high wall...'

'Yes, I couldn't help but notice that.'

'...which was begun early in the seventeenth century, and finally completed just before the dawn of the eighteenth. They didn't rush things in those days, because they liked to make sure they'd got it right.'

'You sound almost nostalgic.'

'There's a lot to be said for the seventeenth century. The people back then didn't have televisions and fridges like we do, but then there's more to life than material possessions.'

They had driven around the side of the house, and were heading down another tree-lined avenue at ninety degrees to the one that Paniatowski had used to reach the courtyard.

'Beyond the walls, there are a dozen tenanted farms – and most of them have been lived in by the same families for around three hundred years,' Bell said. 'What we're approaching now is the East Gate. It's normally locked, but it will be open for the festival, because that's how the visitors will get in.'

Next to the East Gate, a dozen workmen were

involved in erecting the scaffolding which would be the basis of the stage. Further away, to both the left and right, perhaps two dozen more workmen were sinking tall metal posts into the ground.

'You going to fence the whole of the concert area in, are you?' Paniatowski asked.

'Yes.'

'With wire-netting?'

'That's right, except we bought it from America, and over there they call it chain-link fencing.'

'You imported the wire-netting from *America*?'

'American chain-link is supposed to be the best in the world – and the earl always insists on the best.'

'That's nice for him,' Paniatowski said drily.

Bell swung the Land Rover expertly on to the rough track which ran around the inside of the perimeter wall. They passed the deer park, caught a glimpse of two of the follies, and finally reached the wood.

'This is Backend Wood – it's where the security staff will be sleeping,' Bell said.

'They'll be sleeping in the woods?' Paniatowski asked incredulously.

'That's right. We offered them accommodation in some of the outbuildings, but they said they'd prefer to camp in the woods.'

'Just what kind of security company is it that you've employed?' Paniatowski asked.

'It's not a security company as such,' Bell said, a little awkwardly. 'It's a motorcycle appreciation club.'

'You're telling me you've hired a *biker gang*?'

'I really would prefer to use my description of them.'

'And what's the name of this *motorcycle appreciation club*?'

'I believe they're called the DDs,' Bell said evasively.

'And that stands for what?'

'Err ... the Devil's Disciples.'

'That's a nice, friendly name. Don't you think you're taking a bit of a risk by using them as your security?'

'I've been told that similar organizations have fulfilled that role at other festivals.'

'Indeed, they have,' Paniatowski agreed. 'The Hell's Angels are a good example. They were used at the Altamont Free Festival in 1969 – and they murdered a member of the audience.'

'That was the Yanks,' Bell said dismissively. 'You can't see British people behaving like that, can you?'

'America – put your faith in its wire netting, but not in its thugs-on-wheels!' Paniatowski said.

'And not in its hamburgers, either,' said Bell, in a clear attempt to change the subject.

But Paniatowski didn't *want* the subject changed, not if she was to be involved – even peripherally – in the festival's security arrangements.

'Who *was it* who decided to hire the Devil's Disciples to take care of the security?' she asked.

'The earl himself made that decision.'

'And you didn't try to talk him out of it?'

'It's not my place to question the earl.'

'Did you actually just say that it's *not your place* to question the earl?' Paniatowski said, amazed.

'I did.'

'You're the estate manager, for God's sake!'

'And God put my family on this earth to serve the de Courtney family – not to criticize them.'

'You can't be serious!'

'But I am.'

'You're an intelligent man,' Paniatowski protested.

Bell smiled. 'And an educated one, to boot. I have a BSc degree in estate management from Manchester University, and a postgraduate degree from Yale.'

'So what's all this about having been "put on the earth to serve the de Courtney family?" It sounds like something your grandfather would have said.'

'It *is* something my grandfather would have said.'

'And do you seriously expect me to believe that someone like you – a man who's seen something of the wider world – can still have the same vision of that world as his grandfather – a feller who probably went no more than a few miles from the estate in his entire life?'

'You're wrong about my grandfather,' Bell said. 'He served as the earl's grandfather's servant in the First World War, just as my father served as the earl's father's batman in the Second. And when it was all over – when they both *had* seen something of the wider world –

they came back here and resumed the lives they had led before those terrible conflicts occurred.'

'I'm amazed,' Paniatowski admitted.

'That's because you're trying to measure my sense of duty with your own logical yardstick – and it won't work,' Bell said easily. 'I'm not a fool. I know that the world's changed since my grandfather's day. I know most people don't look up to the aristocracy in the way they used to. But my family has cared for this estate and its owners for nearly four hundred years – and duty is in our very bones.'

Perhaps it had been like that for her father, when he had led the cavalry charge against German tanks at the start of the Second World War, Paniatowski thought. His logic must have told him that it was a futile gesture – but his sense of duty had made him do it anyway.

'I never meant to offend you in any way, Mr Bell – and I'm sorry if that's what I've done,' she said humbly.

'You haven't offended me, Chief Inspector,' the estate manager told her. 'As I said earlier, I am not so naive as to expect other people to understand the way I feel. All I ask is that they recognize those feelings as genuine, and show the proper respect for them.'

They had reached the end of the track, and Bell turned the Land Rover on to the south avenue, which led back to the Hall. When they reached the carriage turning circle, Bell pulled up in front of the fountain.

'This is as far as I go,' he said. He checked his watch. 'The earl should be just about ready to

59

receive you now.'

'Won't you be coming inside with me?' Paniatowski asked, surprised.

'No, I haven't been invited to this particular meeting,' the estate manager said. 'Ring the bell at the main door, and the butler will take you to see the earl.'

'Good God, did you actually just say that he still has a *butler*?' Paniatowski exclaimed.

'Yes, I did.' Bell sighed. 'In my grandfather's day, there were over two hundred servants working at the Hall. These days, with all the modern labour-saving devices now available, you could probably maintain the same level of service with about fifty – as long as they were really dedicated workers. But most people don't want to go into service now, so the Hall has to get by with just ten servants, excluding, of course, the ground staff.'

'Of course.'

'The work the servants can't manage themselves is done by contract staff brought in from the outside. They're efficient enough, but they have no real pride in what they do.' He sighed again. 'It's just a job to them.'

'Well, there you go,' Paniatowski said philosophically. 'Life is tough all over – even for earls.'

Edward Bell chuckled. 'Even for earls,' he repeated. 'I'll see you around and about, Chief Inspector.'

Then he slipped the Land Rover into gear and drove away.

She liked Edward Bell, Paniatowski thought as

she watched the Land Rover grow smaller and smaller, and while she still could not quite get to grips with the way his brain worked, she was sure that she could put her absolute trust in him.

Ignoring the heat and stickiness of the cigarette packet, she lit up a Winston, and took her time smoking it.

Then she walked up the impressive double doors at the front of the Hall and rang for the butler.

Paniatowski had told her team that the new DCI would merely be dropping by that afternoon, but, as it turned out, the chief constable had misled her, and even as the team were meeting for a final drink together in the Drum and Monkey, DCI Wellbeloved had been settling into his new office.

As was the usual practice with a newcomer, he'd been allocated an office at the far end – the outer darkness – of the CID suite, but, like a dog marking out new territory by peeing on every wall, he had already taken steps to make it very clearly his own, Beresford noted.

A photograph of a younger Wellbeloved, in military uniform, hung just behind the desk, with a certificate of some kind flanking it to the right, and a framed newspaper article (which no doubt reflected well on him) to the left. A coat stand, topped with deer antlers, had been placed by the door, and a bag of professional-looking golf clubs was very much in evidence in the corner.

Wellbeloved was about his own age, Beresford guessed. He was not particularly tall and had a rugby player's build. His eyes were pale blue, and his cheeks – in contrast – had a permanent slight flush. The blue check suit he was wearing was almost aggressively smart, and he had an expensive-looking signet ring on his index finger.

'As you already know, I'm DCI Wellbeloved,' the new chief inspector said, 'but that's just the name I was born with, not a description of how my subordinates regard me.'

Unsure of whether or not he was making a joke, Beresford risked a modest smile.

'The purpose of this meeting is for me to get to know you, and for you to get to know me,' Wellbeloved continued. 'You joined the force as a cadet, didn't you, DI Beresford?'

'That's right,' Beresford agreed, and then he noticed Wellbeloved's pale eyes harden, and added, 'yes, sir.'

'And yet you weren't promoted to inspector until a little over two years ago,' Wellbeloved said. 'Is that because you're a bit of a plodder?'

'No, I wouldn't say that, exactly,' Beresford replied, slightly awkwardly. 'Most of the inspectors in the Mid Lancs force weren't promoted until they were at least my age.'

'And most of them won't get any higher up the ladder, will they?' Wellbeloved asked.

'Probably not,' Beresford agreed.

Wellbeloved stretched his hands in front of him, as if he were already reaching out for the next rung himself.

'Tell me, DI Beresford, do *you* want to spend the rest of your career as an inspector?' he asked.

'I haven't really thought about it,' Beresford

admitted.

Nor had he. He was a man who had nursed his sick mother throughout his twenties, and only lost his virginity after turning thirty. Now he was making up for lost time in matters sexual, and was still coming to terms with the fact that fresh-faced young officers who he'd never met before automatically called him sir.

Besides, the next step up was DCI, and Monika was the DCI.

Except she wasn't *the* DCI, he reminded himself. There were others – and he was looking across the desk at one, at that very moment.

'You can't afford to stand still in the modern police force, Colin, especially when you have no higher education to speak of,' Wellbeloved told him. 'If you're not careful, you'll have DC Crane as your boss in a few years, and once he's got the power, it'll be payback time for all the resentment he's built up against you while he was climbing the slippery slope.'

First it had been a ladder, and now it had become a slippery slope, Beresford thought. Wellbeloved needed to make up his mind which one it was.

'There'd be no payback time with Jack Crane, sir,' he said aloud. 'He's not like that.'

'We're *all* like that,' Wellbeloved contradicted him. 'It's just that some of us are better at hiding it than others.' He paused, and a sudden and totally unexpected smile came to his lips. 'I can be a bit too blunt, sometimes,' he continued. 'A bit too blunt and, in order to make my point, somewhat over-emphatic – and I'd like to apologize for that, here and now.'

'There's no need,' Beresford said.

'*Of course* you're not a plodder – you're one of those good, solid policemen who make up the backbone of the force. And *of course* Crane isn't the sort of man who would extract his petty revenge the moment the opportunity was presented to him. In fact, from what I've heard so far, you seem to be an excellent team, and I'd like that team spirit to continue now I've taken over.'

'So would I, sir,' Beresford agreed.

'But one thing I learned during my time in the army is that there are two halves to any team – the officers and the other ranks – and the team works best when that clear distinction is constantly reinforced. That's the job of the officers, and they can only do it by working together.' Wellbeloved smiled again. 'What I'm really saying, Colin, is that I need to know I can count on your support, and in return – I promise you – you can count on mine. Any questions?'

Yes, he had a lot of questions, Beresford thought – but none he was prepared to voice at that moment.

'No, sir,' he said aloud.

'Then send in the next one, if you wouldn't mind,' Wellbeloved told him. He waited until Beresford was almost at the door before he added, 'Actually, there is just one more thing I'd like to ask you before you go. What do you know about DS Meadows?'

'I think she's a very good bagman, and should develop into—' Beresford began.

'I'm not talking about how she does her job in

Whitebridge,' Wellbeloved interrupted him. 'I mean what do you know about her *before* she came here?'

'Not much,' Beresford admitted, and was surprised to discover that even *not much* was an exaggeration, and that, in fact, he actually knew bugger all. 'Why do you ask, sir?'

'No real reason,' Wellbeloved said. 'It's just that her record is rather vague. Still, she can probably explain that to me herself.'

'Yes, sir, she probably can,' Beresford agreed.

Though knowing Meadows as he did, he doubted she would.

As Paniatowski was led along the high corridor to the earl's sitting room, she found herself wondering what to expect.

Would Gervaise de Courtney be wearing a flowery shirt and sitting barefoot on the floor, smoking a joint?

Or would he – despite his hippy aspirations – be dressed as his ancestors would have been, in a heavy tweed suit?

He turned out to be neither of those things. He was wearing a pair of faded jeans, a white shirt and a pullover that looked as if it had been bought from a chain store. He was a tall, slender man – so slender that Paniatowski was sure she could have encircled his wrist with her thumb and index finger. His nose was long and thin, his jaw had a soft delicate line, and his pale blonde hair just brushed lightly against his shoulders.

He was not alone. Sitting beside him in his parlour was a woman. She was perhaps a few years younger than him – say, thirty-five – with a good figure, a face which was pleasing rather than beautiful, and long red hair. She was definitely foreign, Paniatowski thought, and probably central European.

As the chief inspector was ushered into the room, the earl stood up and offered her his hand.

'I am Gervaise de Courtney, and this is my wife, Katerina,' he said. 'Do please take a seat.'

Paniatowski sat down in the armchair opposite the two-seater sofa occupied by the earl and the countess.

'The first thing I should make clear is that I am not at all happy about having you here,' the earl said.

'That's not very polite, Gervaise,' said his wife, in a mildly reproving voice and with an accent which confirmed Paniatowski's earlier suspicions.

The earl looked slightly shocked at the idea that his wife – and possibly his visitor – might have misinterpreted his words.

'You should not take what I have just said as implying any criticism of you, Chief Inspector Paniatowski,' he said hurriedly. 'It is merely that I do not trust the police.'

The countess gave an uneasy laugh. 'You're just making things worse, Gerv,' she said.

'Have you had a bad experience at the hands of the police?' Paniatowski enquired.

'Me, personally?' the earl replied. 'Of course not! I am a peer of the realm, and such is the class prejudice in this little country of ours that I could probably shoot someone in front of a dozen witnesses and still get away with it. But I do not trust the police in their handling of the poor, the dispossessed and the merely unconventional – and we are expecting people from all three of those classes to arrive here in the next few days.'

'If I may say so, you're showing a little prejudice yourself,' Paniatowski countered. 'Being a member of the poor, dispossessed or unconventional doesn't automatically imbue you with virtue.'

'I had not expected that sort of response from a police officer – and I take the fact that I am presented with it by you as a sign of sensitivity, which is really quite encouraging,' the earl said. 'You are quite right, of course, DCI Paniatowski. Not all members of those classes are model citizens, but the atmosphere we will create at our RockStately Festival will hopefully neutralize those base, vicious tendencies which run through us all. That is why I do not think we will need any kind of police presence – even *outside* the walls. Unfortunately, the authorities did not take the same view, and in order to get a licence for the festival, I was forced to agree to cooperate with the police.'

'I get the picture,' Paniatowski said.

'I'm not sure you do,' the earl said. 'I would like, if I may, to explain my motives in promoting this festival.'

'That won't be necessary,' Paniatowski said.

The earl looked flustered. 'My doctor says it is good for me to express my feelings,' he told her. 'He says that by explaining things to others, I am helping to explain them to myself.'

'Let him tell his story in his own way,' the countess said softly. 'Please, Chief Inspector.'

'All right,' Paniatowski agreed.

The earl seemed relieved. 'My family have been landowners for over six hundred years, and in that time we have ruthlessly stamped on any-one who tried to oppose us,' he said. 'For the last three hundred years, we have dispatched young-er family members out to the colonies, where they behaved in much the same way as they did at home – except that there, they were exploiting black people and brown people – and all so that we could continue to live in the lap of luxury. And never, in all those years, have we ever attempted to give anything back.'

'Keep calm, my darling,' the countess said soothingly.

'All the time I was growing up, I believed that there was no real purpose to life – or, at least, to *my* life,' the earl continued. 'I served in the army, and found it so brutish that I ... err ... fell ill. Then I joined the diplomatic service and was posted to Prague. The year was 1968.'

'The Prague Spring,' Paniatowski said, starting to understand where he was leading her.

'The Prague Spring,' the earl agreed. 'It was a brave attempt, by a brave government, to intro-duce a kind of socialism with a human face. For the first time since the Second World War, there was no press censorship in Czechoslovakia, and freedom of movement began to be regarded as a right. People were allowed to say what they thought, rather than what Moscow had decreed they should think. You should have been there, Chief Inspector. There was such a feeling of solidarity out on the streets – such a feeling of fraternity. It didn't matter what your background was, you were at one with everyone else, and you were all walking arm-in-arm towards a brighter future.'

'Gervaise is right,' the countess agreed. 'It was exactly like that in my poor country.'

'And then – without warning – the Russians invaded,' the earl said. 'They came overnight – ten thousand rumbling tanks and two hundred thousand foot-stamping soldiers. The tanks crushed the cobblestones in the streets of old Prague – stones which had lain there undisturbed for centuries. But they didn't just crush the stones – they crushed hope.'

'Even when we saw it, we still couldn't believe it was happening,' the countess said. 'It felt so *wrong*.'

'After a while, it put such a strain on me that I was almost taken ill again,' the earl said, 'and I went to America to recuperate. And that was my road to Damascus. That was where I had my epiphany – and it was called the Woodstock Festival. For three days, nearly half a million people endured the most appalling conditions, but instead of turning on each other like rats trapped in a cage, they chose to embrace *love*.'

Paniatowski smiled. 'I've seen the film,' she said.

'When I left that concert, I knew that something had changed forever inside everyone who had been there. We would all be ambassadors of the spirit of Woodstock, I thought, and that spirit would emanate from us and eventually conquer all. Politics could alter nothing, because the forces of repression could crush a political revolt, just as they had done in Czechoslovakia. But they couldn't crush love, because it wasn't just gathered on a street corner holding up placards – it was invisible and it was every-where, and its triumph was inevitable.'

'Are you sure you're all right, my dear?' the countess asked.

'I'm fine,' her husband assured her. 'But I was as wrong about Woodstock as I had been about the Prague Spring,' he told Paniatowski. 'The forces of repression would crush that spirit, too. But they wouldn't use tanks, as they had in Czechoslovakia, they would use the record companies and the mass media. They would drive out the good music – the music of hope and peace – and replace it with garbage which promised nothing but saccharine clichés. Yet, for a moment back then, there was real promise, and what I am offering now, with this festival, is a second chance to get it right.'

He stopped, breathless.

'You have explained it all wonderfully,' the countess said. 'In fact, I have never heard you express it better. But I think perhaps you now need a little quiet time on your own.'

'Yes, you're quite right,' the earl agreed, rising, slightly shakily, to his feet. 'I hope you will excuse me, Chief Inspector.'

'Of course,' Paniatowski said.

FOUR

DCI Wellbeloved leant forward on his desk and ran his eyes quickly up and down DS Meadows' body.

Slim figure, delicate features, and hair cut so unfashionably short it was almost as if she was wearing a velvet cap.

She wasn't the type of woman he'd normally lust after – he tended to favour them big, blonde and straightforward – yet he had to admit there was something indefinably exciting about her.

'What's your impression of DI Beresford, DS Meadows?' the chief inspector asked.

'DI Beresford?' Meadows repeated, as if she really didn't understand the question.

'DI Beresford,' Wellbeloved repeated patiently – because he understood that the lower ranks were very cautious about criticizing one of their superiors to another, and sometimes needed a little encouragement.

'DI Beresford is ... steady,' Meadows said.

Except for the times when he lets his dinosaur/caveman instincts take control, she added mentally.

'Steady,' Wellbeloved repeated, rolling the word carefully around his mouth, as if he were afraid of breaking it. 'That's just the word I

71

would have used myself. And we do need steady officers in the force. In fact, we'd be lost without them, wouldn't we?'

'It takes all sorts,' Meadows said, enigmatically.

'But when I look at DI Beresford, I can find little evidence of the flair and sparkle which were apparent the moment *you* walked into a room,' Wellbeloved told her.

'You're making me blush, sir,' Meadows said, though, if he was, there was no external sign of it.

'The problem is that police officers with drive – and I include both of us in that category, Sergeant – are sometimes resented by our slightly duller colleagues. They see us as a threat – and I got the distinct impression that DI Beresford sees *you* in that way.'

'Is that right, sir?' Meadows asked.

'Yes, it is. You see, Sergeant, he's probably begun to worry that his performance will look bad when compared to yours, and it's my guess that he'll decide to start undermining you, if only to ensure his own survival. Now, to be fair to him – because he seems a decent enough chap – he may not even realize that he's doing it. But whether it's intentional or not, his actions could really damage your career.' Wellbeloved paused again. 'Am I making any sense here?'

'Oh yes, sir, you most certainly are,' Meadows replied. 'In fact, I'd say that listening to you has been a real revelation.'

'Now I can't let your career be damaged – and for a purely selfish reason,' Wellbeloved said crisply. 'Any good DCI needs a good bagman – and I think you fit the bill. Do you see what I'm saying here?'

'Yes, sir – you're saying you'll watch my back.'

'And, in return, I'll expect you to watch mine.'

'That seems fair,' Meadows agreed.

'Excellent,' Wellbeloved said. 'Now there's one other small matter we need to clear up, and that's your record.'

'My record, sir?'

'According to the file, in the two years before transferring to Whitebridge, you worked for the West Midlands Traffic Division as a humble WPC.'

'Yes, sir, I did.'

'So could you explain to me how you managed to jump from uniformed constable to detective sergeant in one mighty bound?'

Meadows shrugged. 'I passed my sergeant's examination, and I'm very good in interviews, sir.'

'You could have passed the exam with flying colours and been positively brilliant in the interview, and you still wouldn't have got such a huge promotion,' Wellbeloved said. He smiled encouragingly. 'Tell me what really happened, Kate. I can assure you, it will go no further.'

'I don't know what to say,' Meadows told him, with a confusion in her voice that Wellbeloved didn't believe for a moment was genuine. 'I applied for the job, and I got it. If you want further details, perhaps you should ask Mr Baxter or the West Midlands Constabulary.'

Wellbeloved glared at her. 'I would have thought, Sergeant, that given the understanding we've just established, you would have been a little franker with me,' he said.

'And, with the greatest respect, sir, I would have thought, for the same reason, that you'd never have asked me that particular question in the first place,' Meadows countered.

'You can go,' Wellbeloved growled.

'Thank you, sir,' Meadows replied.

The countess had insisted that they should take afternoon tea in the rose garden, and Paniatowski had not seen how she could refuse.

There were just the two of them there, sitting on teak garden chairs, with a slatted teak table between them. The air around them was heavy with the heat and soaked with the scent of roses, and Paniatowski felt almost as if she were trapped in an Edwardian engraving.

'Our gardeners are very clever,' the countess said, as she poured tea from a delicate china pot. 'Do you know, they manage to keep some roses in bloom for almost the entire year? I suppose that must be because we grow so many different species here.'

'Yes, I suppose it must be,' Paniatowski agreed.

The butler had brought sandwiches, scones and a variety of cakes, but neither woman seemed inclined to try any of them.

As they sat sipping their tea, Paniatowski said, 'This has all the trappings of a social occasion, but it really isn't one, you know.'

'No, you're quite right, it isn't,' the countess agreed. She took a deep breath. 'What do you think of my husband, Chief Inspector?'

'It's not really for me to express any opinion about him, one way or the other,' Paniatowski replied guardedly.

'Then if you will not tell me what you think, I will tell *you* what you think,' the countess said. 'You see him as a passionate idealist, but also as a rather weak man. You think that if he had not been born rich and privileged, he would have made virtually no impression on the world at all. And you curse the fact that he *is* rich, because that means he can make life more difficult for you. Is that a fair assessment of your thoughts?'

'Now, you couldn't possibly expect me to comment on that,' Paniatowski said.

The countess nodded, as if no comment was all the comment she needed to confirm her suspicions.

'You're wrong about him, Chief Inspector,' she said. 'Gervaise is a sensitive man, but he is also a man of great strength. I first met him in Prague, after the Warsaw Pact army had invaded. My husband – my first husband – was a liberal activist, and he had been arrested. It was pointless to ask the new Czech authorities to do anything about it – they had been hand-picked by Moscow just after the invasion – but one of my husband's grandmothers had been English, so I went to the British Embassy to see if they could help. I was told the ambassador and first secretary would be unable to see me, and I was fobbed off with Gervaise, who held a very low position in the embassy pecking order. He seemed very sympathetic, and he promised he would do what he could, but I thought that was no more than words, and when I left the building, I was in tears.' The countess paused, and an almost blissful smile came to her face. 'But, of course, I didn't know Gervaise then like I know him now.'

'From which I take it that he *did* try to help.'

'He did more than I could ever have hoped for, even in my wildest dreams. In his search of my husband, he went to places where even the bravest of Jan's friends would not have dared to go.' The countess paused again. 'You're thinking it was easy for him,' she said, almost accusingly. 'You're thinking that because he was not Czech and had diplomatic immunity, he was quite safe. Isn't that right?'

'Well, yes,' Paniatowski admitted.

'You're quite wrong, but I can't blame you for that. No one who was not there at the time could ever imagine what Prague was like for those few months in 1968, when the Prague Spring turned into the Soviet Winter.'

Despite the heat in the rose garden, Paniatowski shivered as she remembered the years that she and her mother had spent on the run in central Europe, with both the Russians and the Nazis constantly on their tail.

'So what was it like?' she asked.

'Russia sent in some of its crack troops on the first wave of the invasion. They were well-disciplined, and knew that they had a role to play in the propaganda part of the operation, as well as in the military part. The official version of events, you see, was that they had only invaded to protect the Czech people from a government which had betrayed them, and they acted like kindly liberators, even though they were nothing of the sort. But the elite forces did not stay once resistance had been crushed.'

'Why was that?'

'I suppose – though I do not know it for a fact – that Moscow feared there might be other parts of the empire which would try to follow our example, and those troops were deployed to deter them. At any rate, they left, and the task of keeping the order they had established was put in the hands of other soldiers who had not been so carefully selected.'

'And they caused problems?' Paniatowski guessed.

'And they caused problems,' the countess confirmed. 'They were mostly uneducated conscripts – Ukrainian peasants with the dirt still under their fingernails, Uzbek cotton pickers who had never even seen a big town before, never mind a sophisticated city like Prague. They didn't even know where they were, let alone why they were there. They had been treated brutally during their time in the army, and had become brutal themselves. They looted and raped and were drunk all the time – and they got away with it, for who would dare lodge a complaint against a member of the "liberating" army.'

'I'm getting the picture,' Paniatowski said.

'Moving amongst men like that, a diplomatic passport provided no protection at all,' the countess said. 'Their own world was narrow and ignorant, and I doubt if most of them had any idea of what a diplomat was. Once, a group of them beat Gervaise up badly, and on another occasion, he came within a hair's breath of being stood against a wall and shot. He didn't tell me any of this himself, by the way – I learned it from another source entirely.'

'It must have taken considerable courage.'

'It did – and despite the setbacks and the dangers, he kept on looking until he eventually found out what had happened to my husband.'

'And was he...?'

'He was dead. The authorities said he'd had a heart attack, and perhaps, because of what they put him through while he was in custody, that was, strictly speaking, quite true.'

'How awful for you,' Paniatowski said.

'Yes, it was, though, in a way, it was a relief to know he was gone,' the countess replied. 'You tell yourself he may still come back, but there is a part of you – deep inside – which knows he never will. Yet you can only truly begin to mourn when you know for certain that he's dead.' The countess wiped a tear from her eye with her napkin. 'But this is not about me, and it is not about my first husband. It is about Gervaise. Why do you think he tried so hard to find Jan? Was it out of a sense of duty, do you think – because he was an embassy official and my husband had an English grandmother?'

'No,' Paniatowski said softly. 'It wasn't because it was his duty, it was because he had fallen in love with you.'

She and her mother had been taken under the wing of an Englishman, too, when they were thin and shivering and trying to scratch out an existence in Berlin, just after the war ended. But Lieutenant Arthur Jones hadn't brought them to his own country because of love, he had done it for much darker reasons – and a few years later, when Monika, still a child, had woken up one night and found Jones in her bed, she had finally realized what those reasons were.

'Yes, Gervaise did it because he had fallen in love with me,' the countess said. 'And what a love that was – a love which had, as its only objective, my happiness. A love which knew that in restoring that happiness of mine – in finding my husband for me – it would be denying happiness for itself forever.'

'It's breathtaking,' Paniatowski gasped.

The countess smiled. 'And once I was free to choose, how could I *not* love a man who had loved me like that?' she asked.

It seemed strange for there to be only three of them at the corner table in the Drum and Monkey. But it could have been worse – Wellbeloved could have been sitting in Paniatowski's chair.

'I don't mind the new boss being a bastard,' Meadows said, sipping at her tonic water. 'I can take bastards in my stride. What I don't like is the fact that he's also a complete bloody idiot.'

'What makes you say that?' Beresford asked, reaching for his pint.

'His game plan,' Meadows said.

'His game plan?' Beresford repeated, mystified.

In the good old days – when Monika Paniatowski was still in charge – Meadows would have sighed in theatrical exasperation at Beresford's obtuseness. But these were not the good old days. Paniatowski was gone, and those who survived her needed to stick together – which meant that antagonizing the inspector really wasn't a very good idea.

And so, instead, she turned to Crane and said, 'I'm guessing that when he spoke to you, Jack, he reminded you that you were both university men, and that was bound to cause resentment and downright jealousy among the lesser mortals in the force.'

'He did say more or less that,' Crane confirmed, 'but he couldn't quite disguise the fact that he thought that while a double first from Oxford was all very commendable in its way, a two-year sandwich course in criminology from Birmingham University was of much more use in modern policing.'

Meadows nodded. 'Stupid,' she said. 'And I'd be willing to bet that he told you, sir, that we were after both your jobs, and that people of inspector rank and above need to stick together.'

'Yes, he did,' Beresford said thoughtfully.

'What he was banking on was that we'd feel so insecure about our new situation that we'd lie to each other about what had been said. And with a lot of teams, that would have worked, but in building her team, the boss has taught us how to trust each other, so it hasn't. Still, it was a stupid risk for him to have taken.'

'So his game plan is to turn us against each other, is it?' Beresford asked.

'Yes, but not too much – not so we're going at each other's throats – just distrustful enough to make us all rather dependent on him.' Meadows shook her head. 'It's no good – he'll have to go.'

'How do you expect to get rid of a DCI, Sarge?' Crane asked.

'I don't know yet,' Meadows said, 'but where there's a will, there's usually a way.'

'When he was interviewing me, he seemed a little unhappy about your history in the force before you came to Whitebridge,' Beresford said.

'Did he?' Meadows asked, as if it was of no interest to her.

'Yes,' Beresford persisted. 'Why was that?'

Meadows sighed. 'I suppose it was because my file says I was working for the West Midland Traffic Division.'

'And were you?'

'My file says I was, so I must have been.'

'What were you *really* doing?' asked Crane, who had made it a personal challenge to try and piece together as much about Meadows' background as he possibly could.

What had she really been doing?

She has been undercover for over a year, living among the vicious and cruel, and working so hard at pretending to be one of them that she wonders if she will ever be able to find her old self again.

It took her months to even get on the fringes of the Pagans' motorcycle gang, and it has taken even longer to get close to Doc, the charismatic six-foot-eight giant who leads them. But she has done it, and is not surprised when her handler sends her a message that Chief Superintendent Addison would like to have an urgent meeting with her.

The meeting, under the tightest possible security, takes place in a run-down motel just outside Birmingham.

Addison is in his late forties. He has the body of a rugby prop forward who doesn't get enough exercise any more, and hooded eyes which could be either dangerous or greedy.

He looks more than pleased to see her.

'We've been trying to infiltrate the Pagans for years – and had no luck at all,' he says. 'When your chief inspector said you could do it, I thought he was mad, because if we couldn't even get a man into the charmed circle, how the hell did we hope to achieve anything with a woman? But he was right, and I was wrong. How did *you do it?'*

She shrugs. 'In some ways, being a woman made it easier, because that was the last thing they expected.'

Suddenly, Addison's eyes are alive with excitement.

'You must have had to do some terrible things to get them on your side,' he says. 'Some terrible disgusting things.'

His salacious interest sickens her. Yes, she has had to do some disgusting things, but she isn't

82

going to recount them now just to stoke this man's pornographic imagination, which is already causing his eyes to bulge.

'I did what needed to be done,' she says, and there is an edge to her tone which tells him he will get no more out of this line of questioning.

'Are you sure those fingerprints you gave us were Doc's?' he asks, doing his best to hide his disappointment by changing the subject.

'Certain.'

'We checked them thoroughly. They're not on record.'

'Then he must never have been arrested.'

'And you're sure he's the actual leader of the gang, are you?' Addison asks sceptically.

'He's the leader,' Meadows confirms. 'It's beyond doubt.'

'And yet we know nothing about him.'

'From the odd thing he's let slip, I'm almost certain he was a real doctor at one time,' Meadows says.

'His gang has been causing a great deal of trouble, and the top brass want him banged up as soon as possible,' Addison tells her. 'There's one hell of a lot of pressure on us to put him behind bars. Careers – including yours – may well depend on it.'

'I need more time to collect evidence,' Meadows says.

'There is no more time,' Addison counters. 'The deputy chief constable's applied for a new job, and by the time he goes for interview, he wants a few triumphs under his belt.'

'I'd like to help if I could,' Meadows says,

83

although she couldn't really give a damn about the deputy chief constable's promotion prospects.

'There's been a string of unpleasant attacks on schoolgirls while you've been working under cover,' Addison says. 'One of the victims actually died from the internal injuries she received, and we've been getting considerable flack from the press over it.'

She says nothing – there doesn't seem to be anything to say.

'We'd like to charge your friend, Doc, with those attacks,' the chief superintendent says.

'There are a lot of terrible things Doc would do without even thinking about it – but raping schoolgirls isn't one of them,' Meadows replies. 'He likes his women big. He likes them to be able to give as good as they get.'

'I didn't say he did it,' Addison replies, with a chill in his voice. 'I said we were going to charge him with it.'

'And what will you use for evidence?'

'The university boys back at headquarters are a bunch of wankers, but they can sometimes be useful. And on this occasion – by using statistical analysis and other such mumbo-jumbo – they've come up with a pattern which ties in the Pagans' movements very closely to the scenes of the attacks.'

'I wouldn't have thought that was enough,' Meadows says.

'It isn't,' Addison agrees. He smiles. 'The prosecution will be mainly based on the testimony of an undercover detective sergeant.'

84

She can hear the words – can understand them perfectly – but she still can't quite believe that they're actually being spoken.

She looks around the motel room. The armchairs are worn and faded. The sheets on the bed have a bleached look, but even the bleach has not succeeded in quite removing the stains of a thousand hasty lunchtime encounters.

The whole place is sordid – but nowhere near as sordid as the proposal that Chief Superintendent Addison is making to her now.

'How can I testify to something I didn't see and don't even believe happened?' she asks.

'You'll be given a good script that will have been written to tie in with circumstantial evidence,' Addison tells her. 'And remember, Kate, Doc might not have done what we'll charge him with, but he'll have done plenty of things that are just as bad.'

'What about the real rapist, who'll still be at liberty?' she wonders aloud. 'What about his future victims?'

'The important thing is to get Doc off the street,' Addison says, and there's an odd tone to his voice now, as if he's just realized she's not quite as intelligent as he thought she was.

'But you'll still be looking for the real rapist, even once he's banged up, won't you?' Meadows asks.

'Of course we will,' Addison says quickly.

Far too quickly!

'I don't see how you'd justify an ongoing investigation, since you'd be claiming to have already caught the guilty man,' Meadows says.

'You're a mere detective sergeant,' Addison says, and there is real ice creeping into his voice now. 'It is not for you to question department policy and procedures.'

'I'll tell you what I think you'll do,' Meadows says. 'I think you'll put the investigation on hold until the rapist strikes again, and you'll claim it's a copycat crime.'

'By putting Doc in gaol, you'll have taken a menace off the streets, and you'll get a promotion for it,' Addison says. 'That really should be quite enough for you, Sergeant.'

'I won't do it,' Meadows says firmly. 'I won't put innocent girls at future risk just so a few fat cats in headquarters can add another scalp to their belts.'

'I don't think you should be so hasty, Kate,' Addison says. 'I really think you should give the matter your serious consideration.'

'I won't do it.'

'Well, in that case,' Addison says, 'the sooner you're transferred out of the West Midland police, the better.'

The transfer comes though – with record speed – two weeks later. It is not good policing to take her off the case at that stage, but this is to do with fear and revenge, rather than policing.

She has turned down an offer which should never have been made, and so that offer itself has had to be written out of history, just as her undercover work has now been written out of her record.

She does not complain, because she knows it

86

would do no good – and because she has come to cherish the police work which has finally given her life some meaning.

'Sarge? Are you all right?' said the voice.

It seemed hollow and unreal – like words spoken into a metal bucket. But it made Meadows realize that for some time – and she had no idea how long – her mind had not been in the public bar of the Drum and Monkey, but back in that sordid Birmingham motel room.

'Sarge?' Crane repeated.

'I can't tell you what I did in the West Midlands, Jack,' she said. 'And even if I could – and trust me on this – you really wouldn't want to know.'

Most nights when she got home from work, Louisa would either be waiting for her in the hallway or doing her school work in the study they shared. And however hard her day had been – and whatever tasks still lay ahead of her – Paniatowski would always find half an hour to spend with her daughter.

Sometimes they would talk about what Louisa had done at school that day. Sometimes – increasingly, now that Louisa was older and had expressed a strong desire to join the force – they would talk in very general terms about Paniatowski's work. And sometimes they would talk about seemingly nothing at all – and have a great time doing it!

That night, there was no healing conversation. That night, Paniatowski was greeted by an empty house, because it was the school holidays, and Louisa was spending a couple of weeks with her great-aunt Pilar in Valencia.

It was as Paniatowski was preparing herself a nightcap that the phone in the hallway rang.

'It's so totally 1950s to have a phone in the hallway, Mum,' Louisa always said. *'Why don't we have one installed in the living room,'* and then she would invariably add cunningly, *'and while we're at it, we might as well put one in my bedroom as well.'*

She *would* have a phone put in Louisa's bedroom, Paniatowski promised herself. She'd do it soon, as a 'welcome back' present. But, in the meantime, it was still in the hall, and she supposed she'd better answer it.

'Hello Monika, it's Reg Holmes here,' said the voice at the other end of the line. 'The reason I'm calling you is that I've just had a briefing session with the chief constable, and it wasn't really very satisfactory at all.'

'Why was that, sir?'

'Well, he explained my own remit to me – keep an eye on the campsite but don't make the police presence too conspicuous unless things start to go wrong, et cetera, et cetera – and then he said that you'll be based at the Hall itself. What I missed – or rather, what Mr Baxter failed to explain – is exactly what your role will be. And when I pressed him on it, he started to get very irritated for some reason.'

He got irritated because he's feeling guilty, Paniatowski thought. He knows he's doing the wrong thing, but he just can't stop himself.

'Are you still there, Monika?' DCS Holmes asked.

'Yes, sir.'

'Anyway, I've been trying to work out for myself exactly what your job will be, and I can't do it for the life of me. I know you won't be in charge of security within the grounds, because I hear they've employed a gang of thugs for that. That is what they've done, isn't it?'

'Yes, that's what they've done.'

'It seems like a bloody stupid idea to me, but it's their stately home, so I suppose it's their business. But all that would seem to leave *you* with is observer status – and that clearly can't be the case, because you're a high-ranking officer. So what exactly *is* Georgie Boy expecting you to do?'

'I'm there as an adviser,' Paniatowski said, thinking, as the words came out, how hollow they sounded.

There was a long pause at the other end of the line – and in the silence, she could almost hear Holmes' brain clicking as he joined up the dots and reached the inevitable conclusion.

Finally, he said, 'Ah, I see. An adviser. Well, thank you for explaining that to me.'

'Are we still on for dinner at the Trocadero, a week on Thursday?' Paniatowski asked – mainly to confirm her own suspicions.

Another pause – even longer this time.

'Actually, my schedule's getting rather jammed up, so we should probably take a rain check on the meal out,' he said finally.

'How about making it the week *after* next,

then? I could ring up and book it, if you like.'

'That's a possibly,' Holmes said vaguely. 'But I wouldn't like to commit myself at the moment. Tell you what – when things become clearer, I'll let you know. All right?'

'All right,' Paniatowski agreed.

'Good night, Monika.'

'Good night, sir.'

He couldn't get off the phone quickly enough, Paniatowski thought, as she replaced her own phone on its cradle.

'When things become clearer,' Holmes had said.

But what he really meant was that things were suddenly becoming *very* clear – and that since Paniatowski's career seemed to be heading straight for the rocks, it was time for the wilier rats to start jumping ship.

'I wish you were here, Louisa,' she said to the empty hallway. 'I *really* wish you were here.'

FIVE

Thursday, 5th August

'Where is it you said you were going, Jeff?' Mona Hill shouted from the balcony of the master bedroom, from where she was watching the way that the Filipino maid packed her husband's suitcases.

Jeff Hill, who was sitting on a sun lounger by the pool and smoking a large cigar, looked up, and called back, 'Whitebridge.'

And he was thinking, 'Why must she scream like a fishwife? Does the woman have *no* class?'

'It seems like a funny place to me to be holding a sales conference,' Mona said.

'It's where all the cotton mills are,' Hill told her, adding, almost under his breath, 'you ignorant bitch!'

'I though they'd all moved to India, or somewhere like that,' Mona said suspiciously.

'Most of them have moved, but not all. And people who buy the JHSG brand expect top quality – which means made in Britain.'

Mona retreated back into the master bedroom – no doubt to criticize the way the poor bloody maid was doing her job – and Hill took another generous puff of his cigar.

91

As a matter of fact, he reminded himself, most of his products *were* made in India – it was much cheaper to use child labour thousands of miles away than it was to use adult labour close at hand – but Mona didn't know that, and she was too thick to find out.

There was one school of thought in the footballing world which confidently asserted that Jeff Hill had been the best English player to emerge since the end of the War, and another – equally sure of itself – which contended that he had merely been the dirtiest.

There was something to said on both sides – he had certainly been a hard man on the pitch, but he had also been an amazingly successful one, and the last time he had been transferred (to Honnerton United, in 1969) his new club had paid two hundred and twenty thousand pounds for him, which was a record fee at the time.

Most people thought it was bad luck – though there were those who considered it no more than just retribution – that he should get a serious knee injury only a year into his new contract. The injury had effectively ended his football career, but as one door had slammed shut on him, another had opened, and making use of both the money he had saved and his great national fame, he had launched Jeff Hill Sporting Goods, which soon became one of the leading firms in its sector.

Seeing his wife appear at the patio door and begin to walk towards the pool, Hill sighed and took a sip of his whisky.

'You're not seeing a woman, are you?' Mona

demanded, when she drew level with him.

'A woman?' he repeated. 'Whatever would make you think that?'

'Well, it's not as if it hasn't happened before, now is it?'

Hill did his best to try and look cut to the quick.

'I made one mistake – four years ago – and you won't let me forget it, will you?' he asked, mournfully.

'If it *was* just one mistake,' Mona countered. 'If that hussy wasn't just the last of a long line.'

'I swear to you, she was the only one,' Hill promised.

He would dearly love to get rid of this bloody woman, he thought, but not at the cost of her taking half his assets with her.

'Why don't I come with you to Whitebridge?' Mona suggested.

'We've been through all this before,' Hill said wearily. 'The sales conference is also a trade fair – which means it's strictly business. I'll be involved in some tough negotiations with some very hard men, and in a situation like that, it's the one who blinks first who loses out.'

'I still don't see...'

'Nobody else who's there will be taking their wives with them, and if I take mine, that's as good as saying I'm henpecked. And henpecked husbands don't get offered good terms.'

'But how do I know I can trust you?' Mona asked in that plaintive voice he hated so much.

'Listen,' Hill said, 'if I really was playing around with another woman, don't you think I'd take her somewhere nice – like the South of France? Can you seriously see me having an affair in a dull, grimy town like Whitebridge?'

'No, I suppose not,' Mona admitted.

Idiot! Hill thought.

When Linda Davies examined her life so far – all seventeen years of it – she felt compelled to give it a mixed review. On the one hand, she had been blessed with the voice of a Southern share-cropper – a voice which was harsh and powerful, passionate and angry, yet could be so softly beautiful that it could bring grown men to tears – and all without the necessity of ever visiting the USA or picking cotton. On the other hand she had been cursed with parents who were middle class and – what was even worse – liberal.

It wasn't that she didn't love her parents. She really *did* love both of them. But through their kindness and compassion, they were making it very hard for her to grow into being a real rock star.

Harsh, conservative parents would have been much easier to handle. She could have run away from home, and slept in doorways until she was discovered by a travelling band which was desperately in need of a singer.

Uncaring, neglectful parents would have been better, too. She could have endured an unhappy childhood which might have left her with mental scars, but would have made her performances even more gut wrenching.

Instead, she had Tom and Helen Davies!

'We only want what's best for you, darling,'

her mother had said, two years earlier, when she'd announced that she wanted to join the Midnight Crawlers. 'Your happiness is really all we care about.'

'Does that mean you're going to try and stop me being a singer?' she'd asked, half-hoping they'd finally give her something to rebel against.

'Of course not, sweetheart,' her father had said soothingly. 'You have a wonderful voice, and while we can't say we're entirely happy about the songs you choose to sing—'

'They are rather depressing,' her mother had interrupted. 'Couldn't you find something a little more cheerful?'

'A *happy* blues, do you mean?' Linda had asked. 'The "Life Is Wonderful And Everything's Coming Up Roses" blues, for example?'

'...and while we can't say we're entirely happy about the songs you choose to sing,' her father ploughed on, regardless, 'we can both see that it would be a shame not to use that voice.'

'So what are you saying?' Linda had asked.

'That we're perfectly willing to allow you to play your "music" with your friends...'

'They're not my *friends*, for goodness sake – they're my *band*.'

'...with your band, then. But you're still very young and we need to be sure you're being looked after.'

'Are you saying that every time I play a gig you'll want to come with me?' Linda had asked.

'No, we're not saying that at all. We're not quite as out of touch as you seem to think, and we realize that having us tag along would prove to be something of an embarrassment for you.'

'Well, thank heavens for that.'

'But when you do a show which takes you away from home overnight, I'm afraid we're going to have to insist that either Dominic or Charles goes along as a chaperone.'

She'd agreed to pay her parents' price, and every time the Midnight Crawlers had played a gig outside the London area, one of her two brothers had been there by her side.

The band never said anything about it – they couldn't afford to, because they knew that with her they were going places, and without her they were going nowhere – but she was certain that they were laughing at her behind her back.

As the band's fame had spread and they spent more and more time touring, it became plain that the arrangements simply couldn't stay as they were, and the elder of her two brothers, Dominic, had become her manager.

He was working for *her*!

She was paying *him*!

At least, that was how it looked on paper. But in practice, Dominic was not so much a manager who also happened to be her brother as a brother who did a little managing on the side.

And so it was that on stage she could be a second Janis Joplin – a mesmerizing force of nature – but once she walked off stage again, she became – under Dominic's watchful eye – Little Miss Perfect.

But that was all about to change. The Rock-Stately Festival was the biggest venue the Midnight Crawlers had ever played, and she knew she would be a sensation. And when she climbed down from the stage, she would still be the same person she had been while she was dominating it – and if Dominic didn't like that, he could just go and get stuffed.

Paniatowski looked around the small room in the west wing of Stamford Hall. The place was crammed with television monitors.

'So what do you think of my electronic control centre,' asked Edward Bell, giving the last three words a slightly mocking tone which didn't quite hide his sense of pride.

'It's very impressive,' Paniatowski said. 'Who came up with the idea? Was it you? Or was it the earl?'

'Neither of us, actually,' Bell admitted. 'The original idea came from a very bright young chap who came to see me shortly after the first advertisements for the RockStately Festival appeared. He said he wasn't really interested in selling the equipment – he was more what you might call a researcher – but he wondered if we'd do him a favour.'

'Oh yes?' said Paniatowski, who could smell a sales technique from a mile away.

'Apparently, his company had been looking around for somewhere suitable to test out all the new surveillance equipment they'd developed, and they almost couldn't believe their luck when they heard about the festival. Anyway, he asked if he could set up a couple of cameras – just to show me what they could do – and I have to say,

I was most impressed.'

Paniatowski suppressed a smile. Edward Bell might be both intelligent and educated, but he was scarcely sophisticated, and it was plain that he'd been as dazzled by the 'very bright young chap' as one of his ancestors would have been by an itinerant magician.

'So what happened next?' she asked.

'I agreed to let him set up a system which covered the whole estate – a *comprehensive* system, he called it. Well, it seemed the least I could do, after he'd gone to so much trouble.'

'And all this was free?'

'Absolutely free. Of course, once the festival is over, I'll have the opportunity of buying the equipment, but since it will be good publicity for the company to have their cameras installed in one of the finest stately homes in England, he's promised me I can have it at a very substantial discount.'

The bright young chap is banking on the fact that once you've got used to it, you'll wonder how you ever managed without it, Paniatowski thought.

'So everybody wins,' she said aloud.

'Well, exactly,' Bell agreed. 'Let me show you how it works.'

He flicked a switch on the control board. One of the screens lit up to reveal a panoramic view across the grounds towards the East Gate, where the builders were putting the final touches to the stage.

'And when you get bored of looking at that, you can look at this,' Bell said, flicking a second

98

switch.

A second monitor covered the section of the park which led down to Backend Woods.

'Where are the actual cameras?' Paniatowski asked.

'All over the place,' Bell told her. 'Most of them have been set up on things that were already there, or, to put it another way,' he grinned, 'they've been "deployed on pre-existing natural or man-made objects".'

'They would be the bright young man's words, would they?' Paniatowski asked, grinning back.

'That's right,' Bell agreed. 'There are cameras mounted on some of the follies and in the trees. They're not exactly hidden, but if you didn't know they were there, you probably wouldn't notice them. That, according to our young friend again, is to make them blend in with their environment.'

'I'm impressed,' Paniatowski said.

And also a little envious, she thought.

The Mid-Lancs Police could use this kind of set-up, but given the budgetary restraints, it was as unlikely to get it as it was to discover that Superman had signed up as a special constable.

'Maybe I can persuade your bright young man to use the centre of Whitebridge as his next testing area,' she said, whimsically.

'Well, you can but ask,' Bell agreed. 'I certainly feel happier in my own mind now that I've got these cameras.'

'Or perhaps I could borrow yours, because – after all – the Devil's Disciples are providing you with all the security *you* could possibly need,' Paniatowski said, teasing him a little.

But then she saw just how uncomfortable her remark seemed to make Bell feel, and she was sorry she'd spoken.

'It's just a bit of extra insurance,' Bell said awkwardly.

'Yes, I can see that,' she agreed readily.

In his position, Bell needed to be a real mental gymnast, she thought. There was a part of his brain which insisted – which *had* to insist – that the earl's judgement was not to be questioned. But at the same time, there was another part of it which knew that if you relied solely on the Devil's Disciples for your security, you were asking for trouble. And somehow – except when some smart-arsed detective chief inspector made a thoughtless remark – he managed to keep these two parts of his brain from talking to each other.

'The reason I've shown you this set-up is because I thought you might like to help me out,' Bell said.

'Help you out?'

'Yes. I haven't got the manpower to have the cameras monitored round the clock, so what I thought I'd do instead was to come up here whenever I have the chance, and review the tapes.'

'That sounds like a sensible plan.'

'And I was thinking that perhaps – if you can spare the time – you'd do some of that monitoring for me. After all, you're the one with the trained eye, so you'd probably spot things that I'd miss.'

The suggestion was an act of kindness on his

part, she thought – an attempt to make her feel useful – but if even people *outside* the force were starting to pity her, then she was really up Shit Creek without a paddle.

Jane Lewis watched as her husband packed his suitcase. He was making a bit of a mess of it – she could have fitted things in much more neatly – but since he'd lost his job, he'd been insisting on doing any number of things he'd been quite happy to have her do previously. It all came down to the fact that now he was no longer providing for his family, he had to prove himself useful in other ways, she supposed, but really, there was no need for it.

'You still haven't told me where you're going,' she said, as she watched him packing shirts in a way which would virtually ensure that they would come out of the case looking as if they'd been slept in.

'I'm going to Whitebridge,' Terry replied, not looking up.

'And why are you going there?'

'I'm following a lead.'

'What kind of lead?'

'I don't want to go into that, now.'

It hadn't been his fault he'd lost his job on the Globe, Jane thought – or at least, she added in fairness, not entirely his fault. The problem was that he was too easily led – that though he'd never instigate anything dubious himself, he found it hard not to go along with it once someone else had.

'Have you got a commission for this story

you're chasing down, Terry?' she asked.

Now, her husband *did* look up – and there was anger in his eyes.

'Of course it's not on a bloody commission,' he snorted. 'Who would give a marked man like me a commission?'

'So how are you...?'

'I'm paying my own expenses – if that's what you're asking.'

'You mean that *we* – the family – will be paying the expenses,' Jane said quietly.

'Anything we've got, we've got because I earned it!' Terry said hotly. Then, a look of shame swept across his face. 'I'm sorry. I should never have said that. We're a partnership. I've earned the money, you've made a home for the family – and a wonderful home it is.'

'It's just that we have hardly any savings left,' Jane said. 'Certainly not enough to throw away on some story that may, or may not, come to anything.'

'It's not just *any* story,' Terry told her. 'It's huge. If I can land it, all the editors on Fleet Street will be biting each other on the leg to get it, and I'll be pretty much able to write my own ticket. A month from now I'll have a staff job again – a much better one than I had before.'

'*If* you can land it,' Jane said.

'I will,' he promised her. 'I'm ahead of the game on this one. No other hack will be able to steal the story from me this time – because no-body else even knows there *is* a story.'

'I'm worried about you being away on your own,' Jane said.

'You mean, you're worried I might drink myself into a stupor?'

'Yes.'

'I promise you, there'll be no drinking on this trip. It's far too important.' Terry looked down at his suitcase. 'I seem to have made a real mess of that,' he said. 'There's no chance you could re-pack it for me, is there?'

She smiled at him. It seemed a long time since that had happened.

'Of course I'll repack it,' she said. 'But I might have to *re-iron* some of the stuff first.'

Terry's lower lip quivered. 'I love you, you know,' he said.

'I know you do,' Jane replied. 'And *I* love you.'

The Devil's Disciples were on the move up the M6 motorway – forty-three powerful bikes in a convoy led by Badger, with his two lieutenants, Chainsaw and Sharkteeth, immediately behind him.

Spike was somewhere in the middle of the column, but that had not always been his place.

In the early days, when he had only recently been through the initiation ceremony, he had ridden at the tail end, forced to suck in the exhaust fumes of more fortunate men.

Now, he could turn around and see all the newer recruits behind him – and when he did, he experienced a rush of pride even more invigorating than the wind which was ruffling through his hair.

It was a wonderful thing to be part of something much bigger than you were, he thought – it was a wonderful thing, after all that had happened in his life, to finally *belong*.

They were approaching a motorway service station. Badger signalled he was about to turn, and behind him a line of indicators rippled like the muscles on a large and dangerous snake about to strike.

The gang saw the other motorbikes the moment they pulled in to the car park. In fact, it would have been hard to miss them, since there were over forty machines in all. They were parked some distance from the café, and each had a red dragon displayed prominently on its petrol tank.

'Christ, it's the Welsh Dragons!' Spike said softly to himself.

The Devil's Disciples had many enemies up and down the country – 'You can tell how important you are by the number of gangs that want to kick your heads in,' Badger always said – but the Dragons were one of the most formidable.

Twice, during Spike's time with the Disciples, they had clashed with the Dragons. Twice, both sides had taken a bloody beating. And the beatings hadn't been the end of it. The battles had been so fierce that they hadn't even broken up when the police in riot gear had arrived, and several Disciples and several Dragons had ended up serving short prison sentences.

The Dragons had left no one guarding their bikes – to have posted a guard would have been to suggest they were worried someone might be brave enough to damage their hogs – and so there was nothing to prevent Badger riding up to them, which was exactly what he did.

Badger dismounted, put his bike on its stand, and looked around. To his left, several large lorries were parked. To his right, there were a few mid-range cars, probably being driven by commercial travellers. And just beyond the café, there was a grassy area with picnic tables.

He's picking out his spot for the rumble, Spike thought, and though he personally would have preferred not to have to fight at all, he felt his adrenalin start to pump.

Several Dragons had already appeared in the café doorway and were watching with keen interest, but they would not attack yet – not as long as the Devil's Disciples were so close to their machines.

Chainsaw and Sharkteeth had dismounted, and were in consultation with their leader.

And it was then that one of the newer members of the gang – a lad called Ferret – decided to do something that he probably thought would show initiative and might even attract admiration.

Getting off his own bike, he strolled up and down in front of the bikes belonging to the Dragons.

'Poxy Welsh bastards!' he shouted in the direction of the café. 'Call these hogs – I wouldn't put my granny on one of these.'

And leaning forward slightly, he spat on the petrol tank of the nearest bike.

Badger swung round and squared up to him.

'What the bloody hell do you think you're doing, you stupid dickhead?' he screamed.

'I ... I...' stuttered Ferret, who realized he had made a mistake, though he had no actual idea what that mistake might be.

From the moment Ferret had spat on the bike, the Dragons had been tensing up for a charge. They didn't want to fight so close to their own machines – of course they didn't – but there were some insults they simply couldn't allow to go unchallenged.

Now, however, seeing the way Badger was reacting, they held back, and waited to see what would happen next.

'The Dragons might be shit, but their bikes aren't – and the bikes deserve your respect,' Badger bawled at Ferret.

'I'm sorry, I didn't...' the boy mumbled.

Badger hit him in the stomach. Ferret sank to his knees, Badger followed through with a boot to the chest, and Ferret was lying on the ground, his body in a fetal position, his hands covering his head.

Badger walked around him several times, lashing out with his foot as he circled.

'You don't...' (kick) '...disrespect the bikes...' (kick) '...you don't...' (kick) '...disrespect the bikes...' (kick) '...have you got that?'

Ferret groaned.

'Get him up,' Badger said.

Chainsaw and Sharkteeth hauled Ferret to his feet. Despite Ferret's efforts to protect his head, Badger had managed to catch him a blow in the face, so his right eye was almost closed and his cheek was already turning purple.

'Let go of him,' Badger said.

Chainsaw and Sharkteeth released their grip. It looked as if Ferret would fall over again, then, by a massive effort, he managed to retain his balance.

'Clean that machine,' Badger said, pointing to the petrol tank that Ferret had spat on.

Ferret moved unsteadily to the motor bike and raised his arms, as if he was about to rub his sleeve along the tank.

'Not with your colours, you bastard!' Badger yelled. 'Use your bloody tongue!'

Ferret hesitated, as if he were about to appeal against his punishment. Then – perhaps accepting that any attempt at appeal would only make matters worse – he leant stiffly forward and licked the tank.

Twice, Ferret looked up from his task, his eyes wide with doglike pleading, in the hope that his leader would say he'd done enough. Each time, Badger shook his head.

Then, finally, Badger tapped Ferret on the shoulder, to signal that the humiliation was over.

'Can you still ride your machine?' Badger asked, when Ferret had straightened up. 'Because if you can't ride, I'll leave you here for the Dragons to deal with.'

'I can ride,' Ferret groaned.

'Get on your bike, then,' Badger said. He turned to the rest of the gang. 'We're moving out.'

Spike did his best to analyse what he had just witnessed. He strongly suspected that Badger had not been anything like as angry and outraged as he seemed to be, that it had, in fact, all been a pretence brought on by his need to find an excuse – any excuse – not to have to fight the Red Dragons.

But why wouldn't Badger *want* to fight the Dragons? Spike had never known him to back away from a confrontation before. Usually, it was quite the reverse – usually, he went out of his way to provoke other gangs.

The only possible explanation was that he didn't want the Disciples getting into any trouble with the police at that time. And the reason he didn't want trouble – the reason he was prepared to run the risk of being mocked as a coward by the Dragons, and perhaps even by his own members – was because he didn't want to be late for the RockStately Festival.

And that meant that, for some reason Spike couldn't even begin to guess at, the festival was very important indeed to Badger.

The Devil's Disciples moved out. The Red Dragons did not jeer at them for retreating. In fact, they seemed to have appreciated Badger's gesture, and raised their arms in what could almost have been a token of friendship.

And that was what made Badger a great leader, Spike thought – he knew exactly when to push things, and how hard that push had to be.

SIX

From the monitors in the control room, Paniatowski and Bell watched the column of motorcycles arriving at the East Gate.

'There's over forty of them,' Paniatowski said.

'Forty-three, according to what I was told in
advance,' Bell told her. 'That's not a lot, really,
when you consider they'll have to control upwards of a hundred and fifty thousand people.
Still, if the earl's right – and I'm sure he is – it'll
all be peace and love once the festival's started,
so they shouldn't need much controlling at all,
should they?'

The column came to a halt, and the lead motor-
cyclist dismounted and approached the gate. A
man appeared at the other side of the gate, and
they seemed to be exchanging words.

'That's the head gardener, Walter Brown,' Bell
explained. 'He's a responsible chap – well, he
has to be, to control a team of eleven other
gardeners – and I've put him in charge the gate
during the festival. I'm sure he'll do a good job,
and he's very eager to help – like me, he wants
the festival to be a big success, if only for the
earl's sake – but he's already fretting about
having to desert his greenhouses.'

The head gardener opened the gate, and then

109

walked back to his Land Rover. When he pulled off, the Devil's Disciples followed.

'He's taking them straight to Backend Wood. I'll give them a bit of time to settle in, then I'll pay them a visit – just to let them know what's expected of them and what their duties will be.'

'I'll come with you,' Paniatowski said.

Bell shook his head, almost mournfully.

'I'm afraid that won't be possible, Chief Inspector,' he said.

'What do you mean – *it won't be possible?*'

'The earl doesn't want you to have any contact with the gang. They don't like the police, and he thinks it might upset them.'

'What if I insist?' Paniatowski asked.

But she knew that she *couldn't* insist. This was private land – in the most literal sense of the word – and on it, the earl's word was absolute law. If she disobeyed him, the earl would ask her to leave, and she would have to go. That would give George Baxter a reason for accusing her of not doing her job properly, and it would be another nail in the coffin he was building for her career.

'You're not *going to* insist, are you?' asked Bell, offering her a way out.

'No,' she said, grasping it gratefully. 'If those are the earl's wishes, then I suppose we must respect them.'

'By the way, where's your bag?' Bell asked.

'My bag?'

'The one with your clothes in it.'

'I have no idea what you're talking about.'

'Oh,' Bell said, confused. 'I was told you'd be staying here, round the clock, for the next five days.'

'*Who* told you that?'

'I got a call from your headquarters. I assumed, of course, that you knew all about it, but ... err...' The estate manager was growing more and more uncomfortable. 'Anyway, if you decide to use it, I've had a room made up for you in the east wing. I think you'll find it very comfortable.'

'I didn't ... I haven't...' Paniatowski spluttered.

Why was this move to marginalize her – more than any of the other strokes that George Baxter had pulled in the previous two days – having such an effect on her, she wondered.

Perhaps it was because the chief constable now seemed to think that he'd pushed her so far out on a limb that he didn't even need to speak to her directly any more.

She felt both insulted and humiliated to learn what his orders were through a civilian – and that was exactly what she had been intended to feel!

She took a deep breath. 'If you'll excuse me, Mr Bell, I think I need a little fresh air.'

She rushed out the room, down along a corridor, and out through one of the numerous narrow side doors which had been installed in previous centuries to enable the servants to move around freely without having to cast their unworthy shadows over those of their betters.

She was planning to head for the nearest bushes, but her stomach was not prepared to wait that long, and before she was even halfway there, she doubled up and vomited.

'It's only a job,' she told herself, as her stomach heaved. 'Things could be much worse. You could have cancer! Louisa could have cancer! You don't *have to be* a police officer.'

But she *wanted* to be a police officer, she thought, as she straightened up. Being a police officer was the second most important thing in her life.

A sudden flash of light from above distracted her from her misery, and she looked up. The flash had come from the roof, but she couldn't actually see what had caused it.

There was a second flash, a little to the left, and she saw a man standing close to the edge of the roof and holding a pair of binoculars. He was only there for a second, then he moved closer to the centre, and she lost sight of him. She couldn't be sure, but she thought it was the earl. And though she couldn't know for certain why he had gone up there, either, she guessed it was to track the progress of the Devil's Disciples through the estate.

'Nasty thing, an upset stomach,' said a voice to her left, and turning, she saw Edward Bell examining her pile of vomit.

'I ... I'm sorry,' she gasped.

'You don't have to apologize for catching a bug,' Bell said easily. 'And it won't take one of the staff more than a minute to clear it up.' He looked her up and down. 'You're very pale. Would you like me to show you where your room is, so you can lie down for a while?'

Paniatowski's legs had turned to water, and her head was swimming.

'Thank you,' she said weakly. 'I'd appreciate that.'

The row of Jaguars, lined up and awaiting valet parking, made Jeff Hill, sitting behind the wheel of his own XJ6, frown with displeasure.

There had been a time when driving a Jag had meant something, he thought, but now every little jumped-up market trader and sports socks manufacturer seemed to be able to afford one – which meant that it was time for him to get shut of his Jag, and buy a Lamborghini or a top-of-the-range Mercedes.

'But if you do that, Bloody Mona will automatically assume you've done it to impress women,' he said aloud.

As if a sporting hero like him needed a big car to talk a bit of loose into his bed!

One of the garage staff – a lad of around eighteen – tapped on his window, and Hill opened the door with such speed that the boy had to jump back to avoid being hit by it.

'Does that window look like a door knocker to you, you bloody idiot?' Hill demanded.

'No, sir, but...'

'Then don't bloody knock on it. I'm the customer here, in case you hadn't noticed, and if you want to speak to me, you stand where I can see you, and wait until I'm ready.'

'Sorry, sir,' the boy said. 'I only came to tell you I'm ready to park your car now.'

'And not before bloody time,' Hill growled, climbing out of the Jag and holding out his car keys.

'Wait a minute,' the boy said, taking the keys. 'Aren't you Jeff Hill?'

'That's right.'

'My dad took me to see the '68 Cup Final. Watching you slam that second goal in was the best moment of my life.'

Hill had been inclined to dislike the boy at first, but now he was warming to him.

'Sorry I snapped at you just then, son,' he said, 'but it's been a very long day.'

The youth grinned. 'Don't worry about it – it's an honour to be bawled out by you, Mr Hill,' he said.

Well, of course it was, Hill agreed silently.

He reached into his pocket, pulled out his billfold and peeled off a five pound note.

'Look after my car properly,' he said.

'I don't want your money, Mr Hill,' the boy said.

'Take it,' Hill said, stuffing the note into the boy's top pocket with one hand, and ruffling his hair with the other.

Feeling better about himself – and about the world in general – he walked around the car, and entered the hotel through the main door.

A large sign, stretched across the top of the reception desk, said: 'The Royal Victoria Hotel welcomes the British Sports Manufacturers Association.'

He looked around, and saw Baby Doll – looking as luscious as ever – sitting near the entrance to the bar, drinking a gin and tonic. Once he had established that she was there, he looked straight through her, which was no mean feat, given that, the moment she'd spotted him, she'd rapidly adjusted her position to show him a generous length of thigh.

The mistake that most men made with their bits of stuff on the side was to pretend that the two of them were just friends or close acquaintances, he thought, as he walked up to the reception desk. And the *reason* it was a mistake was that once they'd established that connection, other people paid them extra attention, just to see if there was more to it than that.

That was why a clever man – and he considered himself, looking at the matter objectively, a *very* clever man – maintained a much greater distance from whoever he happened to be poking at the time.

Certainly, he'd spoken to Baby Doll in public – they were in the same business, so there was no use pretending he had no idea who she was – but no one had ever seen them doing any more than exchange passing pleasantries.

If they were drinking in the same bar, they sat at opposite ends of the room. If they were in the same restaurant, they made sure they were facing in different directions.

And that distance helped make the whole affair even better, because by the time they did get together – late at night, in one of their rooms – they'd been waiting for so long to touch each other that the sex was red hot.

It was a perfect system, and if Mona was hoping to catch him at it again – and thus take an arm and a leg off him in the divorce court – then she was due for a big disappointment.

* * *

'George Baxter speaking,' said the voice at the other end of the line.

'It appears you intend me to stay at the Hall for the whole of the festival,' Paniatowski said.

'Yes, I thought I'd already made that plain,' Baxter replied.

Like hell he had!

'There's no point in me being here all the time,' she said. 'They're taking care of their own internal security – and, the way things stand, I have absolutely no authority to do *anything*.'

'Not even *moral* authority?' Baxter taunted. 'Most police officers – most *good* police officers, I should say – consider moral authority to be one of the strongest weapons in their armoury.'

'Listen—' Paniatowski began.

'No, *you* listen, Detective Chief Inspector Paniatowski,' Baxter interrupted her. 'The earl will allow me to have only one officer within the grounds, and you are the officer that I have selected. I want you there, for the whole period, in case anything goes wrong, because if something *does* go wrong, I'll need a credible witness – by which I mean a fairly high-ranking officer – to testify that, given the restrictions imposed on me by the earl, there was simply nothing I could have done about it.'

It sounded plausible – but it wasn't true. What Baxter really wanted, if anything went wrong, was someone to take the fall.

She could almost hear him addressing the disciplinary board – 'I posted DCI Paniatowski to Stamford Hall because she had an excellent record. We now know that she was no longer up to the job. I accept responsibility for failing to notice that, though I feel I must add, in my own defence, that rather than coming to me and expressing her doubts about her ability to handle the situation, she chose instead to carry on as normal.'

He *wanted* something to go wrong, she suddenly realized – he was *praying* for something to go wrong.

'Listen to me, George,' she said. 'Please listen to me. It wasn't my fault that Jo died. I had nothing to do with it.'

There was a sudden loud thud at the other end – as if Baxter had slammed his fist down hard on the desk, or perhaps thrown something against the wall – and then the line went dead.

If the Devil's Disciples' camp were to be viewed from the air, it would look like a random scattering of tents, Spike thought, but there was nothing random about the way that Badger set up camp.

He would always start by selecting a clearing which would be the centre – the heart – of the camp. It would be at this central point that all the communal activities – the gang-bangs, the drinking sessions, the arm-wrestling competitions – took place. It would be, in other words, a sort of peripatetic clubhouse, which both proclaimed the Devil's Disciples' identity and reaffirmed it.

The tents would fan out from this clearing, with roughly a quarter of them going in each direction. No one tent would be that close to any other tent, not because the Devil's Disciples cherished their privacy – a Disciple *had* no privacy, everything he was and everything he owned was no more than part of the large, dangerous beast which was the gang. No, it was done purely on strategic grounds, because, with no focal point for an attack, an enemy – and the Devil's Disciples had plenty – could not deliver a quick knockout blow.

Even here at Stamford Hall, surrounded as they were by high walls, Badger took the same precautions he always did, Spike noted. Even here, he had not neglected to post a couple of sentries at the edge of the woods. And this caution of his was just as admirable, in some ways, as his obvious bravery in battle.

Once the tents were all pegged down, Badger called the gang to the clearing. The other Devil's Disciples sat down on the ground, but Badger remained standing, with his two lieutenants flanking him – a clear indication that this meeting was about 'official' business, and therefore carried with it the force of law.

'This isn't the first time we've worked security,' Badger told the other Disciples. 'Most of you will remember how we "kept order" at the crappy old house in Derbyshire.'

Oh yes, I remember it, Spike thought.

The 'crappy old house' had been a rather fine – though somewhat dilapidated – Georgian mansion. It could have been truly beautiful if it had been lovingly restored, but the owners, a property development firm, were not in the least bit interested in restoration.

The meeting takes place in an out-of-the-way pub called the King's Head, which is run by an old woman who is both deaf and has a pronounced limp. It is a cold, unwelcoming place, and there are very few other customers, which is probably why this particular venue was selected.

There are three Devil's Disciples at the meeting – Badger, Chainsaw and Spike. Spike knows why he is there – Badger is assessing him to see whether or not he has the potential, at some time in the future, to become a lieutenant – and he is bursting with both pride and apprehension.

The other two men at the table both have hard, uncaring eyes, and are wearing flashy – though obviously expensive – Italian suits. When they reach for their drinks, Spike notes that while the older one is wearing heavy gold cuff-links, the younger has opted for little links with diamonds in them.

It is the older of the two who makes the running.

'It was a sweet deal we'd got going for us,' he says. 'We were going to knock the building down, throw up half a dozen executive-style houses which look pretty good on the surface, and then sell them on before the roofs started leaking and the doors began to warp.'

He's not bothering to lie to us, Spike thinks. With most people he'd at least make some pretence of being an honest business man, but we're not even worth that small effort.

And then he thinks, but why should he lie to us? We're the Devil's Disciples – and we don't play by normal rules. Isn't it really a compliment that he's being so frank with us?

'Things were going beautifully,' the second man – Diamond Cufflinks – says. 'We spread a bit of money round in the town council planning committee, and we got their permission to knock the place down.'

'But then the local conservation society stuck its oar in,' Gold Cufflinks continues. 'They claimed it's a listed building.'

'And is it?' Spike asks, before he can stop himself.

Both suits glare at him.

'What's that got to do with anything?' Gold Cufflinks asks.

'Nothing,' Spike mumbles, aware that Badger's eyes are on him, and that the look in them is not one of approval.

'Anyway, they file an appeal, and in the meantime they take out an injunction to stop us demolishing the place. Now normally, we'd have ignored that. Once the building's gone, it's gone, and by the time they get around to fining the company for knocking it down without permission, that company doesn't exist any more – we've already filed for bankruptcy, and we're off running some other business entirely,' Diamond Cufflinks says.

'But this conservation group's smarter than most,' Gold Cufflinks says. 'It's organized a human chain to stand around the building – and that chain's there twenty-four hours a day.'

'They'd soon shift themselves if they saw the bulldozers coming at them,' Badger says.

'Maybe they would,' Gold Cufflinks agrees. 'Or maybe they'd decide to call our bluff. And we can't risk one of them getting killed, because that would really sink the deal.'

'On the other hand,' Diamond Cufflinks says, 'we've got no objection to a few of them getting hurt.'

It is late afternoon. A dozen Devil's Disciples are sitting on their machines at the crest of a small hill, on the road which descends to the old mansion. The wall around the mansion has already gone – knocked down before the conservationists really realized what was happening – but it has been replaced by a human chain which is keeping the bulldozers at bay.

The chain is made up of all kinds of people. There are old ladies in Burberry overcoats and green Wellington boots. There are middle-aged men smoking pipes and reading newspapers (probably the Guardian, Spike thinks) and middle-aged women who have learned how to knit while standing up.

But it is the line of around fifty young people – the boys mostly long-haired, the girls all dressed in smart casuals – that attracts Badger's attention.

'Students!' he says.

And the word comes from deep in his throat, like the growl of a dangerous dog.

He really hates students, Spike realizes. They represent everything he isn't, and he takes even their presence there as a personal insult.

'Leave the old bags alone,' Badger says, as he

pulls his bandanna up to cover his mouth and nose. 'It's them hippy bastards we'll go for. And no knives, no razors – just fists.'

The Devil's Disciples go down the hill at full throttle, heading towards the students. Even from a distance, Spike can sense the panic among the young people, and it is no surprise at all that the line breaks up to allow the Devil's Disciples through.

The bikes are going at some speed when they reach the bottom of the hill, and Spike is forced to slam on his brakes to avoid smashing into the side of the house. He goes into a back-wheel skid, but he had expected this, and so is ready to ride with it.

The bike stops moving, and Spike stamps his left foot down hard on the ground, to hold it. Around him, he can see half a dozen other Devil's Disciples doing the same.

The whole thing has been much easier than he had thought it would be, and no one has got hurt. He feels a great sense of relief – and then he looks over his shoulder, and sees that the students have regrouped.

Badger has already dismounted from his machine, and is walking towards the line, screaming obscenities at the top of his voice. He sounds angry, but Spike doesn't think he is. All he is really doing is hyping himself up for battle – and he is glad the line has chosen to resist.

As Badger gets closer to the line, several of the male students adopt a fighting stance. Perhaps some of them really do know how to fight – perhaps some have even boxed for their college

– but it won't do them any good.

They should attack him now, while they still have the advantage of numbers on their side, Spike thinks. But the students just stand there, waiting for Badger to make the first move.

Badger raises his fist, as if he is about to lash out at the student directly in front of him, then twists to the side, and kicks one of the other boys on the kneecap. The boy howls in pain, and goes down, but before he hits the ground, Badger has kicked him again, this time in the face.

There are perhaps four or five seconds when the students surrounding the fallen boy gape at him in stunned silence. And when they do start to move – to help their wounded colleague or perhaps defend him from further harm – it is already too late.

The rest of the Devil's Disciples attack the same part of the line – gouging, kicking, punching. More of the students drop to the ground.

Further down the line there is confusion, and the chain splinters and young men and women turn to look at the violence which is being enacted a few yards from them – a violence which is nothing like the violence they have seen in the movies, but involves cracked bones, broken teeth and real blood.

It only takes a few of the students to retreat for the retreat to become a stampede.

In the background, the bulldozers roar angrily into life, and start to edge forward.

The Devil's Disciples step back, and allow waiting building workers to carry away the injured, leaving a clear path for the heavy machines.

By the time the bulldozers reach the old house, there is no longer a protective chain, merely a mass of dazed individuals, well away from the action, who still can't believe what they've just seen.

The first bulldozer reaches the house. Its blade smashes into the wall, and two hundred and fifty years of history is turned to dust.

Later, when the Devil's Disciples are back at their camp, celebrating with the beer the property developers' money has bought for them, Spike finds a quiet corner of the woods in which to do some thinking.

What had happened that afternoon was a very different thing to the pitched battles the Devil's Disciples had with other gangs, he thinks. It was somehow less honourable.

But there were more of them than us, he argues. They outnumbered us ten to one.

Yes, but you could put ten novices on one side of a chess board and a grand master on the other, and that still wouldn't make it a fair fight.

He wonders if he should leave the Devil's Disciples. But he has never stuck with anything – seen it through – in his entire life, and this may be his last chance. Besides, he does not want to disappoint Badger, who is grooming him.

The students could have fought back and they could have run away right at the start, he tells himself, but they did neither, so what happened to them was entirely their fault.

The crisis of conscience he has been experi-

encing is banished for the present – but it will return.

Spike was not sure how long he had been on his trip back through time, but Badger was still speaking, so it might have been only a few seconds.

'When we did them students, we were paid to hurt them,' Badger was saying. 'This time it's going to be very different – this time we're being paid to *stop* them getting hurt.'

Several of the Devil's Disciples looked puzzled – perhaps even perplexed – because what their leader was outlining seemed almost *law-abiding.*

'We're going to play it straight,' Badger continued, expanding on the point. 'We're going to do the job they want us to do. And there'll be other changes this time, as well. Normally, it's Chainsaw and Sharkteeth who run things when I'm not around to do it myself, but they'll be busy this weekend, so I'm putting Lobo and Spike in charge.'

The words echoed around Spike's head.

I'm putting Lobo and Spike in charge.

I'm putting Lobo and Spike in charge.

He had never been put in charge of anything before, and he was both proud and terrified.

He wanted to tell Badger how honoured he was.

He wanted to jump up and down, like an excited kid on his birthday.

But he knew he couldn't do either of those things, so instead he just nodded, as if it was all

125

in a day's work.

'Lobo and Spike will be in charge of actual security, but I'll still be there, watching you,' Badger said gravely. 'And here's what I'll be watching for – I'll be watching for you getting drunk, I'll be watching for you starting fights, and I'll be watching for you messing with the hippy chicks. Anybody who does any of those things will have to deal with me.' He paused, and looked down at Ferret. 'Do you understand that, Ferret?'

The warning wasn't really aimed at Ferret at all, Spike thought. After what had happened outside the motorway café, it would be a long time before Ferret contemplated stepping out of line again.

No, it wasn't aimed at Ferret – instead, it was Ferret *himself* who was the warning. It was the left side of his face, now a deep purple, which would serve as a reminder of what could happen if you didn't do exactly what Badger said.

'Five days isn't too long to have to behave yourself,' Badger said, his voice now more reasonable and persuasive, 'and I promise you that once we're out of here, we'll have a real week of ... What was that fancy word you used the other day, Spike?'

A sudden chill ran down Spike's spine. He had thought that Badger either hadn't heard, or failed to register, the 'fancy word' he'd used – but Badger didn't miss a thing.

'Well, what is the word?' Badger demanded.

'Mayhem,' Spike said.

'That's right,' Badger agreed. 'We'll have a

whole week of pure bloody mayhem.'

The use of the word at that particular moment had been no coincidence, Spike told himself.

It had been a warning to him, as much as Ferret's battered face had been a warning to the others.

It had said, 'I know you're a bit bloody odd, and I'll be keeping an eye on you.'

That was the way Badger worked – perhaps the way all leaders worked – using both the carrot and the stick.

The carrot – I'm promoting you.

The stick – if what's different about you becomes a problem, it will be dealt with.

It made Spike uneasy to have both these things hovering above his head at the same time – but it was still a marked improvement on his childhood, when there had *only* been the stick.

PART TWO

'Rock 'n' Roll Suicide'

6th–9th August

SEVEN

Friday, 6th August

Jeff Hill was trying to work out how he'd got inside this room that seemed to have no window and doors, but the bloody ringing in his ears was making it very difficult to think.

He'd been at the sales conference's opening night drinks' party.

He remembered that.

Baby Doll had been there, too, and when he'd bumped into her – totally accidentally, as it had happened – he'd said, 'Nice to see you,' in a disinterested, couldn't-wait-to-get-away tone.

Clever Jeff – clever little sporting hero!

The problem was that the fleeting contact had sent his libido into overdrive, and several times during the course of the evening, he'd caught himself looking at her lustfully – which wasn't clever at all.

He supposed that was when he had starting drinking heavily, in some sort of attempt to assuage the impatient demon that lived in his underpants, but that – of course – had only made matters worse.

So what had happened next?

The party slowly fizzled out – as such parties

tended to – until the only people left were a small group of men who spent much of their free time fighting a valiant battle against encroaching middle age. One of the members of this group – more aware than the rest of the growing hostility of the waiters whose shift had officially ended half an hour earlier – had finally suggested that they wrap up the evening with a nightcap in the bar, and it would have been highly suspicious if jovial Jeff Hill – who was well known to be always up for a drink – had said no.

So he *hadn't* said no. In fact, he had been so enthusiastic about the idea that by the time they reached the bar, most of the revellers were convinced it had been Jeff's idea in the first place.

They'd had three or four before they finally called it a night. Was *that* when he ended up in this windowless room?

No. What he'd done after that was go up to his *own* room – and he'd made sure his drinking companions had *seen* that that was where he went.

And then?

Then he had waited for half an hour – fighting off the urge to fall asleep – before making his way down to Baby Doll's room on the floor below.

Had they done the dirty deed once he was there? He didn't know for sure, but he suspected they hadn't.

But none of that came even close to explaining the closed room or the ringing sound.

He looked up and saw a great hollow metal

object swinging to and fro above his head.

A bell! He was inside a bloody bell!

But how could he even *see* the bell, when he knew for a fact that his eyes were shut tight?

He opened his eyes – for real, this time – and then quickly closed them again when they found the light too painful.

He wasn't in a bloody bell at all. He was in a bloody bed – probably Baby Doll's bed.

He opened his eyes again – more cautiously this time – and tried to focus on the alarm clock which had so disturbed his dreams.

Seven thirty-five!

Shit, he had his first meeting of the day in less than an hour. And worse – far worse – than turning up late for that meeting, was the fact that, at seven thirty-five in the morning, there were probably already quite a lot of people moving around in the hotel.

He hit the alarm clock button with the palm of his hand, and climbed out of bed.

'Well, you weren't much good last night,' said a sleepy voice from beneath the covers.

'What time did you set the clock for?' he demanded.

'What?'

'The alarm clock! What time did you set it for last night?'

'Half past six, like you asked me to.'

He had slept through nearly an hour of the bloody thing, he thought, searching around the room for his clothes. How could he have been so stupid?

His suit and his shirt were on the chair, his

socks, vest and underpants were strewn on the floor. He had no idea where his shoes were, but he'd worry about that once he was dressed.

Baby Doll got out of bed and went into the bathroom.

Hill dressed at high speed, then looked around for his shoes. They didn't seem to be anywhere.

Baby Doll came out of the bathroom again, wearing a white hotel dressing gown.

'I can't find my shoes,' Hill said.

'Have you checked under the bed?'

'Now why – in God's name – would my shoes be under the bloody bed?' he asked, irritably.

But that was where they were.

He slipped on the shoes, laced them up, and moved over to the door. There was no noise in the corridor outside, so maybe he'd get lucky.

'Sorry about my performance last night,' he said. 'I'll be back on form tonight.'

'You'd better be, or I'm trading you in for a new – younger – model,' Baby Doll told him.

He put his hand on the door knob.

The most dangerous moment of his escape was the one in which he left Baby Doll's room and exposed himself to the wider world, he thought. And the second most dangerous moment came immediately after it – walking along the corridor on a floor where he had no business to be.

After that, it was a doddle. Once he had reached the emergency stairs at the end of the corridor – once he was actually *on* them – he could have come from anywhere and be going anywhere, and there would be nothing at all to tie him to Baby Doll.

He listened for a second, with his ear pressed up against the door, took a deep breath and turned the handle.

It was as he was stepping into the corridor that he saw the man turn the corner. He was a pretty average-looking feller – around thirty-five, brown hair, maybe five feet nine – and yet there was something vaguely familiar about him.

To retreat into the room would be fatal. There was nothing for it but to try and brazen it out.

Hill headed down the corridor towards the man – walking neither too slow nor too fast, and trying to look like someone who had so much on his mind that he was hardly registering the fact there was anyone else there.

The two passed each other, and he was almost at the fire doors when he heard a bedroom door back down the corridor open, and a woman's voice call, 'You've forgotten your tie, Jeff!'

He turned around. Baby Doll – the stupid bitch – was actually in her doorway, waving his tie at him. And not only that, but the other man had turned around too, and was taking in the whole scene.

There were a number of things he *could have* said, some of them smart and some of them stupid. But if he'd sat down and thought about it for a long, long time, he could not possibly have come up with anything quite as stupid as what he *did* actually say.

'You've made a mistake,' he told her. 'My name's not Jeff.'

He turned again, and strode quickly down the

corridor. And with each heavy footfall, a single word was reverberating around his head.

'Shit, shit, shit, shit, *shit.*'

Chief Superintendent Holmes had never ridden in a helicopter before, and every time it banked he made a mental resolution never to ride in one again. Yet despite his growing belief that he should never have put his faith in aeronautical science, he was forced to admit that being up in this rattling death machine did give him a wonderfully strategic view of the area around Stamford Hall, and made policing the flow of traffic so much easier.

The festival-goers – or the scruffy, layabout, dope-smoking sex mad students, as he preferred to think of them – had started arriving in the afternoon of the previous day. Some had come in beaten-up vans with crude logos daubed on their sides, some on motorcycles, and some in cars (which they had no doubt cajoled their weak-willed parents into lending them). The majority, however, had reached the site via the special buses which were running a shuttle service between Whitebridge railway station and the Hall.

Official police estimates were that around thirty thousand had reached the site by the time night fell, and the tent city they had thrown up was already covering several fields which, in Holmes' opinion, could have been put to much better use.

And it would only get worse, he thought. Already, the roads around Whitebridge were becoming clogged, and this was only Friday.

136

Come Saturday, when the other scruffy lay-abouts – the ones who pretended to work for a living – were free, there would be a positive deluge.

He didn't see the point of the festival at all. If the layabouts wanted to listen to loud jungle music, why didn't they just stay at home and turn their gramophones up to full volume?

The helicopter swooped over the Hall, and he found himself thinking about Monika Paniatowski, trapped – with no real job to do – inside the walls. She was being badly treated – very badly treated – and she had his sympathy. He would have liked to help if he could, but – when all was said and done – a man with his own career to think of didn't want to make any waves.

A solid metal turnstile had been installed at the East Gate, and after passing through it, the fans would be inside the wire-netting enclosure. The stage stood at the opposite end of the enclosure from the gate, and it was planned that the acts would enter it through the back, from the part of the grounds which hadn't been fenced off.

'Everything seems to be moving along exceptionally smoothly,' Edward Bell said to Paniatowski, as they stood on the stage, looking down. 'The festival starts at six o'clock. The opening act, by the way, is called Long Sad Day. Have you ever heard of them?'

'No,' Paniatowski admitted, 'I can't say I have.'

'Neither had I, until just before I booked them,' Bell said.

'*You* booked them?' Paniatowski asked, surprised.

'That's right,' Bell agreed. 'It turns out that, as well as all the other things that I do around Stamford Hall, I'm also a rock concert promoter. Whoever would have thought it?'

Paniatowski grinned. 'You're not being serious, are you?'

'No, not entirely,' Bell said. 'The earl had a few acts he particularly wanted to appear, and I got in touch with them myself, but an agency in London organized most of it, from contacting the groups to handling the ticket sales. Still, I *am* the one who had the final say – because I'm the one who signed the cheques.'

'How much did the whole thing cost?'

'You really don't want to know,' Bell said, with a slight shudder. 'But as I told the dowager countess when she asked,' he continued, sounding more optimistic, 'with a bit of luck we might just break even.'

It was a pointless exercise to be standing there on the stage at all, Paniatowski thought, because Edward Bell was right – everything was running smoothly without her having to lift a finger.

And even if things *ceased* to run smoothly, there was nothing she could do, without the necessary authority, to make things right.

She couldn't even talk to the motorcycle gang, for Christ's sake, because the earl – in his infinite wisdom – had decided that it would be far too upsetting for a hardened bunch like the Devil's Disciples to actually come into contact with one unarmed police officer.

So, if she couldn't be of any use where she was, why didn't she simply go back to the Hall?

Because there was no point in *that*, either!

Say she did go back to the Hall – what would she do once she was there?

Go up to the room that Edward Bell had allocated her?

Lie on the bed, in a fetal position, feeling even sorrier for herself than she was already?

Bell looked at his watch. 'Do you fancy a bite of lunch at the Lodge, Chief Inspector?' he asked.

'Where's the Lodge? Is it a pub?'

'Bless you, no – it's where I live.'

Paniatowski hesitated. 'I wouldn't like to intrude.'

'It'll be no intrusion,' Bell assured her. 'It was my missus who came up with the idea of inviting you round, and she'll be expecting you.'

Jeff Hill knew where he had seen the man in the corridor before. It had been a little more than a year earlier – in the divorce courts.

Hill is there as a character witness for his mate, Dave Langtree, another ex-footballer who has made good after leaving the game, though in his case it is as the host of a nationally televised chat show.

Hill has already given his evidence, under oath.

'I cannot swear that Dave Langtree has not committed adultery,' he has testified. 'How could I, unless I was with him twenty-four hours a day, every day of the year? But I will say this, the

139

Dave I know has never had eyes for any woman but his wife.'

He's been lying, of course – Dave Langtree is, and always has been, randier than a stoat in heat – but the lie had been delivered with complete sincerity and conviction, and if you can't take the word of a sporting hero, then who can you believe?

Terry Lewis takes the stand. Under the guidance of Elaine Langtree's barrister, he outlines how – in order to obtain a story for the Sunday Gazette, the newspaper he worked for – he had secretly followed Langtree around for several weeks.

'And what did he see, during that time, which is of any relevance to this hearing?' Elaine's barrister asks.

'On five occasions, I saw him enter a motel room with a woman I now know to be Lucy Hetherington,' Lewis answers.

Elaine's barrister nods complacently, and sits down.

Dave's barrister rises to his feet.

'You have no proof of these wild accusations you've just made, have you?' he asks.

'I had proof at the time,' Lewis answers.

'At what time?'

'At the time I made them – the time when we were planning to run the story in the Gazette.'

'And what was the nature of this proof?'

'I'd taken several dozen time-stamped photographs of them entering and leaving the motel rooms I mentioned earlier.'

'Then perhaps you can show these "several

dozen time-stamped photographs" to the court.'

'I said I had them at the time – I don't have them now.'

'Why not?'

'I gave them to my editor.'

'Then perhaps he can show them to us.'

'He denies ever having received them.'

'Ah, I see!' the barrister says. 'No further questions.'

'Three days after I gave him the photographs, Dave Langtree agreed to write a weekly column for the Gazette,' Lewis blurts out.

'I said, no further questions,' the barrister reminds him.

'All the papers in Fleet Street were desperate to have him writing a column for them, and he'd turned every one of them down. So why did he agree to write for the Gazette? There can be only one reason. He did it because he was black-mailed into doing it.'

'You should be more careful with the words you use, or the next time you appear in court it will be because you're being sued for slander by either your editor or Mr Langtree himself,' the judge warns him.

'With your lordship's permission, I think I will ask a few more questions after all,' the barrister says.

'After that extraordinary outburst from the witness, I think you're certainly entitled to,' the judge agrees.

'You got fired from your job on the Gazette, didn't you, Mr Lewis?' the barrister asks.

'Yes.'

'*And why was that?*'

'*Because Dave Langtree* wanted *me off the paper as revenge for me putting him in such a difficult position. I think it was part of the deal he struck with my editor when he agreed to write the column.*'

'*Really? That's what you think, is it? Well, I put it to you that that was not the case at all. I put it to you that you went to see Mr Langtree, and threatened him that if he didn't give you a considerable amount of money, you would go to his wife and tell her the same cock-and-bull story you've just told to this court. But Mr Langtree, who had done absolutely nothing wrong, refused to be intimidated. And being the nasty, vindictive sort of person you are, you went to see Mrs Langtree anyway – and* that *was when your editor fired you.*'

'*I did go to Mrs Langtree,*' Lewis admits, '*but only* after *I'd lost my job – and I never asked either of them for a penny.*'

'*So, two conflicting stories, then – yours and Mr Langtree's,*' the barrister says. '*I wonder which one the court will believe.*'

Elaine had not got her divorce on that occasion, though later Dave had agreed to one based on the 'no fault' principle. She'd walked away with a fraction of the money she would have got if the adultery had been proved, and Dave had become a real hero with his drinking mates.

But not every story could have the same happy ending, Hill thought. Lewis might not have any proof *this* time either, but he'd only to drop the whisper in Mona's ear and she wouldn't rest until she'd found enough proof herself to take him for everything he owned.

So Lewis had to be dealt with. One way or another, he simply had to be dealt with.

Edward Bell's cottage – the Lodge – was near the North Gate. It was a rectangular building, redbrick and grey slate, two stories high. The windows were smaller than those in modern houses, and the window frames, like the doors, were made of solid oak. Running along the side of the house there was a vegetable garden – as neat and tidy as any ever shown on a television gardening show – and just beyond it there was a small orchard.

Bell parked the Land Rover close to the back door – which was open – and immediately two small brown dogs appeared from inside the house, wagging their tails and barking furiously.

'Well, here it is, home sweet home,' Bell said, as he fussed over the dogs. 'What do you think?'

'Very nice,' Paniatowski replied.

Bell laughed. 'What you're really thinking is that it's a bit small – and maybe a bit humble – for a man with a couple of university degrees who runs an estate worth millions of pounds.'

'I wasn't thinking that at all,' Paniatowski lied.

'Every year, the earl offers me a bigger house, and every year I point out that if my ancestors – who sometimes had as many as nine or ten children – could live in this house, then it should be more than comfortable enough for a man who only has two kids.'

'Well, as long as you're happy with it,' Pania-towski said, feeling a little inadequate.

'It's not so much that I'm happy with it as that I'd be miserable *without* it,' Bell confessed. 'My family's history is steeped into these bricks. Their presence is in the very air.' He paused. 'My great-grandfather was nearly a hundred when he died. He was a wonderful man, and when I was a very small child, he used to sit me on his knee and tell me stories about the old days. Some-times, when the kids are asleep, and the missus has finally gone upstairs to bed, I still sit in that same armchair and talk to him. And, do you know, it's not hard to imagine that he's talking back.'

'Are you telling her about Grandad Joshua?' asked a voice from the doorway.

'No, I...' Bell said awkwardly.

'He always tells people about Grandad Joshua,' the woman said. 'There are times when I think the best thing I could do with him would be to have him locked up for his own safety.'

'Now don't go showing me up in front of the company, love, or she'll be starting to regret hav-ing accepted your invitation to lunch,' Bell said with mock severity. He turned back to Paniatow-ski. 'In case you haven't guessed, this is my wife, Rosie. Rosie, this is DCI Paniatowski.'

'Monika,' Paniatowski said.

Rosie had been appropriately named, she de-cided. She had cheeks like apples, and the coun-try air had given them a warm, red glow. It would have been inaccurate to call her fat, but she was certainly ample, and had the sort of hips that her peasant ancestors would have balanced heavy buckets on.

'The food will be on the table in five minutes,' Rosie said. 'I hope you've brought your appetite with you, Monika.'

And Paniatowski, catching a whiff of what was being prepared in the kitchen, was surprised to discover that she had.

Terry Lewis chose a seat at the back of the bus, and sat there quietly turning over in his mind what he had learned that morning. He'd known immediately that it was Jeff Hill he was walking towards in the corridor of the Royal Victoria, but when he'd heard the woman shout that Hill had forgotten his tie, he'd automatically assumed she was *Mrs* Hill. Then Jeff had made that stupid comment, and he'd felt his tabloid journalist's instinct tingle.

So where did that leave him?

He'd no proof that Hill was having an affair, so there was no way he could sell the revelation to one of the more salacious papers. And anyway, he reminded himself, he was trying to leave that type of story behind him and move into more serious, hard-hitting copy.

So, all in all, it might be better to just forget the whole thing.

And then he remembered the broad smirk on Jeff Hill's face as Dave Langtree's barrister had torn him apart in the witness box – and with that came a wave of shame and humiliation.

That barrister had called him a blackmailer. It hadn't been true, but everybody in the court had believed it.

If he *had* been a blackmailer – if he'd actually asked Langtree for money – he had no doubt that the man would have paid up, so he would have both kept his job and been given a great wad of cash.

It had taken him a long time to learn a simple truth, but now he finally realized that black-mailers – like the editor of the Gazette, who *had* blackmailed Langtree – prospered, while people who tried to do their honest – if slightly seedy – job as best as they could, ended up getting shaft-ed.

Well, from now on, things would change. He would not give up his quest to become a better, more respected reporter, but if, along the way, he was presented with the opportunity to squeeze cash out of people who wanted to protect their sordid secrets, he would grab it with both hands.

And he would start with Jeff Hill.

They dined on shepherds' pie, followed by baked apple. It should, in theory, have been too heavy a meal for a hot day in summer, but Paniatowski had no difficulty at all in clearing her plate.

When the meal was over, Rosie Bell insisted that she – and she alone – should clear away and wash up.

'I get very nervous over the idea of guests coming into my kitchen,' she said.

'You get very nervous over the idea of any-body else at all in your kitchen,' her husband told her.

'That's true enough,' Rosie agreed.

146

When she'd gone, Paniatowski said, 'Rosie had no idea I was coming to lunch, had she?'

'What makes you say that?' Bell wondered.

'When you reminded her that she'd invited me, I could tell from the expression on her face that it was complete news to her. That look wasn't there for long – but it was there long *enough*.'

'I knew it wouldn't be a problem,' Bell said. 'Rosie always cooks too much food.'

'So why *did* you invite me?'

'I thought you could do with a bit of cheering up. Do you want to talk about it?'

'I don't think so,' Paniatowski said cautiously.

'It'll go no further,' Bell promised her.

And almost before she realized she was doing it, she was telling him the whole thing, starting from her affair with Baxter all those years ago, and ending with Jo's death and the way Baxter had treated her since.

Bell was a good listener. He didn't interrupt while she was speaking, but once he was sure she'd finished, he said, 'The chief constable seems to have behaved very badly.'

Paniatowski felt a sudden pang of guilt.

'You've only heard my side of the story,' she said. 'I'm sure George Baxter would give you a completely different picture, and – who knows – his version of events may be more accurate than mine.'

'Us men are such weak creatures,' Bell said musingly, as if he hadn't really heard her last comment at all. 'We act on instinct a lot of the time, and sometimes it seems as if we've got no more control over our feelings and actions than

147

animals. But what makes us different from the beasts of the field is that we know when we've done wrong, and – if we're any kind of men at all – we're willing and ready to take the consequences.' He paused. 'I'd like to think that if I'd been in his shoes when his wife died, I wouldn't have blamed anyone else for her death. I'd like to think that if I'd been George Baxter, I'd have picked up a shotgun, gone into the orchard, and blown my own bloody head off.'

He was serious, she thought – he really was serious!

Bell saw the expression on her face, and smiled.

'Of course, the other thing about all men is that we're perfectly capable, on occasion, of talking a complete load of old bollocks,' he said. 'Shall we get back to work?'

'Yes,' Paniatowski agreed. 'I think that would be a good idea.'

Sitting outside his tent, Spike thought about how he hated being back in Lancashire, and how he hated being in these particular woods – which he knew so well – most of all.

The trees were not *just* trees to him, but living monuments to some of his past failures.

This oak represented the misery of his ninth birthday.

That elm embodied the humiliation he had felt when he had realized that there were other sorts of lives to be led out there in the wider world – but that those lives were not for him.

The previous evening, when Edward Bell had

come to the woods to talk to the Devil's Disciples – and make it perfectly clear what he expected of them – Spike had hidden himself away like a small, frightened child. And later, once Bell had gone, he had sat shivering, fearful that some other phantom from his past might make an appearance and expose him as both a fraud and a failure.

Yet even as wrapped up in his own suffering as he was, he still couldn't help noticing that Badger and his two lieutenants had been behaving very strangely since they'd pitched camp in Backend Woods.

In many ways, the Devil's Disciples were like the sort of medieval court that he had learned about in school. Badger was the monarch – there was no doubt about that. But Chainsaw and Sharkteeth were important too, and other members of the gang tended to cluster around them as minor lords had once gathered around royal dukes. Normally the two accepted it as their right, and seemed to revel in the attention, but the moment they had arrived in the woods, they'd thrown up an invisible shield around themselves.

The other Devil's Disciples had all sensed this, and wisely decided to keep their distance, and while the rest of the gang had spent the evening drinking beer in the middle of the camp, Badger and his lieutenants had drunk as a lonely trio in front of Badger's tent.

And then, that morning, while everyone else was sleeping off the booze, Chainsaw and Sharkteeth had ridden out of the camp and been away for more than two hours.

Where had they gone, Spike wondered.

What had they been doing?

And – in violation of the Devil's Disciples' code – what secret had they been keeping from the rest of the gang?

Because there had to be a secret, didn't there? It was the only explanation for their behaviour.

The phantoms had not come for him the night before, Spike thought, but they *would* come eventually. And Badger's secret – whatever it was – would lie there and fester, until it had poisoned everything the Devil's Disciples had ever been.

It would all end badly – it simply had to.

Time-keeping being the true rock and roller's Antichrist, the RockStately Festival did not start at the advertised time, but by six fifteen there were some signs of activity from the technicians, and at a quarter to seven, four long-haired young men walked on to the stage, and peered out at the crowd, which had now swelled to about fifty thousand.

The singer walked up to the microphone. 'We're LSD and we're here to blow your minds,' he announced.

The crowd cheered and whistled and clapped, the drummer launched a vicious assault on his drums which lasted for almost a minute, and then the guitars joined in, weaving in and out of the beat like electric worms.

The earl's own version of Woodstock had begun.

EIGHT

Saturday, 7th August

By the time DS Meadows arrived at Crook Lane
– a narrow alley that ran between Whitebridge
High Street and Accrington Road – the police
operation was already well under way.

There were patrol cars parked at both ends of
the alley, and beside them stood uniformed constables who had strict instructions to move on
any passer-by who had got it into his or her head
that murder was a spectator sport. An ambulance
had arrived and was ready, the moment Dr Shastri gave the word, to whisk the dead body to the
mortuary. And in the alley itself, floodlights had
been erected, so that even though it was one
thirty in the morning, the whole area was as
bright as day.

When Meadows arrived at the scene, she found
Wellbeloved and Beresford standing next to the
corpse, and though that was exactly who she'd
been expecting to find there, it still came as a
slight shock not to see Paniatowski, too.

The dead man was laying face down, next to a
row of dustbins. As near as she could tell, he was
in early middle age, and even without getting too
close, she could see that the back of his head was

151

a real mess. He was dressed only in his under-pants and vest, and, despite the fact there'd been no rain, the vest was soaked.

'What happened to the vest?' Meadows asked.

'I don't know,' Wellbeloved replied, though it was obvious that he did. 'Maybe you could explain it, Mr Grimshaw.'

He was talking to a little old man in a cloth cap, who was standing just beyond the circle of light around the body.

'Well, it's like this,' the old man began, ner-vously licking his lips. 'I was on my way home from the George and Dragon when I was sud-denly caught a bit short.' He paused. 'And the ... err ... the reason I happened to be coming back from the pub so late was because—'

'Because there'd been a lock-in,' Beresford interrupted him. 'We're conducting a murder in-quiry here, Mr Grimshaw, in case you hadn't noticed.'

'Yes, I ... err...'

'And *because* we're conducting a murder inquiry, we've absolutely no interest at all in prosecuting the landlord of the George and Dragon for serving a few drinks after hours.'

'Right,' said Grimshaw, looking relieved. 'Anyway, as I said, I was caught a bit short. I did go to the toilet *before* I left the pub, but my bladder's not what it used to be and—'

'Get on with it!' Wellbeloved said impatiently.

'I could have had a pee on the High Street – it was nearly one o'clock, and there was nobody around – but I thought, no, that's not really very salubrious, so I came down this alley.'

'And pissed all over our murder victim,' Well-beloved said.

'There was no light in the alley,' Grimshaw explained. 'I didn't even know he was there, though I must admit, it didn't sound as if I was peeing on cobblestones. Anyway, this car came down the High Street – so it was just as well I'd decided not to have a slash there – and as it drew level with the top of the alley, the driver must have realized he was going in the wrong direction, because he slowed down and did one of them three-point turns. The headlights shone down the alley, and that's when I saw the body.'

'And you phoned us straight away?' Beresford asked.

'As soon as I'd finished peeing,' Grimshaw said. 'Well,' he added, obviously feeling the need to defend himself, 'once you've started, you can't stop, can you? And I did turn away, so I wasn't peeing on him any more.'

'Most considerate of you,' Wellbeloved said drily.

'Go back up to the top of the alley, and tell the constable on duty there that you need a lift home,' Beresford said.

The old man turned to go, then hesitated.

'Will my picture be in the papers?' he asked.

'It's more than likely,' Beresford told him.

'And will it ... will it mention how I discovered him? Because if my missus found out that I'd been...'

'We'll ask the reporters to keep quiet about that bit of the story,' Beresford promised.

The old man nodded gratefully, and took his

153

leave. Halfway down the alley, his path crossed that of Dr Shastri, who was coming from the opposite direction.

Shastri first looked down at the body, and then across the circle of light at Colin Beresford.

'Where's DCI...?' she began, making the same mistake as Meadows earlier, but in her case starting to put it into words, and only pulling back in the nick of time.

'Where's DCI *who*?' Wellbeloved asked.

'Ah, it is plain from the commanding tone in your voice that you are the chief inspector to whom I was about to refer,' Shastri said, with a neat bit of verbal footwork which both Beresford and Meadows couldn't help admiring. 'You are Chief Inspector Well-Below, are you not?'

'The name is Wellbeloved, doctor.'

'A thousand apologies, Mr Wellbeloved,' Shastri said. 'For a simple Indian like myself, your English names are often so confusing. Would you like me to examine the body now?'

'If it wouldn't be too much trouble, Doctor,' Wellbeloved said, with an edge of sarcasm to his voice.

'It will be no trouble at all, Chief Inspector,' Shastri replied, pretending not to notice his tone. 'In point of fact, it is what I am paid to do.'

She walked over to the corpse, and crouched down next to the head.

'This man is dead,' she announced. 'I would stake my professional reputation on that.'

It was vintage Shastri, and both Meadows and Beresford grinned. Wellbeloved, on the other hand, did not look the least amused.

'Death was almost certainly caused by a blow to the back of the skull, but I can't confirm that definitively until I've cut him open,' Shastri continued. She stood again. 'There's no more I can do here, so could you please arrange for the cadaver to be taken to the mortuary.'

'When can I expect your report?' Wellbeloved asked.

'I see you inherited your predecessor's impatience,' Shastri said. 'I will go home now and get a few hours much-needed beauty sleep, but the moment I awaken I will rush to the mortuary, reach for my trusty scalpel, and carry out the post-mortem with great alacrity. If all goes well, you should have my preliminary findings by lunch-time.'

The ambulance men – who had been having a quiet smoke at the end of the alley – were summoned to take the body away, and it was after they had turned the corpse over and were lifting it on to the trolley that Meadows noticed there was something tucked into the waistband of the dead man's underpants.

'What's that?' she asked, pointing.

'Looks like a wallet,' Beresford said.

And a wallet was what, indeed, it was.

By two o'clock, the team – which now included DC Crane – were back in Wellbeloved's office.

Beresford took his packet of cigarettes out of his pocket, and looked around for an ashtray. There wasn't one. And that was when he noticed that Wellbeloved was glaring at him. He put the cigarettes back in his pocket.

'You have my permission to smoke if you want to, Inspector Beresford,' the chief inspector said, producing an ashtray, a lighter and a box of small cigars from his desk drawer with a magician's flourish.

He placed the ashtray in the centre of the desk, lit up one of the cigars, and took a deep drag on it.

'If the wallet belonged to the dead man – and we have every reason to believe that it did – then his name was Terry Lewis and he was a journalist,' he said exhaling the cigar smoke in a series of wavering rings. 'The wallet contained, from our perspective, a number of useful things. There's a driving licence, which has on it his address in Manchester. There's a photograph of Lewis with a woman and two children – presumably his wife and kids. There's a National Union of Journalists membership card, and a key for a room at the Royal Victoria Hotel.' Wellbeloved paused. 'Have you anything to add on the last point, DS Meadows?'

'I called the hotel, and it confirmed that a Mr Terry Lewis booked in the day before yesterday,' Meadows said.

Wellbeloved nodded.

'And finally, there's twenty-seven pounds in cash,' he said. 'Now, given that there's absolutely no forensic evidence to point to his having been killed in the alley where he was found – no blood, no bone shards, no signs of a struggle – what questions should we be asking ourselves?'

'If that wasn't where he was killed, why did the murderer choose to dump his body there?'

Beresford said. 'It was a risky thing to do, because even though the centre of town is pretty much deserted by one o'clock, it's not entirely so – Mr Grimshaw and the driver of the car who pulled the U-turn are proof of that. It would have been much safer for him to dump it out on the moors.'

'And there would have been another advantage – quite apart from avoiding the risk of being spotted – to disposing of the victim that way,' Meadows said. 'If the murderer had left the body on the moors, it could have been days – or even weeks – before it was found. And it's common knowledge – even among civilians – that the longer we take to find out about a murder, the less our chances are of tracking down the killer.'

'But not only did he leave the body where it would be found, he left the wallet to make identification easier,' Beresford pointed out.

'Exactly,' Wellbeloved agreed. 'So why did he do that?'

'Maybe he wants us to catch him,' DC Crane suggested. 'Some murderers do.'

'That's certainly one theory,' Wellbeloved said. 'And if it's correct, all we have to do is sit on our arses and wait for him to send us some more clues. But let's assume that *isn't* the case – what other explanations for his behaviour can we come up with?'

'Turning Crane's idea on its head, the killer *doesn't* want us to catch him, but he's giving us every chance to,' Meadows said.

'Why would he do that?' Wellbeloved asked.

'Because he wants to show us just how clever

he is, and how stupid we are. If he makes it almost impossible for us to find him – if, for example, he buries the body on the moors – there's no fun in it. If, on the other hand, he gives us a massive clue right at the start of the investigation, and we still can't track him down, that proves he's so much better than we are.'

'He'd have to be incredibly arrogant to think in that way,' Beresford said.

But they all knew that many killers *were* that arrogant – that arrogance was there right from the start, in the assumption that they had the *right* to take another person's life.

'He wants to be caught or maybe he just wants to taunt us,' Wellbeloved said, summing up. 'Any other ideas?'

'Perhaps the killer wanted to make a point, or to send a message,' Beresford said.

'A message to whom? And what kind of message?'

'A message to all journalists everywhere. And that message would be, "This is what happens to you when you start trying to stick your nose into matters which are no concern of yours".'

'It's a possibility,' Wellbeloved conceded. 'But why strip him down to his vest and underpants?'

'Maybe that was all he was actually wearing when he was killed,' Jack Crane said.

'Then where's the blood?' Wellbeloved asked.

'I'm sorry, sir?'

'When he was hit over the head, blood would have come spurting out, and at least some of it would have found its way on to his vest. The fact that there is none would suggest that he was wearing something else – possibly something quite thick – which absorbed that blood.'

'You're right,' Crane said.

'Maybe the killer stripped him down to his underwear to humiliate him,' Beresford said.

'But it's not really that *much* of a humiliation, is it?' Meadows argued. 'Now if he was completely naked, and his body had been mutilated in some way, I'd say you were on to a winner, sir, but as it is...'

'So we've got a lot of questions – which is a positive thing – but no real answers, which is not quite so good,' Wellbeloved summed up. 'Does one of you have any useful contacts in the Manchester police?'

'I worked with a Manchester DI called Henry James on a case last November,' Beresford volunteered.

'And what was he like?'

'He was a good bloke – very helpful.'

'You got on well, then?'

'Yes, sir.'

Wellbeloved nodded. 'Then I want you down in Manchester first thing in the morning. Reestablish contact with James, and take him with you when you go to talk to Lewis' widow.'

'Err ... I normally coordinate the door-to-door operations, sir,' Beresford said.

'I'm sure you do,' Wellbeloved said, 'but the Manchester police could be crucial to this investigation, and since you've already established a good relationship with one of its officers, you'll be of more use to me down there.'

'That makes sense,' Beresford agreed – though

he was reluctant to surrender the role he had made pretty much his own.

'DS Meadows can take over the coordination of door-to-door inquiries,' Wellbeloved said.

'That's normally an inspector's job, sir,' Meadows pointed out.

'I know it is, but I think you're perfectly capable of doing it, and the experience will be good for you,' Wellbeloved told her. 'I want all the streets within a quarter of a mile of the crime scene canvassed, Sergeant. I want every single householder questioned to find out if they noticed anything last night. I also want all the staff and guests at the Royal Victoria put through the mill. Did they see much of Lewis – maybe even talk to him? Was there anything about his behaviour that struck them as odd? Did he seem to be associating with anyone in particular?'

'Got it,' Meadows said.

'And as from tomorrow night, I want police roadblocks set up on the High Street and Accrington Road – and maybe even beyond that, if you've got the manpower available. I'll want to know who uses those roads late at night, and whether *they* saw anything.'

'Check,' Meadows said.

'As for you, DC Crane, the moment we've finished here, I want you to get on the phone and drag the editor of the local rag out of his bed. Tell him we've got a picture of our victim, and we want it prominently displayed on his front page tomorrow morning.'

'The paper will already have gone to press, sir,' Crane said.

'Then they'll just have to start the presses again and re-do the four outside pages, won't they?' Wellbeloved said. 'And if the editor argues with you, you might point out to him that we live in a you-scratch-my-back-I-scratch-yours world, and that if he wants my cooperation in the future, the best way to ensure it is by giving me his now. If it'll help, you can also say that I can be a right proper bastard when I don't get what I want.'

Crane grinned. 'Right, sir.'

'You look like you think I've just made a joke, Crane,' Wellbeloved said, stony-faced. 'Let me assure you, I've done no such thing. I *can* be a right proper bastard, and you'd be well advised never to put yourself in a position in which you'll experience it first-hand. Got that?'

Crane merely nodded – it seemed the safest thing to do.

'I'll handle the local TV news myself,' Wellbeloved continued, 'and before you ask, that's not because I particularly fancy the idea of becoming a Whitebridge celebrity, it's because television people are even cockier than print journalists, and if you're going to try and make them jump through hoops, you'd better make sure you're waving a very big stick.' He looked around the table. 'Are there any questions? Because if you're not quite sure you've got a clear picture of what I want, now is the time to tell me.'

There were no questions.

'Right, that's it,' Wellbeloved concluded. 'Go home and try to snatch a few hours sleep, because there's no saying when you'll get your next opportunity, and I want you hitting the 'deck running, first thing in the morning.'

Beresford and Meadows walked down to the car park together. They obviously both had a lot on their minds, but it was not until they were on the point of going their separate ways that Beresford said, 'Well, what do you think?'

There was no need for Meadows to ask what the question was specifically referring to.

'He's sneaky and he's underhand, and – for all I know – he may rape baby bunnies on his day off,' Meadows said. 'And I didn't like that trick he pulled of waiting until you'd put your cigarettes back in your pocket before giving you permission to smoke. That was just bloody-minded gamesmanship.'

'But...?' Beresford asked.

Because there clearly was a 'but'.

'But he's nowhere near as stupid as I used to think he was,' Meadows said. 'In fact, though it pains me to admit it, the boss herself couldn't have handled that meeting better than he did.'

'No,' Beresford said gloomily, 'she couldn't.'

NINE

Lawrence Taylor was sitting in the breakfast room of the Royal Victoria, carefully sipping black coffee and wondering if he dared risk eating a little toast.

The previous evening had been one of the most uncomfortable he ever remembered spending. His gut had started issuing warnings at just after six o'clock, and he had thrown up for the first time at around half past. The Napoleon brandy he sent his stomach as a peace offering seemed to quiet it for a while, but by seven thirty it was on the march again, and he was forced to leave the table at which he was entertaining some business associates, and rush to the toilet. When the same thing happened again – half an hour later – and yet again – fifteen minutes after that – Taylor finally admitted defeat and excused himself.

Once up in his room, the toilet bowl had become his closest companion, and it was not until half past two, still crouched over the bowl, that he had finally fallen asleep.

And even now, the morning after, eating toast seemed like a dangerous adventure, on a par with swallowing a buttered razor blade.

Taylor looked up from his coffee cup and saw

Jeff Hill entering the breakfast room.

Bloody hell, he looks worse than I feel, Taylor thought.

And even though he disliked Hill on both personal and professional levels, he couldn't help experiencing a moment of compassion for him.

Hill glanced around the room, and then walked straight to Taylor's table, and sat down.

'I hear through the grapevine that you had a bit of a rough night, last night,' Hill said.

'And you've come to gloat about it, have you?' asked Taylor – though, for once, it looked as if Hill had no appetite for putting the boot in.

'Come to gloat? No, no, not at all. Did you ... did you see anybody last night, after you went upstairs?'

'Not a soul,' Taylor said bitterly. 'I might have expected a few of my so-called friends to come and find out how I was getting on, but I expect they were too busy boozing to spare the time.'

'Good,' Hill said.

'Good?' Taylor repeated.

'Well, no, not good, exactly,' Hill amended, 'it must have been horrible for you. But the fact that you didn't see anybody does mean that you might be able to help me out.'

'Help you out?' Taylor said suspiciously. 'How?'

'I've ... err ... been spending some time with a friend while I've been here, and I have reason to believe that my wife's having me watched.'

'Then you're stuffed, my old son – you're *really* stuffed,' said Taylor, who had decided the morning was starting to look up.

164

'I wouldn't be stuffed if you gave me an alibi for last night – if you said I was so worried about you that I came up to your room at about ten o'clock and spent the night looking after you.'

'True.'

'So you'll give me an alibi?'

'No.'

'Why not?'

'Why should I? What's in it for me?'

'I've just won the franchise for selling the kids' model of the new Whitebridge Rovers winter strip – and I'll cut you in for ten per cent if you'll do me this small favour,' Hill said.

If the bastard was prepared to offer ten per cent of such a lucrative franchise, he must *really* need an alibi, Taylor thought.

'I want forty per cent,' he said.

'That's outrageous!'

Taylor shrugged. 'Please yourself, Jeff – it's not my marriage that's in jeopardy.'

'Twenty-five per cent,' Hill said. 'And that's my final offer.'

It was never a good idea to push Jeff Hill *too* far, Taylor thought.

'Twenty-five per cent, then,' he agreed. 'But I'll want that down in black and white.'

Hill reached into his inside jacket pocket, pulled out what looked like a pre-prepared contract, and laid it on the table.

Only eight hours earlier, the enclosure inside the walls of Stamford Hall had been filled with the sound of a heavy metal group called Crazy Mary. Now, the fans who had been jumping up and down while the band attempted to make their ears bleed, were all recovering from the night's excitement in their tents on the other side of the wall, and – apart from the ground staff who were clearing up the rubbish, and a couple of technicians who were making adjustments to the equipment on stage – Paniatowski and Bell had the enclosure to themselves.

'It went well, yesterday,' Bell said. 'In fact, it went better than I'd ever dared hope it would. There wasn't a riot, nobody got murdered – and the Devil's Disciples behaved in an exemplary way.'

'Since the earl won't let me get anywhere near them, I wouldn't know about that,' Paniatowski said, with a touch of bitterness in her voice.

'In an exemplary way,' Bell repeated. 'While the show was on, they made sure nobody tried to climb on the stage, and once it was over, they controlled the traffic flow through the East Gate to the camp site with all the calmness and patience of school lollipop ladies.'

Devil-worshipping school lollipop ladies,' Paniatowski said drily.

'I had some doubts when the earl first told me that he was going to employ a motorbike gang,' Bell said, choosing to ignore the comment, 'but it just goes to show, doesn't it?'

'Goes to show what?'

'That the earl always knows exactly what he's doing.'

Paniatowski turned away, so that Bell wouldn't see the smile which had come to her face.

The estate manager had claimed he hadn't any

worries about the Devil's Disciples the day before – in fact, he'd expressed his complete confidence in them – and he was only allowing himself the luxury of admitting his earlier doubts now because they had been proven to be groundless.

She wondered what the earl would have to do before Bell would feel entitled to criticize him.

Mow down the entire adult population of Whitebridge and district with a sub-machine gun, perhaps?

No, even then, Edward Bell would probably do his best to find extenuating circumstances!

They had been walking around the perimeter of the enclosure as they talked, and Bell suddenly came to a halt.

'Look at that,' he exclaimed.

Paniatowski crouched down to examine the section of the fence he was pointing at.

A vertical cut had been made in the chain link to a height of about two feet, and another – perhaps eighteen inches long – made horizontally from the top of the vertical one. The result was a flap which could be pushed outwards to allow a man – or woman – to crawl through, but which would spring back into roughly its original position once there was nothing to impede it.

'There's no chance that was done accidentally – or on a whim – is there?' Bell asked hopefully – although it was clear he already knew what the answer was going to be.

'There's no chance at all,' Paniatowski replied. 'You'd need industrial cutters to get through that wire, and since no one habitually carries tools like that around with them, we can assume that whoever cut through the wire came here with precisely that intention in mind.'

'Oh my God!' Bell said.

He was starting to panic, Paniatowski thought. This man – who she was sure would face a bayonet charge without turning a hair – was starting to panic at the thought he might have let the earl down.

True, the festival had not been his idea, and true, it had not been his decision to hire totally untrained security men. None of that mattered. His role in life was to see that everything went smoothly for the earl *whatever* the circumstances, and on this occasion he seemed to have failed.

'Did the Devil's Disciples search the visitors as they came in?' Paniatowski asked.

'No,' Bell said. 'It would have taken too long. Even if they'd started early in the afternoon, half of the audience would still have been on the other side of the wall by the time the concert began.'

'And I take it there was no metal detector on the gate?'

'I never thought to have one installed,' Bell said, in what was almost a moan. 'Why would anybody have done this?'

And what he meant was – how *dare* anybody do this? Didn't the man with the wire cutters know that the earl was special? Didn't he understand there was never any excuse for disturbing the earl's peace of mind?

'You need to calm down,' Paniatowski said

firmly.

'Yes,' Bell agreed, taking a deep breath, 'that's what I need to do. I need to calm down.'

'My first guess would be that the intruder is a burglar,' Paniatowski said. 'The rock concert will have provided the ideal distraction for him. Everybody's eyes – and all the lights – will have been concentrated on the stage. Nobody will have noticed him cutting through the wire. And once he had cut through it, he'd have access to the whole estate.'

'What do I do now?' Bell asked.

'The first thing is to get the Devil's Disciples to search the grounds to make sure the intruder isn't still here,' Paniatowski said. 'The second is to get the staff to check and see if anything has been stolen – because if something has been taken, you'll need to inform the police. And once you've got those two jobs out of the way, we'll take a look at the security tapes.'

'The security tapes!' Bell gasped, as if he'd been drowning, and Paniatowski had just thrown him a rope. 'I'd forgotten all about them!'

There were some women who could detect the smell of tragedy from a mile away, Beresford thought, and the slightly faded blonde woman who answered the door of number thirty-two Elsden Avenue, Manchester – her eyes already wide with fear, her body starting to tremble – was definitely one of them.

'Are you Mrs Lewis?' Beresford's companion asked, holding up his warrant card for her to see.

'Yes, I...'

169

'I'm DI James from the Manchester Metropolitan Police, and this is my colleague, DI Beresford. May we come in?'

Mrs Lewis wiped her hands nervously on her apron, and then brushed some imaginary hair away from her eyes.

'Yes, of course,' she croaked. 'Please follow me.'

She hadn't asked them what this was all about, because she already knew she wouldn't like the answer, Beresford thought.

Mrs Lewis led them into a living room which was almost rigorously neat and tidy, and yet still managed to exude an air of quiet desperation.

'I think it would be best if you sat down before I say anything, Mrs Lewis,' James told her, indicating one of the armchairs, which was patterned with yellow and red roses.

'I can't go doing that,' the woman protested. 'I've still got a lot of housework to do.'

'Please,' DI James said softly, 'it won't take a minute.'

He put his hands on her shoulders, and gently steered her to the chair. He pressed down on the shoulders a little, and she sank on to the cushion.

'Do you know where your husband is, Mrs Lewis?' James asked.

'He's ... he's in Whitebridge.'

'And what's he doing in Whitebridge?'

'He's a journalist.'

'Yes, I know.'

'Well, that's why he's there – he's covering a story up there.'

'What kind of story is it that he's working on?

Do you think you could give me a few details?'

Mrs Lewis shook her head. 'I don't know any more details. I asked him what the story was about, but he wouldn't tell me.'

'Would his newspaper know what the story was about?'

'He doesn't work for the paper any more. He ... he resigned over a matter of principle.'

James nodded, as if he quite accepted as the absolute truth what was so obviously an outright lie.

'I'm sorry to have to tell you this, but I'm afraid your husband has had an accident,' he said.

'Is he ... is he...'

'Yes, I'm afraid he's dead.'

'But he can't be,' the woman said – and by now she was almost in tears. 'He ... just ... *can't* ... be.'

The phone rang in the hallway.

'I'll get that,' Beresford said, before Mrs Lewis had time to become distracted by the ringing.

He stepped into the hall, closed the door tightly behind him, and picked up the phone.

'Could I speak to Mr Lewis, please?' asked the man on the other end of the line.

'Who's calling?'

'My name's Meacham. I'm the assistant manager at the local branch of the Whitehall Bank.'

'I'm afraid Mr Lewis isn't here.'

'Then could I speak to Mrs Lewis instead, please? It really is rather important.'

'She *is* here, but she can't come to the phone at the moment. Can I give her a message?'

'Well, no, not really,' the bank manager said awkwardly. 'It's rather a confidential matter, you see.'

'I'm from the police,' Beresford said. 'My name is DI Colin Beresford, and I regret to inform you that Mr Lewis has been murdered.'

'Oh, good heavens!' the bank manager gasped.

'It might help us in our inquiries if you could tell me now exactly what this confidential information of yours concerns.'

There was a pause on the other end of the line.

'Look, I'm not doubting that you actually *are* a policeman, Mr ... Mr...' Meacham said finally.

'Beresford. DI Beresford.'

'...but in matters of this nature, Mr Beresford, we have to be absolutely sure we know who we're talking to.'

'I understand that,' Beresford said. 'Call Manchester Central Police Station, and ask them where DI Henry James is at the moment.'

'Henry James? But I thought he was—'

'A novelist who most people have never read. Yes, there is certainly that Henry James, but *this* Henry James is a detective inspector with the Manchester Metropolitan Police.'

'I'm sorry, I must sound like a babbling idiot, but it has all been rather a shock to learn that—'

'When you ask them where DI James is, they'll tell you he's here – and the moment they've done that, I'd like you to ring me back.'

'Yes, of course,' Meacham said.

It had been over an hour since Paniatowski and Bell had discovered the gap in the wire-netting fence, and, in that time, the servants had searched the house and the Devil's Disciples had scoured the grounds.

The results had been encouraging. The servants had found no signs of a break-in, and reported that nothing of value seemed to be missing. The Devil's Disciples, for their part, had found no evidence of an intruder.

But it was still far too early to be complacent. In a mansion so stuffed full of treasures, it was possible that the servants had overlooked the fact that one of them was no longer where it should be. In grounds as vast as those belonging to Stamford Hall, it was not *impossible* that a man might have succeeded in keeping his presence hidden from the motorcycle gang.

Even so, it seemed unlikely that the burglar – if that was, indeed, what he had been – had achieved anything during his clandestine visit, and by the time Paniatowski and Bell reached the surveillance control room, the estate manager was finally starting to relax.

'When did the cameras first start rolling?' Paniatowski asked, looking at the bank of monitors.

'I had them all switched on the moment the gates were opened for the visitors.'

'Then that's when we'll start watching. I don't think the intruder will have cut the fence until *much* later, but if he did, we don't want to miss it.'

An image of the enclosure appeared on the monitor. The camera had been set up outside the wire, so everything happening inside the wire was framed by the diamond shapes of its mesh.

Bell set the tape at review speed, and they watched as the fans came through the turnstiles at a speed only previously seen in old Keystone Kops movies.

The tape ran on. The angle of the camera didn't allow Paniatowski and Bell to see the stage, but it was plain from the audience's reaction that the first group had arrived.

The clock at the bottom of the monitor recorded the passing of time.

One hour ... two hours ... three hours...

It was when the clock said three hours and forty-five minutes that the man approached what was *now* a flap in the wire – but certainly hadn't been at the time of the recording.

The man was wearing the sleeveless embroidered sheepskin jacket of the sort which was much in favour with the hippies a few years earlier, and a pair of jeans. He had long dark hair, which partially covered his face.

'Is that the man?' Bell asked, whispering like a child caught halfway between fear and excitement.

'I don't know,' Paniatowski replied, in her normal voice. 'We'll have to wait and see.'

The man was carrying a duffle bag, and now he reached into it and produced a pair of long-handled wire cutters. He worked quickly, snipping a section of wire, straightening up and checking over his shoulder to make sure he had not been observed, bending down and cutting some more, then straightening up and checking again.

174

Judging by how far his head was from the top of the wire when he was upright, it was likely that he was somewhere between five feet nine and five feet eleven, Paniatowski thought.

She wondered if she would recognize him if she passed him in the street – and decided she probably wouldn't.

It took the man less than a minute to finish his work, then he slipped the cutters into the bag, looked around once more, got down on his hands and knees and crawled through the flap.

'I wish we had a clearer view of his face,' Bell said.

'So do I,' Paniatowski agreed.

The man stood up and began to walk quickly away from the fence.

'He's not heading towards the Hall,' Bell said, surprised.

'That proves nothing,' Paniatowski replied. 'He may have decided to skirt it, and then go in from the back.'

Someone coughed in the doorway, and turning around Paniatowski saw an old woman who was wearing a long, black, silk dress and leaning heavily on a carved walking stick. At the sight of her, Bell immediately hit the stop switch, and the screen went blank.

'Who is this person?' the old woman demanded.

'She's Detective Chief Inspector Paniatowski from the Mid Lancs Police, my lady,' Bell said. 'She's advising us on security. DCI Paniatowski, this is the dowager countess.'

'I'm pleased to meet you,' Paniatowski said.

'You didn't tell me about all this,' the dowager countess said, ignoring Paniatowski completely and staring at the row of monitors. 'Had it not been for a remark made by one of the other servants, I would not have even known it was here. *Why* didn't you tell me?'

'I didn't think that you'd be very interested in this sort of thing, my lady,' Bell replied.

'So now you presume to know what will interest me and what will not, do you?' the dowager countess demanded.

'No, of course not,' Bell said contritely. 'You are quite right, my lady – I should have told you it was here.'

The dowager countess was still looking at the monitors.

'It seems like a great deal of unnecessary expense,' she said.

'It wasn't really that expensive at all,' Bell said. 'We haven't paid anything yet, and if we do eventually decide to buy it, we've been offered a very good deal by the installers.'

'In my day, one did not make *deals* with tradesmen,' the dowager countess said. 'One told them what one wanted, and how much one was prepared to pay for it, and they provided it and were glad of the patronage.'

'And it wasn't unnecessary,' Bell said, sounding almost desperate to say something that would meet with the old woman's approval. 'It's designed to keep the Hall safe.'

'I want to see how it works,' the dowager countess said.

'If that is your wish, my lady, of course I will

show it to you, but there really is very little to—'

'Do it now,' the old woman said firmly.

It was over ten minutes before Mr Meacham, the bank manager, called Colin Beresford back.

'I'm sorry if I'd appeared to doubt your word,' he said.

'That's quite all right,' Beresford assured him. 'It's always better to err on the side of caution.'

'It came as such a shock to all of us here at the bank. One of the junior cashiers actually started crying when she first heard the news, and even the senior cashiers—'

'Now that you've had it verified that we actually are police officers, could you tell me the nature of this important information that you had for Mr Lewis?' Beresford interrupted.

'What? Oh yes, of course, I'm so sorry. I was ringing to tell him that we've had to stop paying out the standing orders for gas, electricity, rates, et cetera, because there's no money in the account.'

'So Mrs Lewis, who's only just lost her husband, can expect all her utilities to be cut off soon, can she?' Beresford asked accusingly.

'Well, given the circumstances, I suppose that we might be able to grant her some leeway in the matter, but only if there was a reasonable chance of her being able to pay—'

'There's a large insurance policy on her husband's life,' Beresford interrupted. 'A *very* large one.'

'Are you quite sure about that?'

'I'm holding it in my hand, even as we speak,' Beresford said, glancing down at his empty palm.

'Oh, well, in that case, there's no need to bother Mrs Lewis at all,' the bank manager said.

'I'm sure she'll appreciate that,' Beresford told him.

And he was thinking, she'll have to face up to the problem of having no money eventually, but at least I've bought the poor woman a little space in which to come to terms with her grief.

'Well, if there's nothing more...' the bank manager said.

'They've been struggling to meet their bills for quite some time, have they?' Beresford asked.

'No, not at all. Their savings account has been gradually going down since Mr Lewis lost his job, of course, but until a few days ago, they still had quite a healthy balance.'

'And what happened a few days ago?'

'Mr Lewis wrote out a rather large cheque.'

'How large?'

'Five thousand pounds.'

Beresford whistled softly to himself. That *was* a lot of money – especially for a man with no job.

'You don't happen to know, offhand, who the cheque was made out to, do you?' he asked.

'As a matter of fact, I do. You see, before ringing, I made sure I had all the details at my fingertips, and—'

'Who *was* the cheque made out to?' Beresford interrupted.

'To Mr Harold Elton, who, as chance would

have it, also has his account in this branch.'

'And do you know what this Mr Elton could have done to have merited such a large cheque?'

'No, not exactly. Not in any detail. But according to our records, he's a private detective.'

TEN

'It's very simple really, my lady,' Edward Bell said to the dowager countess. 'There are cameras set up all around the grounds, and they transmit pictures to the monitors which are also recorded on video tape.'

'So you'll be able to look at what's happening now at some later point, will you?'

'Exactly, my lady.'

'Why is that tree moving?' the dowager countess asked, pointing to one of the monitors.

'It's not the tree that's moving, it's the camera,' Bell explained.

'And why should the camera move? Why doesn't it simply stay in one position?'

The old woman was taking a surprising amount of interest in the technical set-up, Paniatowski thought. Maybe that was because watching the world through the cameras was a bit like playing God.

But no, that couldn't be it, since, from the way she was acting, she clearly thought she already *was* God!

'If the cameras were fixed, my lady, we would need a lot more of them,' Bell explained. 'Because they move, they can sweep across a wider area, and each camera can do the work of several static ones.'

'So there are times when parts of the grounds are *not* being photographed,' the dowager countess said.

'Yes, my lady, but not for very long. Look at this screen. The camera is on the orchid greenhouse, and now it moves away, but by the time you've counted slowly to ten, it will be back on the greenhouse again.'

'I have no intention of counting slowly to ten, Bell,' the dowager countess said haughtily.

'Of course not, my lady,' the estate manager agreed.

Of course not, my lady, Paniatowski echoed silently. One has servants to do that kind of thing for one.

'But you do understand what I'm saying, don't you, my lady?' Bell continued earnestly.

'Yes, your explanation was adequate, and so I *do* understand,' the dowager countess said.

She moved further along the line of monitors.

'These two cameras are on Backend Wood, one on the south side and one on the north side,' she said.

'That's right, my lady.'

'And where have those godless heathens with their filthy motorcycles set up their camp?'

'At the north side, my lady.'

'I don't see them.'

'They are camped deeper in the woods.'

'Well, I suppose we should be grateful for that small mercy, at least,' the dowager countess said.

She studied the two screens, watching as the cameras arced back and forth, and as she did, her lips moved slightly.

She *is* counting, Paniatowski thought. She's actually counting *for herself*. Whatever next? Will she be wanting to take over the scullery maid's job?

'There is a broad strip of land in the centre which does not appear on either of the two screens,' the dowager countess said, in an accusatory voice. 'Why is that, Bell?'

'I believe there are technical reasons, my lady.'

'What sort of technical reasons?'

'It's something to do with angles and arcs. I'm not sure I quite understand it myself.'

'In short, Bell, you are contemplating spending a great deal of the family's money on a system that doesn't even do what it's supposed to do. Is that correct?' the countess asked scornfully.

That was why she was showing so much interest in the cameras, Paniatowski told herself. It wasn't that she wanted to find out how they worked. She was more interested in discovering how they *didn't* work, so she would have something to humiliate Edward Bell with.

'I could ask the installers to come back and try and find a way to include that section, if that is what you wish, my lady,' Bell said, clearly flustered.

'Don't bother,' the dowager countess said. 'Hire more servants instead. They, at least, are reliable.'

She turned and – leaning heavily on her walking stick – left the room.

'Do you always do that?' Paniatowski asked Bell, when the old woman had gone.

'Do what?'

'Drop everything – however important it is – in order to cater to her every whim?'

'She *is* the dowager countess,' Bell said, as if that explained and justified everything. 'But even allowing for that, I'd still like to apologize for her being so rude to you.'

'It's not for you to apologize,' Paniatowski said.

Bell sighed. 'All right, I'd like to say I'm sorry for the fact that she was rude to you.'

'But you weren't sorry enough to mention that she was being rude to me while she was still here,' Paniatowski said.

She regretted saying the words the second that they were out of her mouth.

'I should be the one who apologizes,' she continued. 'I know how much you love your work, and how difficult it is for you to balance the various demands that are constantly being placed on you by the family, so I can't really blame you for keeping silent.'

'You have to appreciate the position the dowager countess finds herself in,' Bell pleaded. 'For a long time, she was the mistress of the Hall, and now she's of no importance at all. It's very hard for her to deal with, and if – by lashing out at me occasionally – she finds her disappointment a little easier to bear, then why not? I've got broad shoulders.'

Yes, in a way, she did appreciate the dowager countess's position, because she must feel a little like a DCI who had been suddenly stripped of her power, Paniatowski thought with a shudder –

and a DCI, moreover, who had *also* just used Edward Bell as her whipping boy!

She'd have to tread very carefully, she warned herself, or she'd end up a bitter old woman, too.

'You didn't tell the dowager countess about the intruder, even though that would have shown her, quite convincingly, just how useful the cameras are,' she said to Edward Bell.

'I didn't want to alarm her – or any other member of the family – unnecessarily,' Bell replied. 'If there's a problem, then I will deal with it. It's what I do.'

It would have been pointless to try and shake his conviction of what was right and proper – and anyway, she didn't trust herself not to come out with something else unpleasant if they got into an argument – so she contented herself with saying, 'Shall we go back to the tape now?'

'Yes, that would be a good idea,' Bell agreed.

They tracked the intruder to the edge of the camera's range, and switched to a second camera's recorder which picked him up immediately. And then, suddenly, he disappeared completely.

'It seems there's *more* than one blind spot in the system,' Bell said despondently, 'so maybe the dowager countess was right all along, and it's just a waste of money.'

'There are very few systems that work perfectly all the time,' Paniatowski replied, as she fought the urge to shake him until his teeth rattled.

The sign on the frosted glass door said, 'Knock and Enter', but DI James did not seem to feel

184

under any obligation to follow the first part of the instruction, and walked straight in.

The office contained two filing cabinets, a desk, and three chairs (two in front of the desk, one behind it). The filing cabinets were covered with dust – suggesting that their owner kept most of the information he needed in his head – and the only things on the desk were a telephone and an answering machine. The wall behind the desk had been painted in a rather sickly cream colour, and there was no sign of the framed pictures, certificates and letters of recommendation which most offices displayed to impress clients.

The man in charge of this small, charmless empire was rather fat, and completely bald. When he looked up and saw who had entered the office, he did not seem either particularly annoyed or particularly surprised.

'Morning, Harry,' James said.

The bald man smiled. 'Morning, Mr James.'

'I hear from my usual sources that you've been up to your old tricks again,' James said.

'And what tricks might they be?' Elton wondered.

'Harry here exists on what you might call the fringes of the criminal underworld,' James explained to Beresford. 'He very rarely does anything obviously illegal himself. Instead, he smooths the path for other people who wish to break the law. You could call him a criminal facilitator. Then again, you might choose a more technical term – like evil little guttersnipe.'

'That's libel, that is, Mr James,' the bald man said. 'I could have you up in court for that.'

'First of all, to take me to court, you need witnesses – and you don't seriously think that my
colleague, DI Beresford here, would support
your word against mine, do you?' James asked.
'Secondly, it's not *libel*, its *slander*. Nowhere did
I write down that you're an evil little guttersnipe
– I only said it.'

'I stand corrected,' Elton said.

He opened his desk drawer, took out a bar of
Cadbury's Fruit and Nut, broke off a fair-sized
chunk, and shovelled it into his mouth. A look of
pure ecstasy came to his face.

'I'm surprised you let Terry Lewis pay you by
cheque,' James said. 'I'd have thought you'd
have insisted on cash.'

The abrupt change of subject did not seem to
faze Elton in the slightest.

He munched the rest of his chocolate slowly,
then said, 'I don't see *why* you'd be surprised,
Mr James. I've got to put *something* through the
books, or the taxman will get very annoyed.'

'Five thousand pounds is a lot of money,'
James pointed out.

'Maybe it is – if you have to live on a bobby's
pay.'

'And what did he pay you five thousand
pounds for?'

Elton broke off more chocolate from the bar.

'The client – Mr Terrance Lewis – paid me for
professional services rendered,' he said.

'You wouldn't care to be a little more specific,
would you, Harry?' James asked.

'I'd love to be more specific,' Elton replied,
between munches. 'It's always been my policy to

cooperate fully with the police. But you see, Mr James, I'm bound by client confidentiality.'

'You do know that he's dead, don't you?' James said.

Elton seemed shocked – *genuinely* shocked – and swallowed the remaining Fruit and Nut with such haste that it started him coughing.

'Well, that is a turn up for the books,' DI James said. 'You really *didn't* know, did you?'

'How ... how did he die?'

'The usual way. His heart stopped beating.'

'No, I mean...'

'I know what you mean. Someone who appears not to have liked him very much bashed his head in.'

Beresford found himself wondering why Elton's reaction to the news should be so excessive. Of course, death always came as something of a shock. The bank manager, Meacham, had been quite knocked off kilter when he'd been told of the murder, and he had probably hardly known Lewis. But Elton was not in the banking business. His business – according to DI James – was firmly anchored in the criminal underbelly of society, where murder was regarded as no more than an occupational hazard.

'Could you ... could you give me a few more details about the murder, Mr James?' Elton asked.

James looked to Beresford – whose case it was – for guidance.

Why not, Beresford thought. If Elton had tuned into the news that morning, he'd *already* have the details.

187

'Lewis' body was discovered in the centre of Whitebridge late last night,' he said. 'As DI James has just told you, his head had been bashed in, and he'd been stripped down to his underwear.'

The words had an almost magical effect on Elton. The tension drained from his face immediately, and though his hands were still shaking as he reached into his drawer for a Mars Bar, it was no more than a residual shake.

'Your eating habits are starting to annoy me, Harry,' DI James said, 'and if you feel compelled to unwrap that chocolate, then *I'll* feel compelled to stuff it up your arse.'

Reluctantly, Elton laid the Mars Bar on the desk.

'That's better,' James said. 'Now where were we? Oh yes, since Lewis is dead, client confidentiality doesn't really apply any more, does it? Which means, in turn, that you no longer have any reason for not telling us what you did for him that was worth five thousand pounds.'

Elton looking longingly at the Mars Bar.

'I'm not quite sure that you're right about that, Mr James,' he said. 'And to be perfectly honest with you, I think I'd better talk to my solicitor before I say anything else.'

The general manager of the Royal Victoria Hotel rarely thought about sex any more, but looking across his desk at the slim detective sergeant with the elfin haircut, he couldn't stop himself wondering what it would be like to have her between the sheets with him.

'The reason I've come to see you is that I'd like you to lend me your ballroom,' Meadows said.

'What!' asked the manager, banishing his erotic fantasies to the back of his mind and becoming, once more, the solid, respectable man of business.

'I'd like to borrow your ballroom,' Meadows repeated.

'I'm afraid that's out of the question,' the manager told her. 'I have a hotel to run.'

'So you do – and I have a murder investigation to conduct,' Meadows countered. 'One of your guests has been killed – it really was rather careless of you to allow that to happen, but let's gloss over that for the moment – so we need to question all your other guests and all the hotel staff. We also need to conduct extensive inquiries in the area immediately around the hotel. The ballroom is the logical choice for our centre of operations.'

'I do not wish to be uncooperative—' the manager began.

'Then don't be,' Meadows interrupted.

'—but I have to think of the hotel's image. It's one thing to have one of our guests murdered, and quite another to have Royal Victoria invaded by heavy-booted police officers.'

Meadows sighed. 'Let's cut through all the crap and get straight to the reality of the situation,' she suggested. 'If I insist on requisitioning your ballroom – which under section 32 of the Beresford Act of 1947 I have a perfect right to do – the first thing *you'll* do is get on to your mates on the town council and in the Whitebridge police force and bitch about how totally unreasonable I've been. And then, because you're all probably members of the same lodge of the bare bollock and funny handshakes brigade, all these mates of yours will put pressure on the chief constable, who'll force me into a humiliating climbdown.'

'That's exactly what would happen,' the manager agreed, 'so wouldn't it be better if—'

'But all that will take some time,' Meadows said. 'And before we ever get to that stage, I'll already have got the food inspectors to go through your kitchens with a fine-toothed comb, I'll have had the health and safety mob climbing over your roofs and inspecting your fire exits, and anybody who parks anywhere near the hotel will be given a ticket. I doubt there'll be enough time to persuade the inland revenue to audit you before my boss comes down on me like a ton of bricks, but I'm certainly willing to give it a try.'

'That's blackmail,' the manager protested.

'I prefer to think of it as incentivization,' Meadows said sweetly.

'You'd probably lose your job.'

'Yes, I probably would – which would be handy for you, because it would mean I could save a place for you in the dole queue.'

The manager turned the dilemma over and over in his increasingly panicking brain.

'I suppose that if you used the ballroom, it would make the whole process considerably quicker,' he said, finally.

'Absolutely,' Meadows agreed.

'So rather than further inconveniencing the guests, it would actually make things easier for them.'

'I hadn't looked at it that way before, but now that I have, I think you're quite right.'

'Very well, since one of the things I pride myself on is being civically responsible, you have my permission to use the ballroom,' the manager said.

'That's most gracious of you, sir,' Meadows replied.

The second day of the RockStately Festival kicked off at noon, and the Midnight Crawlers had been the first band to play.

Linda Davies had worn a short, black skirt and sparkly top. She'd performed Grace Slick's 'Somebody To Love', Janis Joplin's 'Piece Of My Heart', a couple of Bessie Smith numbers and a song that she'd written herself, called 'Way Down And Low'.

She thought she'd been sensational, and a sizeable part of the audience had seemed to agree with her, so she was almost floating on air when she came off the stage.

And then she saw her brother, Dominic, standing there, at the foot of the steps.

'That was good,' he said.

'Good?' she repeated. 'It was bloody brilliant!'

'But that skirt's too short.'

'What!'

'Your skirt's too short. Some of the audience could see right up to your knickers.'

'There's at least a couple of dozen girls out

there who are topless,' Linda said. 'There may even be some bottomless ones, for all I know.'

'That's irrelevant.'

'How is it irrelevant?'

'I don't know them – they're not my sister.'

This state of affairs couldn't go on forever, Linda thought. Sooner or later, she and her brother would have to have a bloody big row, at the end of which it would be clearly established who was the boss and who was the employee.

But she didn't want to have that row now, not while – despite Dominic's best efforts – she still had a little of the glow from her performance left in her.

'That security man will take you to the main gate,' Dominic said, pointing to one of the Devil's Disciples, who was sitting behind the wheel of a golf cart. 'He looks a bit rough, but I've been assured he's perfectly safe. When you get to the gate, you'll find a car waiting to take you back to the hotel.'

'Aren't you coming?' she asked.

'No,' Dominic said. 'Ted Harper's backing band has been delayed, and I've promised him that if they don't turn up by the time he's due to go on, I'll lend him the Crawlers. It'll be good exposure for them.'

They're not *your* band to lend, she thought. They're *my* band.

But a little of the glow was still there, and she knew she would lose it if she argued with him.

'You've had an exciting morning,' Dominic said. 'If I was you, I'd have a little rest when you get back to the hotel.'

She didn't *want* to rest.

She wanted to drink tequila from the bottle, and dance across the roofs of a line of cars.

She wanted to throw herself into a swimming pool fully clothed, and then perform an underwater striptease.

She wanted to do rock 'n' roll things, not the sort of things her Auntie Madge might do.

'Well, go on then,' Dominic said.

She walked over to the golf cart, and got in. The Devil's Disciple *did* look rough, but looking rough was rock 'n' roll, too.

As they pulled away, Linda said, 'What's your name?'

'You can call me CS,' Chainsaw replied. 'That was a good gig you just did.'

'Thank you,' Linda said.

'So why aren't you looking happier?'

It was too difficult to explain. 'I'm just not.'

Chainsaw reached into his pocket. 'I bet I've got something that will cheer you up,' he said.

Lawrence Taylor was standing in line in the corridor, along with all the other guests from the third floor. In his hand he held a form he had partly completed himself, and he was waiting to be ushered into the ballroom, where ten detective constables were sitting at collapsible desks and taking statements.

'You can go in now, sir,' the uniformed constable on the door said to him. 'Please go to desk six.'

Taylor went to desk six, sat down, and found himself facing a detective constable who looked as if he'd only just started shaving, and should, by rights, still have been in secondary school.

The boy looked down at the form.

'Are you Lawrence Taylor?' he asked, in a voice that sounded surprisingly authoritative.

'Yes, I am.'

'And you are the managing director and sole proprietor of Lawrence Taylor Sportswear?'

'That's correct.'

'Could you please confirm that your home address and home telephone number are the ones written on the form?'

'They are.'

The form had been sitting in the middle of the desk, but now the detective slid it closer to his side and uncapped his fountain pen.

'I would like you to look at this photograph, and tell me if you have seen the man who appears in it, either at this hotel or anywhere else.'

Taylor examined the photograph. The man didn't even seem vaguely familiar to him.

'I don't know him,' he said.

The detective retrieved the photograph, and wrote something down on the form.

'Would you tell me where you were last night between the hours of eight o'clock and midnight?' he asked.

'I was feeling ill. I spent the entire night in my room.'

'Is there anyone who can confirm that?'

Taylor laughed. 'What, am I a suspect now? Do I look like a cold-blooded assassin to you?'

'Please just answer the question, sir,' the detective said, in a perfectly flat voice.

He had a problem, Taylor suddenly realized. He couldn't tell this lad that he'd spent the night alone now, and later tell Jeff Hill's wife, her private detective – or anyone else who was trying to bring him down – a completely different story. And the deal he'd made with Hill *was* a very sweet one.

'As a matter of fact, there is someone who can confirm it,' he heard himself say. 'A colleague of mine, Jeff Hill, was quite worried about me, and spent the night in my room, looking after me.'

The detective made another note.

'What is your relationship with this Mr Hill?' he asked.

'I've already told you, he's a colleague.'

'I'm not here to judge you, sir,' the detective said.

'And what's that supposed to mean?'

'It means that if your relationship with Mr Hill is of a more intimate nature, I need to know.'

'Are you saying I'm a queer?'

'I'm not saying anything, sir. I'm merely asking you the questions that I'm supposed to ask.'

'Jeff Hill is a colleague of mine. We are both very definitely heterosexual, and when we were single, we both had something of a reputation for our success with the ladies.'

'Fair enough,' the detective said.

'Jeff was concerned that I wasn't feeling well, and he decided to spend the night in my room in case I needed anything. There's nothing more to it than that,' Taylor said firmly.

The detective made a final note, blotted the form, and slid it into a brown folder.

'Thank you, sir, you've been very helpful,' he said.

While DS Meadows' first team was busy questioning the Royal Victoria's guests and staff, her second team – at the other end of the ballroom – had been given two other tasks.

The first was to coordinate the information that was coming in from the officers conducting inquiries out on the street.

The second was to deal with all the phone calls which always resulted from an appeal in the newspapers, in the hope that in amongst the calls made by the fanciful, the deluded and the deranged, there might just be a few solid bits of information which would help to crack the case.

DCI Wellbeloved finally put in an appearance at the ballroom at around one o'clock.

'Impressive set-up you've got here, Sergeant Meadows,' he said. 'Very impressive indeed.'

'Thank you, sir.'

'I could see last night, when I said I was putting you in charge of inquiries, that the other two – and Inspector Beresford especially – had their doubts, but I never thought for a moment that you couldn't handle it.'

'I luxuriate in the warm glow of your confidence in me, sir,' Meadows said, almost under her breath.

'What was that?'

'I said, I appreciate it that you have confidence in me, sir.'

'Yes, well, you're clearly justifying it,' Wellbeloved said. He paused for a moment. 'I've ...

err ... arranged to meet the chief constable later this afternoon, and I'd rather like to have something solid on this case to take into that meeting.'

'Sorry, sir, but – as yet – we've got virtually nothing to offer you,' Meadows said. 'We know that Lewis was in a pub yesterday lunchtime, and that from there he came back to the hotel and went up to his room, but we still haven't been able to find anyone who saw him after that.'

'No one?' Wellbeloved said.

'No one,' Meadows echoed.

'All right then, well, keep plugging at it,' Wellbeloved said.

Without a breaking lead, he was at loss to know what he should do next, Meadows thought, and, to a certain extent, she sympathized with him, because she was not sure that she would know either.

But the boss would have known what to do. The boss would already have been generating new ideas and suggesting new lines of inquiry. And that was what *made* her the boss – what distinguished her from Wellbeloved, who was merely a detective chief inspector.

'Where will you be if I want to contact you, sir?' she asked.

'As I said, from three until possibly four, I'll be in a meeting with the chief constable, and I wouldn't want to be disturbed for any reason.'

'Of course not.'

'And ... err ... after that, I think I'll wander around the area close to the crime scene. Didn't this division have another DCI who used to do that? Someone they called "Cloggin'-it Charlie"?'

'That would be Mr Woodend, sir,' Meadows said. 'He was here before my time.'

But I've met him, she thought – and he is twice the man you are.

'I'd like reports on any findings you've made on my desk by six o'clock,' Wellbeloved said. 'Give me a couple of hours to digest them fully, and then we'll have a meeting to thrash things out. I believe this team normally uses the Drum and Monkey, doesn't it?'

The Drum was sacred soil, and Meadows was tempted to say that while they used to drink there, they went to the Three Tuns now.

But that, she recognized, would be running away – admitting that she was afraid of the effect Wellbeloved might have on the team and its pub.

'That's right, sir, we meet in the public bar,' she said.

Wellbeloved wrinkled his nose. 'The public bar? Is there something wrong with the lounge?'

'Nothing at all wrong with it, as far as I know,' Meadows said. 'But *we* meet in the public.'

'All right, I don't want to fly in the face of tradition,' Wellbeloved said. 'Can I count on you to inform the rest of the team?'

'Of course, sir,' Meadows said, in her best secretarial voice.

ELEVEN

When Monika Paniatowski learned, via local radio, that there'd been a fresh murder in White-bridge, her first thought was to get on the phone to Colin Beresford and ask him for all the details, but her second thought – following close on the heels of the first – was that calling him would be both pointless and pathetic.

She wasn't involved with the investigation – and, whatever happened, she wasn't *going to be* involved with it – so why torture herself?

So instead of making the call, she went back to the control room to continue the work that she and Edward Bell had been doing before the dowager countess – whose wishes must always come first, whatever else was going on – had in-terrupted them.

There were one hell of a lot of tapes to examine – the security company's hard sell had spared no expense – but there was also a logic inherent to the system which made the task a little easier than it might otherwise have been.

When the intruder had gone beyond the range of Camera 3, the logic said, he should, by rights, have reappeared on Camera 4. Since he hadn't, he must have disappeared into one of the blind spots that the technicians simply hadn't calcu-lated for. But unless he'd stayed in the blind spot forever – in which case, the Devil's Disciples would have found him when they carried out their search – he was bound to be picked up by one of the cameras sooner or later – and the chances were, logically again, that it would be Camera 4.

And so it transpired. Camera 3 had lost the intruder at eight thirty-two, and Camera 4 picked him up again at eight thirty-four.

He was still walking in the same general direction – maintaining roughly the same distance from the main house as he always had – but since his intent was to burgle the house, he should soon be swinging to the right.

Camera 4 lost him when he reached the limit of its cover, but Camera 5 picked him up almost immediately.

Paniatowski frowned. Not only had the man proved inept at breaking into Stamford Hall once he was there, but he seemed to have chosen an unnecessarily circuitous way of reaching it.

The intruder suddenly veered to the right.

The Hall had *never* been his destination, Paniatowski realized. His target was – and always had been – Backend Woods.

That made no sense at all! The woods might be of interest to a genuine naturalist, but as far as Paniatowski knew, naturalists didn't make a habit of cutting through chain-link fences during rock concerts.

The intruder had almost reached Backend Woods, and now he came to an unexpected halt, as if uncertain whether or not to go on.

'What's he doing?' Paniatowski asked softly.

'What the bloody hell is he doing?'

The man put his hand on his head, grasped his long hair tightly, and pulled upwards.

And the hair came away in his hand.

A wig! He was wearing a wig!

The man's natural hair was short, but not excessively so, and though it was hard to say for certain on a black-and-white film, it appeared to be a shade of brown, rather than black.

'Turn around,' Paniatowski said, in what was very nearly a whisper. 'Turn around so I can get a better look at you.'

And almost as if he could hear her across space and time, the man did turn around and scanned the path he'd recently been following.

He was too far away from the camera to give Paniatowski a perfect view, but he was close enough for her to see that he had a face which would not stand out in a crowd, and was probably in his mid-thirties or early forties.

The man turned again, and headed towards the woods.

Why was he going there? What possible interest could the woods have for him?

Didn't he know that the Devil's Disciples – an unpredictably dangerous motorbike gang – were camped in those woods? True, they were at the other end – as far from where he was as it was possible to be – but no sane man would take the risk of going anywhere near them, unless he had a very good reason indeed.

Paniatowski's eyes had started to itch, and she switched off the machine. Tomorrow, she promised herself, she would track the intruder's progress from the woods to the point at which he left the grounds. And then she would hand over what she had to Burglary Squad down at headquarters.

She was pleased with the work she had done. It was not like tracking down a murderer, but at least it was something – and when *something* was all you had left to hold on to, you held on to it for grim life.

Ever since he'd seen his statement to the police being slid – finally and irrevocably – into the brown folder, Lawrence Taylor had been worrying about the conversation he'd had with the young detective.

'Would you tell me where you were last night, between the hours of eight o'clock and midnight?'

'I was feeling ill. I spent the entire night in my room.'

'Is there anyone who can confirm that?'

'What, am I a suspect now? Do I look like a cold-blooded assassin to you?'

'Please just answer the question, sir.'

In other words, he *was* a suspect, as was everyone else who was staying or working in the hotel, but there were *some* people who – for reasons that were glaringly obvious to him *now* – were more deserving of the finger of suspicion being pointed at them than others.

As his concern deepened, his need to talk to Jeff Hill became ever more pressing, but though he spent the whole afternoon looking for the bloody man, he was simply not to be found.

It was not until early evening – when Taylor

202

was desperately checking in the bar for the fifth or sixth time – that he finally caught sight of the ex-footballer, sitting alone at a table in the corner of the room, and looking as if he really didn't have a care in the world.

Taylor walked over to the counter.

'I'd like a double Johnny Walker Black Label,' he said to the barman. 'No, make it a treble.'

The barman's bushy eyebrows rose a barely perceptible fraction of an inch.

'A treble, sir?' he repeated, just to make sure he had heard correctly.

'That's right,' Taylor growled.

While the barman was measuring out his drink at the optic, Taylor turned round to look at Hill again.

Yes, there was no doubt that Hill looked relaxed – but that could just be for show.

Taylor picked up his glass, crossed the room, and sat down at Hill's table uninvited. Hill, for his part, seemed no more than mildly interested in his arrival.

'Where the bloody hell have you been all sodding afternoon, Jeff?' Taylor demanded.

'Round and about,' Hill replied, with an irritating vagueness.

Taylor took a sip of his whisky. It should have helped, but it didn't, so he took a second sip and then a gulp.

'I gave my statement to the police,' he said. 'I told them you spent the night in my room.'

Hill nodded. 'Good – I told them the same thing.'

'The thing is, I've been thinking,' Taylor said

awkwardly. 'You told me you had good reason to believe that your wife had someone watching you, and I automatically assumed that that some-one was a private detective. But it didn't have to be a private detective at all, did it? It could just as easily have been a reporter from one of the scandal sheets. In fact, it could have been the reporter who got himself killed last night.'

'You're quite right, it could have been Terry Lewis – but, as it happens, it wasn't.'

'I'm not sure I believe you.'

'I don't really care whether you believe me or not.'

'What's the name of this woman you've been having the affair with?' Taylor asked.

'That's really no concern of yours – and the fewer people who know who she is, the better.'

'I want you to give me her name.'

'Why?'

'I need to talk to her. I need to ask her if you really were with her all last night.'

'And what would you hope to gain from that?'

'If she assured me that you were with her, I'd feel a lot happier in my own mind.'

'Ah – because if she gave me an alibi for last night, it couldn't have been me who killed Terry Lewis!'

'Well, yes.'

'I *was* with her, I *didn't* kill the reporter, and you're *not* having her name,' Hill said.

'In that case, I shall be forced to take some other course of action,' Taylor threatened.

Hill laughed. 'Forced to take some other course of action?' he repeated. 'What other course of action *could* you take, without first admitting to the police that you'd lied to them?'

'I ... I...'

'It's a serious matter – lying to the police in a murder investigation – and I wouldn't be surprised if you went to prison for it.'

'You *did* kill that reporter, didn't you?' Taylor asked.

'Did I?' asked Hill, looking mildly amused and very superior. 'You say I did, I say I didn't – but only one of us will ever really know which is true.'

'This is a bit of a dump, isn't it?' DCI Wellbeloved said, looking around the public bar of the Drum and Monkey.

'We like it, sir,' Beresford said.

But it was more than just *liking* it, he thought – over the years, the bar had become almost a part of the team's personality.

'Yes, well, there's no accounting for taste,' Wellbeloved said, opening his briefcase and taking out a stack of the day's reports.

Now that was bad form, Beresford thought. The team didn't bring documents to the pub. They didn't need to, because they were *living* the case, and all the information was in their heads.

He suddenly remembered the old bobbies that he had known when he was a bright, young constable, and how they had constantly – and bitterly – complained about how things had changed during their time on the force.

'*DCI Archie Compton would never have done things like that,*' one would say.

'And old Bugger-it Bill Wallace would never have had us filling in all these forms,' another would add. 'He was what you might call a real policeman.'

Was he becoming like them?

Was he already looking back at his time working with Monika Paniatowski as the never-to-be-repeated golden days?

Because if that was what he was doing, it was time to start thinking about a new career!

'This is Doctor Shastri's autopsy report on Terry Lewis,' Wellbeloved said, holding up one of the documents. 'It's not an impressive piece of work, by any standards.'

Beresford felt his resentment flaring up again, because – just as George Martin had often been called the fifth Beatle – he regarded Doc Shastri as the fifth member of this team.

'The only three things the doctor has been able to tell us are that Lewis was killed by a blow to the back of the head, that he wasn't killed where the body was found – both of which we could already see for ourselves at the crime scene – and that he'd been dead for a couple of hours when he was discovered,' Wellbeloved continued. 'I can't help thinking that some other doctor would have been able to come up with a great deal more.'

'When you say "some other doctor", I assume you mean one who wasn't either female or Indian,' Meadows said, in a tone which reminded Beresford of a rumbling volcano.

'I didn't mean that at all,' Wellbeloved said, 'though I do feel that a man who had been

206

brought up in the English tradition might have had a better grasp of what we needed.'

'In other words—' Meadows began.

'Shall we move on, sir?' Beresford suggested.

'Yes, by all means,' Wellbeloved agreed. 'Let's look at the facts, shall we? Yesterday lunchtime, Terry Lewis has a pint and a meal in a pub close to the Royal Victoria, then he goes back to the hotel, and that's the last anybody sees of him until he turns up dead in a back alley. So, given that it's highly unlikely he could have left the hotel again without being noticed, the chances are that that's where he was killed, don't you think?'

'I'm not sure that it *is* so unlikely that he could have slipped out without anyone noticing him, sir,' Crane said.

'If you were talking about him slipping out some time late at night after the bar had closed and everyone had finally gone to bed, then I agree with you, it'd be more than possible,' Wellbeloved said. 'The only problem with that theory is that he was dead by then – and we have the autopsy report to prove it! But leaving the hotel unobserved earlier in the day would have been *impossible*. The Royal Victoria has a large number of staff, and they're trained to be observant.'

'Maybe if he was wearing a disguise...' Crane suggested.

'Oh yes, he could certainly have bought one of those plastic nose, glasses and moustache sets from a joke shop and pretended to be Groucho Marks, but I don't think he did,' Wellbeloved

207

said dismissively.

'I wasn't suggesting the disguise he might have used would be as crude as that, sir, but—'

'Thank you, we've had quite enough of that theory,' Wellbeloved said. 'I'm convinced he remained in the hotel until he was murdered, which means that his killer had to be one of the other guests.'

'How did the killer manage to get the body out of the hotel?' Beresford wondered.

'There are any number of ways he could have done it,' Wellbeloved said irritably. 'He could have bribed one of the staff to wheel him out in a laundry basket. He could have taken a chance and carried him down to the underground garage, put him in the boot of his car, and driven him out. That's no more than a minor detail, and I'm sure that as we continue to build up our case, we'll find answers to all the minor details.'

So it would have been impossible for a *live* Lewis to leave the hotel, but a doddle for a *dead* one to be smuggled out, Meadows thought. That was illogical – but, as far as Wellbeloved was concerned, logic didn't seem to come into it.

'He's already got a suspect in mind, and he's not about to let any other evidence get in the way of that,' she told herself. 'So perhaps he is as stupid as I first took him to be.'

'I've been looking through the list of the guests, and one name jumped right out at me,' Wellbeloved continued. He paused, for dramatic effect. 'And that name is Jeff Hill!'

'The ex-footballer?' Beresford asked. 'Honnerton United star centre forward?'

'The very same,' Wellbeloved agreed. 'When I was an inspector in uniform, it used to be one of my jobs to police Honnerton United's home games, and I got plenty of opportunity to study our Mr Hill. He was a dirty player on the pitch, and he was no better off it. The man had a real temper, and violence was second nature to him. He had a couple of fights which would have landed anybody else in gaol, but because he was the team's star player, he could always find a few important people – and I'm ashamed to say there were senior police officers amongst them – to get him off the hook.'

'Even so...' Beresford said.

'The other thing you should know is that he was a real bugger for the women,' Wellbeloved continued. 'If it moved, he wanted to screw it. Are you starting to see how all this fits together?'

'Not entirely,' Crane said.

'We know that Terry Lewis' stock in trade was exposing celebrities who liked a bit on the side, and we know that he hired a private detective called Elton. Now what did he hire Elton to do, Inspector Beresford?'

'Elton wouldn't say.'

'Of course he wouldn't say – but surely you can work it out for yourself! He hired him to un-cover a few sordid little celebrity affairs. And Elton put him straight on the trail of Jeff Hill,' Wellbeloved paused. 'Is something bothering you about the argument I'm building up, Inspector?'

'Only that Elton looked really worried when he learned that Lewis had been killed, but he relaxed as soon as I informed him that when we found the body, it was only dressed in its underwear.'

'So what?'

'Well, it seems to me that he thought that someone else – someone other than the person who did actually kill Lewis – was responsible for the murder. And that really frightened him, because that *other person* really frightened him, and he thought if that person *was* the murderer, he might be next on the list. But the moment I mentioned the underwear, he realized who the real killer was – and the real killer doesn't scare him at all.'

'I still don't see where you're going with this at all,' Wellbeloved said.

'Well, if Jeff Hill was the killer, why would he undress Lewis before dumping the body? And even if he did do that, how would the fact that the body was undressed tell Elton that it was Hill's doing, so he personally would have nothing to worry about?'

'Hill undressed Lewis because he thought that would confuse us – and in your case, Inspector, it certainly seems to have worked,' Wellbeloved said. 'As for Elton, it must have been something else you said which made him stop worrying, or perhaps you're completely misreading what you saw, and he was never really worried at all. I don't know which of the two it was, because I wasn't there.'

'I didn't misread anything,' Beresford said stubbornly.

'You're getting bogged down in irrelevances

now,' said Wellbeloved, who was starting to sound irritated. 'We know what sort of a man Lewis was, we know what sort of a man Hill is, and we know they were in the same place at the same time. And that's all we need to know.'

'It's still a bit tenuous, sir,' Meadows said.

'Then look at his alibi,' Wellbeloved said, waving around the form that one of the young detective constables had filled in earlier. 'He claims he spent last night caring for a sick friend.'

'Maybe he did.'

'Jeff Hill doesn't *have* any friends – anyone who knows him well will tell you that. Jeff Hill doesn't give a toss about anyone else. You can't always have a smoking gun to help you, Sergeant. Sometimes, you have to really *work* to get a result. And that's what we'll do. Tomorrow morning we'll pull Hill and this other man – Lawrence Taylor – in for questioning, and we'll break them down.'

Both Wellbeloved's methods and reasoning were crude, and there were certainly things along the way that were unexplained, but having listened to his arguments, it was perfectly possible that he was right about Jeff Hill, Meadows thought.

And if he *was* right, and if he managed to crack the case within forty-eight hours, he would have attained an almost unassailable position in the Mid-Lancs Police – which would mean that Monika Paniatowski could never return to her old role.

And wasn't that a depressing thought?

When a member of the Devil's Disciples had

completed his initiation ceremony, he became a new man, born in the jaws of Hell and catapulted into the world of mere mortals to drink, steal, rape and maim as he desired. The past was buried for ever, the future was still to be carved out with sharpened bicycle chains, or beaten into shape with baseball bats. Thus, in the gang's mythology, all members of the Devil's Disciples came from nowhere – and yet, despite the mythology, Knuckles, Slash and Wolfman came from Birmingham.

The three of them never acknowledged their common background when the other Devil's Disciples were around, but occasionally they would slink off together and discuss the places they had known and the things they had done as children. They knew it was wrong – a clear breach of the code – yet they felt it gave them something to hold on to in what was otherwise a rootless life.

They were in a quiet part of the woods that night, taking it in turns to relive their individual pasts, and conjuring up familiar images of a city they had all once shared.

It was Knuckles who was speaking at that moment.

'The first time I had it, I was thirteen,' he said. 'Me and three of my mates got talking to this girl. She was an ugly bitch – but then you don't look at the mantelpiece when you're poking the fire – and she was a bit slow. Anyway, we said to her that after it went dark, we'd go down to Wyndley Pool and look at the birds.'

'And she believed that, did she?' Slash asked,

chuckling. 'She really believed you were going to look at the birds *after* it got dark.'

'Like I said, she was mental. And she must have believed it, because when we met up on Sommerville Road, she had a bag of crumbs in her hand to *feed* the poxy birds with,' Knuckles said. 'We took her down to the pool, and one of my mates said she should lie down, because, that way, she wouldn't scare the birds. Once she was on the ground, I put my hands on her shoulders to hold her down, and another lad put his hand up her skirt. She didn't like that, but when we told her it was a game that all lads and girls played, she sort of went along with it. Then she saw that one of my mates was holding his prick in his hand, and she started screaming. Well, we couldn't have that, so I punched her in the head a couple of times and...'

There was a sudden rustling in the bushes, no more than a few yards away from them.

But it was not the accidental rustling made by someone in hiding, who inadvertently makes the wrong move. It was, rather, a rustling they were meant to hear – a rustling designed to attract their attention.

'Who's there?' asked Knuckles, taking his knuckleduster out of his pocket and slipping it on to his fingers.

'Come here,' said a voice which was both calm and commanding.

'What did you say?' asked Knuckles, not sure he had heard correctly.

'I said come here,' the voice repeated. 'I want to talk to you.'

TWELVE

Sunday, 8th August

The day began unexpectedly early for Lawrence Taylor, Jeff Hill and Harry Elton. At five fifteen in the morning, each of them heard a loud knocking on his door, and by five twenty-five, having been given the opportunity to get dressed and collect a few personal possessions together, all three were handcuffed and being assisted into waiting police cars.

By six o'clock, Hill and Taylor were in the custody cells at Whitebridge Police Headquarters. A third cell had already been prepared for Elton, who was, at that moment, being driven up the M6 to Whitebridge.

At seven o'clock, the forensic teams descended on the Royal Victoria Hotel. They had been instructed to conduct a detailed examination of Hill's and Taylor's rooms, and of both their cars, and though their instructions had been general rather than specific, they knew that it would be greatly appreciated if they could come up with a few bloodstains.

Paniatowski tried to ignore the knocking on her bedroom door, but when it graduated from a gentle tapping to a persistent hammering, she gave up and said, 'All right, come in then, if you must!'

The door swung open, and a uniformed maid, carrying a heavily-laden tray, entered the room.

'I thought I made it clear yesterday that I didn't expect – or want – breakfast in bed,' Paniatowski said irritably, and then – because the young maid looked so worried – she added, 'It's really very kind of you, but to honest, I don't feel comfortable about being waited on.'

'Sorry, ma'am, but I get my orders from the housekeeper, she gets hers from the butler, and the butler gets them from the earl,' the maid replied, infusing the last two words with an awe and reverence which suggested there was really no arguing with such a command issued from on high. 'But you don't have to eat it, if you don't want to.'

'What is it?' Paniatowski asked, weakening.

'It's a lightly poached salmon omelette with wild mushrooms,' the maid told her.

Paniatowski felt herself salivating. 'I suppose it would be a waste not to eat it now it's already been prepared,' she said. 'Could you leave it on the bedside table, please?'

'Certainly, ma'am.'

The maid put the tray down, and turned to leave.

'Sorry if I seemed bad-tempered,' Paniatowski said.

'That's all right, ma'am, you get used to bad tempers, working here,' the maid told her.

Then she moved quickly and quietly out of the

room, and closed the door behind her.

It would have been perfectly possible for Paniatowski to have her breakfast lying in bed, but her exposure to life at the Hall hadn't made her quite that decadent – yet – so she got out of bed and carried the tray over to a second small table, by the window.

As well as the omelette and pot of tea, there was a local newspaper on the tray, and the headline on the front page screamed, 'Whitebridge Murder Inquiry Continues.'

She averted her eyes while she flicked the paper open, because she didn't want to learn about the murder – she really didn't.

As she ate the omelette, she glanced through the stories on the inside pages of the newspaper, but when she reached the end of a longish article on the new ring road extension, she realized she had no idea what she'd just read, and that her mind had been on the murder all along.

She looked down at her plate. The omelette was gone, so she must have eaten it, though she had no memory of doing so.

She sighed, and, giving in to the inevitable, turned back to the front page. The newspaper was running the picture of the murder victim for a second day, it said, because though the police thought an arrest was imminent, they were still appealing to the general public for information.

Paniatowski studied the picture of the murdered man. It was clearly an amateur shot – perhaps taken by his wife or a friend. He was looking straight at the camera, and seemed to be trying his best to appear both thoughtful and strong. But he couldn't pull it off. Instead, he gave off the aura of a man who would always be a follower rather than a leader, a man who might aim at being profound, but would ultimately have to settle for being merely competent.

Paniatowski held the newspaper in the air, and examined the picture from several angles.

'Jesus!' she said to herself. 'Who would have thought it?'

Wellbeloved looked across the table at the man who seemed to be trying to shrink himself into invisibility.

'Let's make this as quick and painless as possible, shall we, Mr Taylor?' he suggested. 'Jeff Hill asked you to give him an alibi for the night of the murder, and you agreed. Is that right?'

'No, I...'

'You agreed to do it because of this,' Wellbeloved said, taking a piece of paper from his folder and waving it through the air. 'Tell him what it is, Inspector Beresford.'

'It's a contract between you and Hill, which we found in your room,' Beresford said. 'It was signed the morning after the murder.'

'That's ... that's just a coincidence,' Taylor babbled. 'We'd been talking about signing that deal for weeks, and it just so happened that...'

'Funny how you've never done business with each other before, isn't it?' Wellbeloved asked. 'Or maybe it's not funny at all, because, according to some of your colleagues, who my lads interviewed over breakfast at the Royal Vic, you and Hill couldn't stand each other.'

Taylor's top lip began to tremble. 'If I tell you the truth, will I end up going to gaol?'

'It's possible,' Wellbeloved said, 'though it's much more likely you'll be given a couple of years probation. If, on the other hand, you insist on sticking to this story of yours...'

'It's like you said – he offered me a share of the contract if I'd say he spent the night in my room. But I'd never have agreed to it if I'd thought, even for a minute, that he'd killed anybody.'

'Thank you, Mr Taylor,' Wellbeloved said.

Jean Harris liked to keep her home spick and span at all times, but on Sundays, she always got up early and made a special effort. And it was worth it, she thought, as she looked around at the result of her labours. It might only be a simple farmhouse, but the pans were gleaming, the floor was sparkling, and you wouldn't find a speck of dust if you went down on your hands and knees and searched for it.

She walked to the foot of the stairs.

'Are you nearly ready, Ben?' she called out.

'Yes, Mum,' a young voice called back.

'Only the countess will be here in a minute, and you don't want to keep her waiting,' Jean said.

She looked up at the clock, and thought to herself that it was strange the countess was not *already* there, because she seemed to really enjoy these Sunday morning lessons, and was normally bang on time.

'Her Ladyship didn't ring to say that, what with all that's going on in the Hall, she couldn't

218

make it today, did she?' Jean shouted up the stairs.

'No, Mum.'

Of course she hadn't cancelled.

What was it she had once said?

'When I make a commitment, Jean, I stick to it through thick and thin, because once you start making compromises, you're lost.'

Jean hadn't understood the last bit. At least, she'd understood the actual words, but not what the countess had meant by them.

But then the countess had seen a lot more of the world than she had, so it was only to be expected that even when they were both talking in English, they were not necessarily speaking the same language.

She walked over to the back door, and saw the countess's shiny blue Mercedes Benz parked near the barn.

'She must have driven up while I was still vacuuming,' Jean thought, surprised at how relieved she felt. 'Yes, it's hard to hear anything over the noise of that old Hoover.'

She went back in the kitchen and put the kettle on the range, just in case the countess fancied a good, strong cup of tea before she got started.

Two minutes passed, and, for the first time, Jean began to wonder if something really was wrong.

But that was a stupid thing to think – because this was rural Lancashire, and nothing *could* be wrong.

Still, the feeling would not go away, and after

another two minutes had ticked by, she decided to go and look for herself.

'So, Mr Hill, now that we know you don't have any alibi at all for the night of the murder, what do you think the next step will be?' Wellbeloved asked.

'I do have an alibi,' Hill protested. 'I was with Lawrence Taylor.'

'Ah, but you see, Taylor has retracted that initial statement and written a new one.'

'I don't believe you.'

'How can we convince Mr Hill we're telling the truth, Inspector Beresford?' Wellbeloved asked.

'Maybe we could show him Lawrence Taylor's new statement,' Beresford said.

'Yes, we could do that,' Wellbeloved agreed. He took a piece of paper out of the folder, and slid it to the centre of the table. 'Strictly speaking, I shouldn't be doing this, but if it helps to convince you...'

Hill barely glanced at the statement.

'You have to understand my position,' he said.

'Perhaps we will – if you explain it to us,' Wellbeloved said coaxingly.

'I knew who Terry Lewis was, and when I saw him in the Royal Vic, I knew why he was there. Now, I've made a couple of mistakes in the past, but I love my wife, and I'm prepared to fight to keep my marriage together—'

'Sorry, you've lost me,' Wellbeloved interrupted. 'What's Terry Lewis got to do with your marriage?'

'I've been having an affair.'

'Ah, and when you saw him, you realized he was on to you, and you decided you'd have to kill him.'

'No, I ... I thought I'd have to buy him off, but I never got the chance to, and when I heard, the next morning, that he'd been killed, I panicked – because I knew the way your minds work, and I thought you'd be bound to suspect me. That's when I got Taylor to give me an alibi.'

'You've lost me again,' Wellbeloved told him. 'Are you saying you *didn't* have an alibi for the night Lewis was killed?'

'No, I'm saying I had an alibi I didn't want to use – the woman I've been having the affair with.'

'What's her name?' Wellbeloved said.

'I'd rather not...'

'Tell me her bloody name!'

'Her name's Margaret Rodgers.'

It was the legs that Jean Harris saw first. They were invisible from the house, because of the angle that the Mercedes was parked at, but once you got closer, you couldn't miss them.

One of the legs – the left one – was straight, but the other – the right – was twisted at a crazy angle, and at first Jean thought the whole thing was no more than one of those practical jokes that her older son, Tommy, was always pulling.

But even Tommy would never have considered pulling a joke which involved the countess's car – and besides, the right leg suddenly twitched, and somebody screamed.

She had been walking fast, but now she ran around the front of the car to the driver's side – where the body attached to the legs was lying.

The countess was a mess. Her right leg was broken below the knee, and the bone was poking through. Her face was a bloody pulp. The position of her left arm suggested it had been dislocated at best, but probably – like the right leg – had been broken.

Jean crouched down beside the injured woman.

'Can you hear me, my lady?' she asked.

The countess made a groaning noise that may have been a yes.

'I'm going to have to leave you for a minute or two while I get help, but I'll be back as soon as I can. And while I'm away, you mustn't fall asleep. Have you got that? *You mustn't fall asleep.*'

The countess groaned again.

Jean stood up. In the distance, she could hear a roaring noise. Her passive mind registered the sound, but her active mind made no attempt to analyse it. She didn't even know it was stored for later use, though, of course, it was.

Beresford could quite understand why Jeff Hill should be attracted to Margaret Rodgers. It wasn't just the blonde hair and the ever-so–slightly voluptuous figure – though they were both pleasing enough – there was also an air of earthy sensuality about the woman which very few men would find it easy to ignore.

Keep your mind on the job, Colin, he ordered

himself.

'It was good of you to agree to come in and help us with our inquiries, Miss Rodgers,' he said aloud.

'I'm always willing to help the police in any way I can,' the woman told him. 'I just don't see how I can help you now.'

'We'd just like you to confirm someone's alibi for the night before last,' Beresford said.

Margaret Rodgers looked puzzled.

'Whose alibi?' she asked.

'Jeff Hill's.'

'But how *could* I confirm it?'

'Mr Hill says he spent the night with you.'

'He says *what*?'

'He says he spent the night with you – and the night before that. In fact, according to him, you've been having an affair for the last six months.'

'I have no idea what would ever possess him to say that,' Margaret Rodgers said.

'It's a lie, then?'

'Of course it is. I hardly know the man.'

The man puts his hand on his head, grasps his hair, and pulls. The hair comes away in his hand. He turns around, as if he is checking whether or not anyone is following him. Then he turns again, and heads for the woods.

Stop ... rewind ... stop ... play.

The man puts his hand on his head, grasps his hair, and pulls. The hair comes away in his hand. He turns around, as if he is checking whether or not anyone is following him. Then he turns again, and heads for the woods.

Stop ... rewind ... stop ... play.

The man puts his hand...

'You look like you've found something interesting,' said a voice from the doorway of the control centre.

Paniatowski stopped the tape, and turned around.

'Yes,' she said, 'In fact, I think I've found a lot more than I ever bargained for.' She held up her copy of the morning newspaper for Edward Bell to see. 'Look at this man.'

'That's the journalist who wrote all the smutty stories for the papers, and ended up getting himself killed,' Bell said, giving the picture no more than a passing glance.

'You're not really looking at it,' Paniatowski said. 'I want you to memorize it, so that when you close your eyes, you can *still* see it.'

'All right,' Bell agreed, clearly mystified.

'Now look at this,' Paniatowski said, hitting the rewind button and then the play button.

The man puts his hand on his head, grasps his hair, and pulls. The hair comes away in his hand. He turns around...

'That's him,' Bell exclaimed. 'That's the journalist.'

'That's what I think, too,' Paniatowski said.

'And this was taken the night he died! Doesn't that mean he might have been killed here?'

'I think it's almost certain it does. That's why the killer stripped him down to his underwear before dumping him.'

'Because if he had still been wearing that

224

sheepskin jacket, somebody might have connected him to the RockStately Festival!' Bell said, excitedly.

'Exactly.'

'So we'll have the murder on film.'

'We might,' Paniatowski said cautiously, 'but it's perfectly possible he was killed in one of the blind spots we've already found, or one we don't even know about yet.'

'This will be a real feather in your cap, won't it?' Bell said.

'You'd think so, wouldn't you, looking at it as an outsider?' Paniatowski agreed. 'But I'm afraid I won't get much out of it at all. This isn't my case. In the eyes of the investigating team, I'm no more than a witness who's inadvertently come across some valuable evidence – and all I can do is pass it on to them.'

'That must be a disappointment for you,' Bell said sympathetically.

'Not really,' Paniatowski replied.

No, she thought, it's not a disappointment – its nearly bloody killing me.

'I think we've let Harry Elton sweat for long enough,' Wellbeloved said. 'It's time to stick the boot in.'

'Before we question Elton, I think you should take a look at this, sir,' Beresford said, handing him the photograph which has just arrived from Paniatowski. 'It was taken at Stamford Hall, on the night of the murder.'

'Why are you showing it to me?' Wellbeloved wondered.

'Look at the man, sir.'

'I'm looking at him. I just don't know why.'

'It's Terry Lewis.'

'This is a photograph taken in fading light, from some distance away. I'll admit the man in it bears some resemblance to Lewis, but it could just as easily be anyone else.'

'It's him,' Beresford said firmly. 'Look at the sheepskin jacket that he's wearing.'

'What about it?'

'You remember when we were trying to figure out why Lewis had been wearing only his vest and underpants when he was dumped?'

'Yes.'

'And DC Crane suggested that maybe that was *all* he was wearing when he was killed.'

'Get on with it!'

'You said that couldn't be the case, because the vest would have been drenched in blood. You said he must have been wearing something quite thick.'

'I remember what I said.'

'Something like that sheepskin jacket, for example?'

'Or an overcoat. Or a donkey jacket.'

'Why would he have been wearing an overcoat in the middle of summer?' Beresford asked.

'Why would he have been wearing a sheepskin jacket in the middle of summer?' Wellbeloved countered.

'Because he needed to fit in with a group of people who put fashion before comfort.'

Wellbeloved sighed. 'So tell me, Inspector Beresford, would you be prepared to stand up in a court of law and swear under oath that that's a photograph of Lewis?' he asked.

'Well, no,' Beresford admitted, reluctantly.

'So there you have it,' Wellbeloved said. 'On the one hand, we have a photograph of a man bearing a passing resemblance to Terry Lewis. On the other hand, we've got Jeff Hill's balls in the vice, and all we need to do now is turn the handle just a little more tightly to get a result. Of the two possibilities before us, Inspector, I think I much prefer the latter.'

'In so many ways, you're no more than an innocent party, caught up in something you have no control over,' Wellbeloved told Harry Elton.

'Have you got any chocolate?' Elton asked.

'I beg your pardon.'

'A KitKat? A Bounty Bar? A Turkish Delight? I don't mind what. Anything will do.'

Wellbeloved turned towards the uniformed constable who was standing by the door on the interrogation room.

'Slip down to the canteen and get Mr Elton a bar of chocolate, will you?' he asked.

'Or two bars,' Elton said. 'Two bars would be good.'

The constable left the room.

'As I was saying, I consider you pretty much the innocent party,' Wellbeloved told Elton. 'And Inspector Beresford believes that, too, don't you, Inspector Beresford?'

'I do,' said Beresford, playing along with the game, though his heart was no longer in it.

'You see, we know what you did to earn the

five thousand pound fee that Terry Lewis paid you,' Wellbeloved continued. 'He wanted you to gather some information on a certain person, didn't he? And that's exactly what you did. Now you weren't to know that the certain person would kill Terry – and I don't think anyone can possibly hold you responsible for the fact that he did.'

'Go on,' Elton said cautiously.

'I'm prepared to offer you a deal, Harry,' Wellbeloved said. 'If you give us the name of the person who Terry Lewis paid you to collect the information on, we'll let you go.'

'Terry Lewis didn't...'

'Didn't what?'

'Nothing.'

The constable returned with the two bars of chocolate.

'Put them on the table in front of me,' said Wellbeloved, who had had his hands clasped together for the entire interview.

The constable laid the bars down, and Elton followed their progress with greedy eyes.

'Just one name – that's all I want,' Wellbeloved said.

He unclasped his hands, and with his left one placed the KitKat bar in the palm of his right. Then he stretched his right arm across the table.

'Take it, Harry,' he said coaxingly.

Elton reached across and lifted the bar slowly and carefully from Wellbeloved's palm, as if he suspected it was a trap waiting to be sprung.

But then, even after he'd liberated the bar, his eyes stayed on the hand – continued to look at it

228

for a full three seconds, until Wellbeloved closed it again.

A grin spread across Elton's fat face.

'You want a name, Chief Inspector?' he asked. 'I'll give you a name – Jeff Hill.'

'Thank you, Mr Elton,' Wellbeloved said. He stood up. 'Now if you'll just excuse me for a minute or two...'

As he left the interview room, his right hand was firmly inside his trouser pocket.

Beresford counted to ten, and then stood up himself. As he reached the corridor, Wellbeloved was already disappearing into the nearest Gents, and by the time Beresford got there, the chief inspector was vigorously washing his hands under the tap.

Wellbeloved jumped slightly when he saw the other man standing in the doorway.

'Why the sudden need to wash your hands, sir?' Beresford asked.

'Don't *you* ever feel the need to cleanse yourself after spending time with scum like that?' Wellbeloved said uncomfortably – and he continued to scrub away.

'Scum like that?' Beresford repeated. 'Oh, you mean Harry Elton, the man you've just given a free pass to.'

'He's given us valuable information,' Wellbeloved said. 'And on the other matter, I wasn't aware that I needed your permission to wash my hands, *Inspector* Beresford.'

'No sir, of course you don't,' Beresford replied. 'A man should be free to wash himself any time he feels dirty.'

Then he turned and left – not quite trusting himself to say any more.

The earl was pacing up and down the corridor in Whitebridge General Hospital, and the expression on his face said that while he was determined to retain his grip on his own mental stability if at all possible, he wasn't holding out very much hope that he'd succeed.

'I came as soon as I could, my lord,' George Baxter said. 'How is the countess?'

'Her leg has been set, and she's been given some stitches,' the earl said. 'They tell me her condition is painful, but not life threatening, and I suppose I should be grateful it wasn't worse. Indeed, I *am* grateful – but if I ever find the man who did this to her, I will kill him.'

They all said that in situations like this one, Baxter thought, and it was perfectly understandable.

The earl smiled weakly. 'That's nonsense, of course. I don't believe in the death penalty, and even if I did, I'm not the kind of man who could ever bring himself to inflict it. But I *do* want this man caught, chief constable, and when he is caught, I want him to be subjected to the full rigour of the law.'

'We'll catch him,' Baxter promised – though he was not entirely sure it was a promise he could keep. 'I'll assign a chief superintendent to head the team, and the case will be given top priority.'

'I want Detective Chief Inspector Paniatowski to be the one who investigates it,' the earl said.

230

And I *don't* want her to be the one, Baxter thought, because I've got her nicely hemmed up in a box, and I intend to bloody keep her there.

'With the greatest possible respect, sir, I think I'm in a better position than you are to decide who should head the team,' he said.

'I know Chief Inspector Paniatowski, I like her, and I trust her,' the earl said. 'And I want her – and no one else – to be in charge.'

It was never wise to cross anyone who was probably on first name terms with the Lord Lieutenant of the county, Baxter thought.

'Very well, my lord, I will assign DCI Paniatowski to the investigation, if that is your wish,' he said.

'It is my wish,' replied the earl, with a tone of absolute certainty in his voice which would have made his autocratic ancestors proud of him.

Beresford, Meadows and Crane sat huddled together at a table in the corner of the police canteen. It looked like a meeting of Paranoiacs Anonymous – and that was what it felt like, too.

'When we went into that interview, Wellbeloved already had Hill's name written on the palm of his hand,' Beresford said. 'And the moment he'd got Elton to read that name, he washed it off.'

'You're sure of that, are you?' Crane asked.

'I'm bloody certain of it.'

'But you can't prove it, can you?'

'Of course I can't prove it! If I could *prove* it, I wouldn't be talking to you two, I'd be talking to the chief constable.'

'So where does that leave us?' Meadows asked.

'I couldn't say whether or not Wellbeloved thinks Hill is guilty,' Beresford said, 'but there's no doubt in my mind that he's determined to pin the murder on him – whatever it takes.' He paused. 'Before we go any further, I'd like to know if either of you think there's a reasonable chance that Hill did actually commit the murder.'

Meadows and Crane shook their heads.

'If he'd done it, there'd have been forensic evidence – maybe not a lot, but some – at the Royal Vic, but the lads have been working on both his room and his car all morning, and they've come up with bugger all,' Crane said.

'Besides, that photograph clearly suggests that Lewis was killed either at Stamford Hall or pretty damn close to it,' Meadows added.

'So Wellbeloved hasn't really got a case, has he?' Crane asked.

'He hasn't got a case *yet*,' Beresford said. 'But who knows how much more evidence he's going to doctor before he's through?'

'Still, without the forensics, he's never going to make it stick in court,' Crane said.

'Without the forensics, it'll be more *difficult*, but far from impossible. You have to bear in mind that most juries aren't comfortable with forensics – they get confused by all the science. On the other hand, they love circumstantial evidence, especially if it's fed to them by a good barrister, because it's something they can relate to in their everyday lives. All of which means that there's a good chance Hill will be found guilty.'

'So what do we do?' Crane asked. 'Take everything we have to the chief constable?'

'Everybody knows how loyal we are to Monika Paniatowski, so how would it look if we went to George Baxter and complained about our *new* boss?' Beresford asked.

'It would go down like a cup of cold sick,' Meadows said.

'I still don't see any alternative,' Crane said.

'I do,' Beresford told him. 'The thing that links Hill to Wellbeloved is that they were both in Honnerton at the same time. So one of us – probably you, Jack, because your absence will be less noticeable – needs to drive over there and find out exactly what Wellbeloved has got against Hill. Once we know that, we'll have something to fight back with.'

'You are aware that investigating your boss is considered very, *very* bad form, aren't you?' Meadows asked.

'I am,' Beresford replied.

'And that if things go wrong, we could face disciplinary action, and might even be kicked off the Force?'

'Yes.'

Meadows smiled. 'Well done, Colin, I'm really proud of you,' she said.

THIRTEEN

'I'd spoken to the countess before, because once a year all the tenants and the staff are invited up to the Hall for a big dinner,' Jean Harris said, 'but it wasn't until we ran across each other at the county agricultural show that we really got talking.' She hesitated. 'To be honest with you, I think it was not so much a case of us just "running into" each other as it was of her seeking me out.'

'Go on,' Paniatowski said.

'She asked me about my two boys – she knew both of them by sight – and she was particularly interested in how they were getting on at school. I said they were doing fine – both of them are near the top of their classes – but she didn't seem happy with that as an answer. Does either of them have a subject he's a little weak in, she asked. Well, yes, I admitted, Ben's struggling a bit with his French. I could help him out with that, she said. My French is very good. And it is – at least as far as I can judge – but, do you know, even if I'd mentioned a subject she wasn't good at, she'd have offered to help – and by the time she gave the first lesson, she'd already have been working hard at *making herself* an expert.'

Jean Harris was no fool, Paniatowski thought –

in fact, she would probably have made a cracking police officer.

'Do you think there was any special reason the countess was so eager to come here?' she said aloud.

'I think she feels a bit lonely up at the Hall. The servants flatly refuse to call her Katerina, but I call her that – at least, when I can remember to – because even though my husband is only one of her husband's tenants, and it felt a little awkward at first, it was what she wanted. And then, of course, there's my kids. She hasn't got any of her own – nor is she likely to have, as far as I can see – but she loves being with mine, and they adore her.'

'You know why I'm asking these questions, don't you?'

'You're trying to find out if anybody hates her enough to have done that terrible thing to her.'

'And is there anyone?'

'You'd have to go a long way to find somebody who even mildly dislikes her. Our Ben isn't the only one she's helped out, you know. She's done countless little kindnesses for the other tenant farmers. And she's not done any of it in any grand lady-of-the-manor patronizing way – she's done it as a neighbour. We respect the earl – he's an honourable, caring landlord – but we look on Katerina almost like she was one of our own.'

'Is there anything you can tell me about the attack?' Paniatowski asked. 'Anything you might have noticed which was unusual?'

'I'm sorry, but I can't,' Jean confessed. 'Everything was just as it normally is on a Sunday morning – apart from the fact that poor Katerina was lying there half battered to death.'

'I want you to do something for me,' Paniatowski said. 'I want you to close your eyes tightly and take yourself back to the last minute or so before you found the countess.'

Jean closed her eyes.

'What are you doing?' Paniatowski asked soothingly.

'I'm walking down the steps from the kitchen to the yard.'

'And what can you see?'

'I see the legs. I think they're a dummy's legs at first, and then I know they can't be, and I feel sick.'

'And what can you *hear*?'

'I hear motorbikes, roaring away in the distance.'

'Open your eyes again,' Paniatowski said. 'Was it *motorbikes* you heard, or just *a* motorbike?'

'It was motorbikes,' Jean Harris said.

Crane's car had been climbing for some time, but once he reached the top of the Pennines, it was downhill all the way to Honnerton.

When you crossed these hills, you were entering a different world – or at least, a different history – he thought. Lancashire folk had spun cotton for over a hundred years, but Yorkshire folk had been weaving wool since the Middle Ages, and had, it seemed to him, a greater sense of permanence – and perhaps even complacency

– about themselves than their neighbours had.

He turned his mind to how he would handle things once he had reached Honnerton itself.

'I can't just walk into the local nick and ask them what they can tell me about Wellbeloved, a man who used to be one of their own, now can I?' he had asked Beresford, before he left White-bridge.

'No, I don't suppose you can,' Beresford had agreed.

'So how am I supposed to get the dirt on what happened between Hill and Wellbeloved?'

'I suggest you follow the sound advice of the legendary Charlie Woodend.'

'And what might that be?'

'Charlie always used to say that if you wanted to find out what had happened in a place, you were wasting your time going to the police station or the council officers. The local news-paper, he said, was marginally better, but if you wanted rock-solid information, you were most likely to find it at the pub – as long as it was the *right* pub.'

'So where's the right pub to find out about what went wrong when Hill was a star football player and Wellbeloved was a uniformed inspec-tor?' Crane mused, as he drove past the sign wel-coming him to Honnerton.

It was the Midnight Crawlers' second gig of the festival, and Linda Davies was feeling not just great but *rock 'n' roll great* as she climbed on to the stage. This was going to be the best perform-ance she had ever given, she thought. It was going to be the best performance anybody had ever given.

She looked out at the audience, and was shocked to find that their heads were sort of wavy and swirling, like the picture on a television which wasn't quite tuned right.

It was the excitement, she told herself. She was just so excited that it was warping everything.

Behind her, she could hear the band striking up the opening to 'Downhearted Blues', and she suddenly realized – with horror – that she couldn't remember any of the words.

Her legs were feeling wobbly now, and there seemed to be something going on in the rest of her body that she really didn't like.

Suddenly the fear swept over her – a fear which told her that her life was about to end before it had ever really begun.

'Help me,' she croaked.

And then her legs gave way under her, and she crumpled on to the stage like a rag doll.

There was a collective gasp from the audience, and her band mates stopped playing and crowded around her.

'Get back – all of you!' screamed her brother, Dominic. 'Give her room to breathe!'

Two St John's Ambulance volunteers came out of the wings, carrying a stretcher.

One of them bent over Linda.

'She's still breathing,' he said.

The two men lifted the girl on to the stretcher, and carried her to the ambulance waiting on standby behind the set.

The compère appeared on stage. 'Get your lads

238

off,' he said to the Midnight Crawlers' drummer. 'Get them off *now*.'

He walked over to the microphone into which – less a minute earlier – Linda Davies had been preparing to sing her heart out.

'Linda's going to be all right,' he assured the audience, 'and I know she'd want us to carry on as normal, so I'd like you all to give a really big hand for Venus Flytrap.'

And by the time the ambulance was pulling away, Venus Flytrap were already singing about the hard-hearted woman who ruined their lives.

The countess's leg was in plaster, and was raised above her head by an elaborate pulley system. There were stitches in her cheeks and on her forehead, and in her hand she held a button which would activate the morphine delivery.

'She can talk – but not for long,' the doctor said. 'Five minutes at the most. And if you start to upset her, I'll cut you off immediately.'

'Understood,' Paniatowski said.

She opened the door, and stepped into the room. From the bed, the countess smiled weakly at her.

'Hello Monika.'

'Hello Katerina,' Paniatowski said softly. 'Would you like to tell me what happened?'

'I'd gone to the farm to give Ben his French lesson. I parked in front of the barn, and then there was this car, pulling up beside me.'

'A car?' Paniatowski asked. 'You're sure it was a car?'

'Yes.'

'What kind of car?'

'A ... a blue Ford Escort.'

'What happened next?'

'A man got out. He was wearing a handkerchief over his face. He didn't say anything. He just attacked me.'

'What did this man look like?'

'I don't know. It all happened so quickly.'

'Was he tall? Short? Skinny? Thickset?'

'I'm sorry, I just don't know.'

She was a very bad liar, Paniatowski thought.

'I'll tell you what I think happened,' she said. 'It wasn't a man in a car at all. It was two Devil's Disciples on motorbikes.'

A fearful look filled the countess's eyes.

'You mustn't think that,' she pleaded. 'You mustn't.'

'Did they threaten you?' Paniatowski asked. 'Did they say that if you told the police what had happened, they'd come after you again?'

'It wasn't them.'

'I can understand you being frightened of them...'

'After my husband – my first husband – was arrested, the StB – the Czech secret police – pulled me in for questioning,' the countess said. 'They held me for three days. They made all kinds of threats – and I told them nothing!'

'I don't see...'

'If fearsome secret police like the StB couldn't frighten me, do you really think that three thugs on motorbikes could?'

'So there were *three* of them,' Paniatowski said.

The doctor, who had been monitoring the conversation through the window, opened the door.

'That's it,' he said.

'I need another couple of minutes,' Paniatowski told him.

'I said that's it – and I meant it,' the doctor told her.

There was little point in arguing.

'Get as much rest as you can,' Paniatowski said to the woman in the bed. 'Your friends on the farms will be thinking of you – and so will I.'

'There is only one thing I *am* frightened of,' the countess said, as if she hadn't heard the words. 'And do you know what that is?'

'No,' Paniatowski admitted. 'I don't.'

'I am frightened of my own ability to destroy the things I love.'

Chief Superintendent Holmes was taking a break from the command post outside the East Gate of the Hall, and was in his office – with his feet up – when Inspector Mitchell came to see him.

Holmes did not like Mitchell, partly because the man was an out-and-out Methodist. There was nothing wrong with religion, of course – Holmes himself made a point of being seen at church nearly every Sunday – but he saw no need to take it quite as seriously as Mitchell seemed to.

'The girl – Linda Davies – is dead, sir,' Mitchell said. 'The doctor thinks it was an overdose of heroin – there were needle marks in her arm – but whether she took too much, or it was simply a bad batch, we won't know until after the autopsy.'

'Write it up for me, will you?' Holmes said.

Mitchell waited for his boss to say more, and when it was clear that Holmes wasn't about to, he asked, 'What are we going to do about it, sir?'

'Do about it?' Holmes repeated.

'There's someone in the grounds of Stamford Hall selling heroin, sir,' Mitchell said.

'Yes, there probably is,' Holmes agreed. 'It's what tends to happen when you get a large number of degenerates crowded into one small area. Although, for all we know, the girl might have brought the stuff with her.'

'So shouldn't we be making an effort to arrest the heroin pushers?' Mitchell asked.

'And how do you propose we do that? Send the lads in?'

'Well, yes, sir.'

'And have them search nearly two hundred thousand people?'

'No sir, we obviously couldn't do that, but I thought we could round up the suspicious-looking ones—'

'They *all* look suspicious,' Holmes interrupted him. 'And even if it was possible, there's a more-than-even chance that the mere sight of policemen would be enough to make some of those animals go on the rampage.'

'But sir—'

'Just think about it for a minute, Inspector. Are you really asking me to risk my men – and my own reputation – on the slim chance that we might be able to arrest a few sleazy drug peddlers.'

'I thought we were supposed to protect the innocent, sir,' Mitchell said. 'I thought that was what we were paid for.'

Holmes gave him a hard stare. 'If you ever wish to rise above your present rank, Inspector Mitchell, you'd better start learning the difference between what we're *supposed* to do and what we *can* actually do. And as far as I'm concerned, if some of those *innocents* inside that enclosure are willing to run the risk of killing themselves, then good luck to them. They won't be missed.'

Badger had been in the concert enclosure for most of the festival – leading from the front, Spike thought, with his customary admiration – but now he was sitting in front of his tent, looking mildly worried.

'Chainsaw told me you wanted to see me,' Spike said.

'That's right, I did,' Badger agreed. 'We may have run into a bit of a problem.'

'What kind of problem?'

'Linda Davies, the lead singer with the Midnight Crawlers, has died from an overdose of heroin.'

'Yes, I heard. She was so young. What a terrible waste.'

'She got the stuff from us.'

Spike thought he must have misheard.

'She got the stuff from us?' he said. 'We're selling heroin?'

'That's right,' Badger agreed. 'We've made a lot of money out of it in the last few days. No more squats for us when winter comes – we'll be able to buy a club house.'

'So that's why you got us this job in security?' Spike said. 'That's why you backed away from the fight with the Red Dragons?'

'I didn't want us to end up in gaol when we could have been making money,' Badger said.

It couldn't be true, Spike told himself. There was no harm in selling a bit of pot, but heroin was evil. Heroin killed people – young, innocent people like Linda Davies. And he refused to believe that his leader – the man who, for all his faults, he almost worshipped – could ever have become involved in anything so vile.

It was a test, he decided. He didn't know what Badger was testing – or how he was supposed to react – but it simply had to be a test.

'You're joking, aren't you?' he said.

'I don't think the police *are* going to bother us, but you can never be too careful,' Badger said. 'And if they *do* come into these woods with sniffer dogs, they'll find the stash wherever we've hidden it.'

Not a test, then. Not a joke at all.

'Why are you telling me this?' Spike asked.

'Because there's one place they definitely won't be allowed to search, and that's in the Hall itself. And you can do something the rest of us *can't* – you can get inside.'

The words hit Spike with all the force of a knuckleduster.

'You ... you know about me,' he said.

'Go to the top of the class.'

'How *long* have you known?'

'Only since I had my first little chat with that bald git, Harry Elton. You're the only reason that we got this gig, Spike. I thought you would have guessed that by now.'

'I never...' Spike said. 'It didn't even cross my mind that...'

'Anyway, I'll give you the stuff, and you can take it up to the Hall,' Badger said. 'All right?'

'No, not all right. I won't do it.'

Badger's eyes hardened. 'You're a Devil's Disciple,' he said, 'and when another Devil's Disciple asks you to do something, you bloody do it.'

'Not any more,' Spike told him.

He walked over to his own tent, at the other side of the clearing. For a minute, he thought of packing up his stuff, but then he realized he didn't *want* his stuff. He didn't want anything associated with the Devil's Disciples – not even his bike, once it had served its purpose in getting him away from there.

He mounted his bike and kicked it up.

'If you ride out now, you can never come back, you know,' Badger shouted at him.

Spike put his bike into gear, and pulled off.

The pub was a stone's throw from Honnerton Police Headquarters. It was called the Fireman's Bucket, but – as far as he knew – Crane had yet to see any firemen drinking in it. Bobbies were quite another matter. Even though it was Sunday, and there were, presumably, pubs much closer to their homes, the Honnerton police seemed to be drawn to the Bucket like iron filings to a powerful magnet.

Sitting quietly at the bar, Crane had already discovered much about the local force. He knew, for example, that their rugby team's first eleven had a good chance of winning the league that year, provided, of course, the referee chose not to turn a blind eye to the tactics of 'them cheatin' bastards from Halifax'. He had learned that one of the local magistrates was a bleeding heart liberal who would have let Jack the Ripper get away with a slap on the wrist, and that while the chief superintendent might not *actually* be a 'big puff', he certainly behaved like one.

But as illuminating as all this gossip might be, it told him absolutely nothing on the thorny question of why DCI Wellbeloved seemed to have it in for Jeff Hill.

His best hope of coming away with something useful lay in Tom, the barman, who was middle-aged, good-natured and had sharp, intelligent eyes. The two of them had been chatting – on and off – for over an hour when the pub had quietened down a little and Crane decided it was time to make his move.

'How long have you worked here, Tom?' he asked casually.

'It must be eleven years now,' the barman replied. 'No, I tell a lie – it's twelve.'

'In that time, you must have seen a lot of people come and go.'

'A fair number, I suppose.'

'You don't happen to remember an Inspector Wellbeloved, do you?'

The barman put down the glass he was

polishing, and looked Crane straight in the eyes.

'A friend of yours, is he?' he asked, somewhat suspiciously.

'Not exactly a friend, no,' Crane admitted. 'He's recently started going out with my sister.'

'And this would be where?' the barman asked.

'Over the border – in Whitebridge.'

'And you just happened to be in Honnerton, and thought you might ask a few questions while you were,' the barman said. 'Is that what you're trying to tell me, Jack?'

Crane grinned. 'I might have done, if I thought you'd believe it – but the simple fact is that the only reason I'm here at all is to find out what I can about Wellbeloved.'

The barman nodded. 'I guessed as much.'

'The thing is, she's my *big* sister and she looked after me while I was growing up,' Crane said. 'And now I'd like to return the favour.'

'Fair enough.'

'Her last boyfriend was a real swine, you see. He really broke her heart – and I wouldn't like to see her make the same mistake again.'

'So you thought you'd pump Tom, the jovial barman, and see if you could find out whether it *would* be a mistake?'

'That's right. Do you have any objection to that?'

The barman shrugged. 'Not really. After all, it helps to pass the time, doesn't it?'

'So what can you tell me about him?'

'I don't think you need worry about him treating your sister badly – he's not that sort of feller – but if she's hoping to be swept off her feet, then she's due for a real disappointment with your friend Wellbeloved.'

'Tell me more,' Crane encouraged.

'He was always a bit awkward with women. Some men are, but in his case, it was so bad that I began to suspect that maybe he was a homo. As it turned out, I was quite wrong.'

'I'm still listening,' Crane said.

'This was about six or seven years back, now,' the barman said. 'There was a crowd of girls used to come in here, and one of them was called Maggie Thorpe. She was cracking looking, but – for some reason – she seemed almost as unsure about herself as he was about himself. In fact, if you ask me, she was still a virgin – and that's rare enough in this day and age.'

'Yes, it is,' agreed Crane – and he thought about Inspector Beresford, who most people now referred to as Shagger Beresford, but who hadn't lost *his* virginity until he'd turned thirty.

'Anyway, for the first few weeks he just sat there looking at her across the bar, but then he finally worked up the nerve to talk to her. It went on like that for a while. They'd just chat, as casual acquaintances who quite liked each other sometimes do. But he was still holding back, to such an extent that I'm not even sure she knew he fancied her. And it was more than just fancied her, in my opinion – I think he was madly in love with her.'

'Did he ever make his move?' Crane asked.

'No, he didn't. I think he was about to, but he left it just that little bit too late, and somebody else waltzed in and swept her off her feet. Of course, that particular romance ended badly – very badly indeed.'

'Who was it who swept her off her feet?' Crane asked.

Though he thought he already knew the answer.

'No chance of a bit of service, is there, Tom?' asked a voice from the other end of the bar.

'Coming right up,' the barman said. He turned to Crane. 'Be back in two shakes of a lamb's tail.'

The last song of the day had been sung as darkness fell, and the audience, marshalled by the Devil's Disciples, had left the grounds and returned to their canvas city. Some – exhausted by ten hours of heavy rock – had crawled into their tents and fallen instantly into a deep sleep. Others, reluctant to come down from their electronic high, sat in front of their tents, talking about this festival, and other festivals they had attended, and smoking a little dope.

It was still the day on which Linda Davies had died, but that already seemed so long ago – a little bit of rock and roll history about which, in later years, they would be able to say, 'Yes, I was there.'

Jimi Hendrix, Janis Joplin, Linda Davies – they had all been soldiers in the war against mediocrity and conservatism, and, as in all wars, you just had to expect casualties.

Paniatowski was pacing her bedroom in Stamford Hall, trying to exhaust herself so that she could grab a few hours sleep. But her body was too tense – her mind too active – to surrender to pain-free unconsciousness.

She had absolutely no idea why three of the Devil's Disciples had beaten up the countess so viciously. Perhaps it had been nothing more than a totally random, mindless attack, fuelled by drugs. Perhaps they simply hated her for who she was, and what she had. But whatever the reasoning behind the attack, she was convinced that the Disciples *were* responsible for it.

Even more puzzling than why she'd been attacked was the question of why the countess should have denied they had done it – why she should have been terrified, in fact, at even the *thought* of them being blamed.

Had the Devil's Disciples also killed Terry Lewis?

The circumstantial evidence all seemed to be pointing that way.

He had been in the Backend Woods, they had been in the Backend Woods – and now he was dead.

But why had they run the risk of dumping his body in the centre of Whitebridge, instead of merely burying it in the woods, where – since no one seemed to even know that Terry Lewis had gone to the Hall – it could have lain undisturbed for years?

If she had been in charge of the murder investigation, and if the earl had given her permission to interrogate the Devil's Disciples, she might already have had answers to some of her questions. But she *wasn't* in charge, and the

250

earl *wouldn't* let her talk to the Devil's Disciples.

She would go to the woods herself, she decided, and get as close to the Devil's Disciples camp as she dared. The Disciples would all be drunk – or high – by the time she got there, and as they sat talking, she just might overhear something which would give her a clue as to what exactly had been going on.

It wasn't a good plan, she told herself – in all honesty, it was a rubbish plan – but it was the only plan that she had.

She was still some distance from the Devil's Disciples' camp when she saw the light bobbing up and down like an ambitious firefly.

It was an electric torch, she thought – held by someone who was attempting to both provide illumination and do something else with his hands.

She moved slowly closer to the light, testing each step carefully before she took it, in case she might step on a twig and signal her presence.

She could hear one of the men talking.

'A hundred for me, a hundred for you, a hundred for Knuckles ... a hundred for me, a hundred for you, a hundred for Knuckles...'

The man sounded drunk, she thought. But there was more to it than that. There was an almost-hysterical excitement in his voice.

'A hundred for me, a hundred for you, a hundred for Knuckles ... a hundred for me, a hundred for you, a hundred for Knuckles...'

She was close enough now to be able to see what was going on. The two men were no more than dark shapes, but the space between them was lit up by the torch, and in that space, there was a great deal of money.

'A hundred for me, a hundred for you, a hundred for Knuckles ... a hundred for me, a hundred for you, a hundred for Knuckles...'

She became aware that someone was creeping up behind her only a split-second before he hit her on the back of the head, and once he *had* hit her, she was aware of nothing at all.

Paniatowski slowly began to regain consciousness. She was lying on the ground, she thought, and her head hurt.

And then she realized it was not only her head which was causing discomfort, but the area between her legs, which seemed to be on fire.

She began to be aware of more things about her condition. She had lost her shoes, her skirt was up around her waist, and her breasts felt as if they had been put through a mangle.

She groaned.

'Can you hear me, bitch?' asked a disembodied voice.

She said nothing.

'Tell me you can hear me, or I'll hurt you again,' the rough, drunken voice told her.

'I ... I can hear you,' she gasped.

'Good, then listen carefully! You're probably thinking of going to the police, to report what's happened, but I wouldn't do that if I was you. And do you know *why* I wouldn't do that?'

She didn't answer.

'Do you know why?'

'No, I...'

'Because, if you do, the police won't believe you. They'll think that you came here looking for a bit of fun, and that it was only when it got out of hand that you decided you didn't like it. They'll think you're just a slag – no different to all the other slags we've screwed.'

'Yeah, just like all the other slags that we've screwed,' said a second voice.

'And even if they do believe you, it won't get you anywhere,' said the first voice. 'We weren't here at all, we were in the camp – and all the other Devil's Disciples will *swear* we were in the camp. So if I was you, bitch, I'd just put it down to experience.'

'And let's be honest,' said the second voice, 'you must have enjoyed being shagged by three *real* men for a change.'

Then they were gone – crashing through the woods, making their way drunkenly back to their camp.

FOURTEEN

Monday, 9th August

They were five simple words – 'I won't be reporting it' – and once they were out, that should have been the end of it.

But the words wouldn't go away. They were trapped in an echo chamber which may have been an examination room, but could just as easily have been Monika Paniatowski's mind.

I won't be reporting it ... I won't be reporting it ... I won't be reporting it ... I won't be reporting it...

'You can get dressed now, Monika,' said a soft, caring voice that she recognized as belonging to Dr Shastri.

'Thank you.'

'Would you like me to help you down?'

'No, I can manage.'

As Paniatowski eased herself off the examination table, a little sunlight managed to ease its way through a gap in the blinds.

It seemed wrong that even the weather should be mocking her like this, she thought.

The sky had no right to be such a brilliant blue. It should be filled with dark, heavy clouds, and thunder should roll between them like the grumblings of an angry giant.

But she was not living in the middle of a Shakespearean tragedy, she reminded herself – and almost laughed at her own inflated fancy.

She was no Othello or King Lear. She was a Polish immigrant who, through some luck and a little judgement, had made a modest success of her life. And now that luck had run out, and that judgement had failed her.

She padded, barefoot, across the room to the chair on which her clothes were hanging.

'Monika...' Dr Shastri said tentatively.

'I don't want to talk about it.'

'But you *must* talk about it. And you *must* report it. You're not *just* a victim in this case, you know, you're also a senior officer in the White-bridge Police Force. It's your duty to report it!'

'You're asking me to confess to making a huge error of judgement – an error that no one in my position should ever have made,' Paniatowski said.

'Anyone can make a mistake.'

'It would ruin me.'

'Surely not.'

'Do you know how hard I've had to work to get into the position I'm in now? Can you even begin to grasp how difficult it is to earn respect in a world dominated by men?'

'I know it hasn't always been easy...'

'Well, once I report the rape, all that will be gone. I'd get sympathy, that's true, but there'd be derision as well. There would be some bobbies – maybe quite a lot of bobbies – who'd be laughing behind my back.'

'It wouldn't be as bad as that,' Shastri said.

'It would. Male officers don't get raped – so they can't really understand how it could happen to a female officer. Remember, I've been on the force a long time, and I've seen some of my so-called colleagues sniggering in corners about rape victims. "Maybe it was what Paniatowski wanted," they'll say. "Maybe she went to the Devil's Disciples' camp because she secretly fancied a bit of rough."'

'But, surely, people who know you could never believe...'

'It would give George Baxter the excuse he's been looking for to take me out of front-line policing forever. And if – by some miracle – Baxter was replaced, it wouldn't make any difference. The new chief constable would take me out of front-line policing, too. And he'd be right to do it – because if I couldn't command the respect any more, I couldn't do the job. And so I'd end up as DCI in charge of paper clips and luncheon vouchers. And I couldn't stand that.'

'Monika...' Shastri implored.

'Besides, rape's not exactly a new experience for me, is it? My stepfather raped me regularly, throughout most of my childhood.'

'But that was different,' Shastri said. 'It was a long time ago, and you've managed to put it behind you. This new attack—'

'It wasn't a long time ago, and I haven't put it behind me,' Paniatowski said angrily. 'Arthur Jones didn't just rape me thirty years ago, he raped me yesterday, and he'll rape me tomorrow – because it never really goes away. And what

256

happened last night won't go away either, but if I don't report it, at least I'll still have the chance to try and patch up my life again. And that matters to me, Doc – because, for all its drawbacks and frustrations, I still like that life.'

'And so you're going to let your attackers get away with it,' Shastri said.

'That's right,' Paniatowski agreed. 'I'm going to let the bastards get away with it.'

Most of the salesmen at the sportswear conference seemed to be young, aggressively dynamic and clean-shaven, but the one who approached Beresford in the foyer of the Royal Vic had been cast in an entirely different mould. He was older, and had a bushy white beard, and while it was hard to imagine him in a no-holds-barred business negotiation, it would have been an absolute doddle to picture him as a department store Father Christmas.

'Studying human nature, Inspector?' the faux-Santa asked.

No, Beresford thought, I'm standing here wondering where the bloody hell we go next with this investigation.

But it was much easier simply to agree.

'Yes, Mr Blair,' he said, glancing down at the man's badge. 'That's exactly what I'm doing.'

'When these young men get up in the morning, the first thing they do is look in the mirror and say, "You're the best salesman who ever drew breath, and today you're going to make a big killing",' Blair said, 'whereas *I* look in the mirror and think, didn't you used to be younger?'

Beresford grinned, but said nothing.

'Have you still got Jeff "Hard Man" Hill banged up at the police station?' Blair asked.

'I wouldn't describe him as "banged up", but yes, Mr Hill is still helping us with our inquiries,' Beresford said cautiously.

'I can't see him killing this man, Lewis, myself,' Blair said. 'I mean, Jeff's a complete shit, but I don't think he's a murderer.'

'As far as I can recall, I never actually said that he *was* a murderer,' Beresford replied.

'What I don't understand is why he doesn't just get Margaret Rodgers to tell you they were up all night making the beast with two backs,' Blair said.

'I hardly know the man,' Margaret Rodgers had said.

'Are you telling me that they've been having an affair, Mr Blair?' Beresford asked.

Blair chuckled. 'During my years in this business, I've seen countless colleagues having a bit of nooky on the side. And do you know what most of them had in common?'

'No, I don't,' Beresford said dutifully. 'What did most of them have in common?'

'They thought they were being so clever about keeping it hidden from everyone else. But, of course, there were always those little looks and gestures which gave it all away. So, in answer to your question, Inspector, yes, they've been having an affair. It was an open secret among the cognoscenti.'

Beresford confronted the woman just as she was

258

coming out of the breakfast room.

'I'd like a word with you, Miss Rodgers, if you don't mind,' he said.

'And what if I *do* mind?' Margaret Rodgers asked, glancing down at her watch.

'I'd like a word anyway,' Beresford said firmly.

With his hand on her arm to guide her, he led her into a quieter part of the lobby.

'Why don't you take a seat?' Beresford suggested, pointing to one of the easy chairs.

Margaret Rodgers ran a hand nervously through her blonde hair.

'Look, I've got a very busy morning ahead of me...' she said.

'Sit!' Beresford said – and this time, it was an order.

Margaret Rodgers sat down with some show of reluctance, and Beresford took the seat opposite her.

'The last time we talked, Miss Rodgers, you told me you hardly knew Jeff Hill,' he said.

'That's right, I don't,' she agreed.

'But apparently, it's common knowledge in the sportswear world that you've been having an affair with him.'

'Common knowledge? It can't be!'

'I can assure you, it is.'

'But that's simply not possible!' Margaret Rodgers protested. 'We've always been so...'

'So *what*?' Beresford asked.

'Nothing.'

'You've always been so *careful*?'

'Look, I'm planning to get married in six

months time,' Margaret Rodgers said.

'And rather than have your fiancé find out that you've been having a last fling with another man, you were perfectly willing to let Jeff Hill go to gaol for a murder he didn't commit?'

'I knew you'd never have enough evidence to charge Jeff with the murder. How could there be any real evidence when he'd ... when he'd...'

'When he spent the night of the murder in your bed?'

Margaret Rodgers looked down at the floor.

'Yes,' she said, in what was almost a whisper.

Beresford stood up. 'You'll be called to police headquarters to make a second statement,' he said, 'and this time, make sure it's a truthful one.'

'Will I be charged with something?' Margaret Rodgers asked, on the verge of tears.

'Do you think you *deserve* to be charged with something, Miss Rodgers?' Beresford asked unsympathetically.

DCI Wellbeloved was surprised when all three members of the team walked into his office, but even more surprised by the look on all their faces, which was somewhere between apprehension and steely determination.

'Jeff Hill didn't kill Terry Lewis,' Beresford said. 'You're going to have to let him go.'

'I should be the judge of whether or not that happens, don't you think?' Wellbeloved replied coldly.

Beresford shook his head.

'You're in no position to make that kind of

judgement,' the inspector said. 'Your own personal history with Jeff Hill means it's impossible for you to see things clearly.'

'Have you been *spying* on me?' Wellbeloved demanded.

'We prefer to think of it as doing the necessary background research, sir,' Crane said.

'I'll have your jobs for this,' Wellbeloved growled.

'Really?' Meadows asked, with studied unconcern. 'And there was us thinking quite the reverse was about to happen.'

Beresford shot Meadows a look which said she should shut up and let him handle things.

'You honestly should listen to what we have to say about the matter, sir,' he told Wellbeloved.

The chief inspector glanced at the door, as if he were about to order them to leave, then changed his mind.

'All right, I'll give you a chance to dig yourselves into an even deeper hole – but make it quick!'

'You used to have an infatuation with a girl called Maggie Thorpe,' Crane said.

A look of deep pain flashed across DCI Wellbeloved's face, and then was gone.

'I used to *know* a girl called Maggie Thorpe – but I've no idea if it's the same one you're talking about,' he said.

'Your relationship with her never actually went beyond friendship, but who knows how far it might have gone if Jeff Hill hadn't come along,' Crane continued. 'Hill was at the height of his fame at that time – Honnerton's sporting hero.

Maggie knew he had a wife, but she told her friends that he'd promised he was going to get a divorce and marry her. Then he damaged his knee, and his footballing career was over. Honnerton wasn't the right place to start up his sportswear business, and he began making arrangements to move away from the town, and that – I assume – is when Maggie began to insist he started his divorce proceedings.'

'You're assuming a *great deal*,' Wellbeloved said.

'Hill told Maggie it was never going to happen, and Maggie went into the woods alone one night, and hanged herself from an oak tree,' Crane continued. 'According to the coroner's report, which I read in the *Honnerton Chronicle*, she was pregnant at the time of her death. Not unnaturally, you've had it in for Hill ever since, but it wasn't until this murder investigation that you got the chance to do anything about it.'

'I admit I used my previous knowledge of the sort of man that Hill was as a pointer in this investigation, but the investigation itself was based on sound police work,' Wellbeloved said.

'Yes, it did look like that at the start,' Beresford admitted. 'But then forensics found no evidence where there certainly should have been some if Hill was guilty, and you refused to even consider the picture of Lewis walking around the grounds of Stamford Hall.'

Wellbeloved looked up at the clock, and then at the door again, as if he were expecting reinforcements to arrive at any minute and rescue him.

'You're building up your whole case against

me on supposition and conjecture,' he said.

'Maybe,' Beresford agreed, 'but given the way you've gone after Hill, it's enough to ruin your career.'

'If you try to take me down, I'll drag the three of you with me,' Wellbeloved threatened.

'No, not the three of us,' Beresford corrected him. 'If anybody tries to take you down, it'll be just me.'

'So the other two, your *so-called* colleagues, are prepared to let you – and *only* you – stand right in the firing line, simply because they haven't got the guts to back you up,' Wellbeloved mocked.

'Ah, the good old divide-and-rule tactic,' Meadows said. 'You haven't used that for days.'

'The reason it will be just me is that I won't *allow* the other two to back me up,' Beresford said. 'I'm the senior man, and it's my responsibility. Isn't that right, Sergeant?'

'Yes, sir,' Meadows replied – and the respectful tone in her voice was, for once, quite genuine.

'But the thing is, we don't *want* to ruin your career,' Beresford told Wellbeloved.

'No?' the chief inspector asked.

'No. We think you're basically a good bobby who's simply not temperamentally suited to CID work. We think you'd be better off in the uniformed branch.'

'Where you couldn't do anything like as much damage,' Meadows said.

'Shut up, Kate!' Beresford said harshly. 'So here's the deal, sir. You take a back seat, and let us conduct this murder inquiry ourselves, and when it's over, you put in a transfer request and go back into uniform.'

Wellbeloved glanced at the door for a third time. There was still no sign of the US Cavalry.

'This isn't about me at all, is it?' he asked. 'It's DCI Paniatowski.'

'It's partly about her,' Beresford admitted, 'but it's also about having the *right* people in the CID.'

'I've only been here a few days, but even in that short time, I've heard enough to realize that the chief constable positively loathes Paniatowski,' Wellbeloved said. 'So do you seriously believe that even if I went, he'd ever allow her to come back to her old job?'

'If we could solve this murder – and find some way for her to get the credit – he wouldn't have much choice,' Beresford said.

But there was the rub, wasn't it, he thought. They'd been on a wild goose chase for three days, and during the time the trail which led to the real killer had been growing colder and colder.

It was just twenty-five past twelve when Meadows entered the public bar of the Drum and Monkey, and ordered her customary bottle of bitter lemon.

In another half hour, the bar would be full of office workers and shop assistants, but for the moment, the only other customers were three old-aged pensioners, who were playing a vicious and unyielding game of dominoes in the far corner of the room.

Meadows sat down and waited for an inspired thought – an idea that would help solve the case and pull Paniatowski out of the shit – to come to her, but inspired thoughts seemed to be in short supply that Monday lunchtime.

'My dear Kate, what a delight to see you,' said a woman's voice. 'Are you waiting for someone?'

'I'm meeting Beresford and Crane,' Meadows said, looking up. 'But what are *you* doing here, Doc?'

'I believe it is perfectly legal for a single Indian doctor to visit a public house whenever she wishes to,' Shastri said, with a smile.

'Oh, it's legal enough,' Meadows agreed. 'But when was the last time you visited the Drum?'

'It was quite some time ago – possibly several years,' Shastri admitted, sitting down opposite her. 'But I am here now, and since I find you alone, let us grab the opportunity to have a real girl-to-girl chat with both hands.'

'A girl-to-girl chat?' Meadows repeated, and wondered if someone else – a mad scientist or an alien, perhaps – had taken over Shastri's brain for the day.

'Just so,' Shastri agreed. 'A cosy little talk would be most pleasant, don't you think?'

'Absolutely,' Meadows agreed, though she still had no idea what was going on. 'Can I order you a drink, Doc? A glass of white wine, perhaps?'

'Thank you. I do normally drink white wine, as you have so cleverly remembered, but on this occasion I rather think I would like a glass of vodka. In fact, I would appreciate you making it a double.'

So that was what all this was about, Meadows thought – or rather, that was *who* this was all about.

The waiter brought the vodka, and Dr Shastri knocked half of it back in one gulp.

'I have always admired you, Kate,' she said. 'You appear to be a very practical woman, who will always find a way to do what needs to be done, and unlike most of your otherwise estimable colleagues, you do not seem unduly bound by rules and regulations.'

Curiouser and curiouser, Meadows thought.

'Most people would consider a disregard for regulations to be something of a failing in a police officer,' she said.

'Indeed, society would not work at all if most of us did not obey the laws,' Shastri said, 'but there is still room for a few mavericks – a few idiosyncratic superheroes, if you like – who can correct the balance when society itself fails to do so.'

Meadows grinned. 'I can't say that I've ever thought of myself as a superhero.'

'Well, you should,' Shastri urged. 'I myself am very conventional – and rather dull – by nature, and if that were not bad enough, I have had imposed on me, by my profession, a code of ethics which I ignore at my peril. I suppose I am like a priest in that way.'

'Oh yes?' Meadows said, non-committally.

'Monika had a case – I think it was about two years ago now – in which a murderer confessed

266

to her priest, and because he was bound by the seal of the confessional, the priest was forced to jump through all kinds of intellectual and moral hoops in an effort to point the police in the direction of the truth.'

'Are you saying that someone's gone and confessed a murder to you?' Meadows asked.

Shastri laughed. It was her special laugh, which Paniatowski always said reminded her of the gentle tinkle of temple bells.

'Good heavens, no,' she said. 'Why would anyone confess to having committed a murder to me? Besides, that is very specific, and we are talking in general and hypothetical terms, are we not?'

'And all within the context of a girl-to-girl chat?' Meadows asked.

'Exactly,' Shastri agreed. 'Let me give you a hypothetical example of a moral dilemma I might possibly encounter. Say, for example, that a woman – for the sake of argument, let's call her a detective chief inspector – say this woman came to me because she'd been raped by three members of a motorcycle gang who had been employed to provide the security for a – oh, I don't know – a rock concert at a Queen Anne mansion. And say this woman – who could quite easily be of Polish extraction – told me she was not intending to report the rape because it would damage her career. Now I might think she had made the wrong decision – I might, indeed, be very angry that these creatures would be getting away without *any* kind of punishment – but there would be nothing I could do about it.'

'Yes, it would be a dilemma, so it's just as well that that sort of thing *has* never happened to you,' Meadows said.

'Well, exactly,' Shastri agreed, swallowing the rest of her vodka.

'The good news is that we won't be charging you with murder after all,' Beresford told Jeff Hill. 'The bad news is that we *will* be charging you with conspiracy to pervert the course of justice.'

'Why would you want to do that?' Hill asked, as if he found the whole idea of prosecuting a sporting hero like him very puzzling. 'What's in it for you?'

'You committed a crime, and we put you on trial,' Beresford said. 'It's sort of what we're here for.'

'Suppose I pleaded guilty?' Hill asked, as a cunning look came to his eyes. 'What would I get?'

'Well, judges always look sympathetically on people who save the court time by admitting their guilt,' Beresford said, 'and if you happen to come up before a judge who's a football fan – and that can be arranged – you may well get away with probation.'

Hill grinned. 'I'd appreciate that,' he said, 'and if there's anything I can ever do for you – tickets to the Cup Final, a big discount on the police football team's strip, something like that – you've only got to give me a call.' His grin widened. 'That doesn't sound like an attempt to bribe you, does it?'

'Certainly not,' Beresford assured him. 'You'd

just be showing your appreciation, like you said.
Of course, as part of your plea, you'll have to say
how sorry you are for misleading the police.'

'Naturally.'

'And you'll have to explain why you did it.'

'Are you saying...?'

'I'm saying you'll have to admit that you spent
the night – and a number of other nights before
it – with Margaret Rodgers.'

'But if I come out with that in a court of law,
then my wife's bound to find out.'

'I wouldn't worry about her finding out as a
result of the court proceedings,' Beresford said.

'Ah, you mean you'll have a quiet word with
the journalists and make sure it never gets in the
papers,' Hill said, grinning again. 'I really will
be in your debt, won't I?'

'No, I didn't mean that at all,' Beresford said.

'Then what *did* you mean?'

'I meant she won't find out from what goes on
in court, because she already knows enough to
work it out for herself.'

'You're joking, aren't you?'

'I'm afraid not. We haven't released your name
to the press – all we've said to the reporters is
that a man is helping us with our inquiries – but
someone must have rung her up and told her it
was you, because she's waiting for you down-
stairs.'

Hill went white.

'You did it!' he said. 'You've had it in for me
from the start, you bloody bastard.'

'You're taking it far too personally,' Beresford
told him. 'I feel about you what I imagine you

269

felt about Maggie Thorpe – I wouldn't go out of my way to harm you, but if you do fall headfirst into the shit, I'm not particularly bothered.'

Jesus Christ, he thought, that sounds just like something *Meadows* could have said!

When Beresford arrived at the Drum and Monkey, he found Meadows gazing at the wall, as if there was a message on it that only she could read.

'Penny for your thoughts,' he said.

'I have to go away,' Meadows told him. 'I shouldn't be gone for more than twenty-four hours, but I'll need you to cover for me while I'm not here.'

'And what does that mean, exactly – you'll need me to cover for you?' Beresford wondered.

'It means you'll have to *lie* for me,' Meadows said. 'It means you'll have to say I'm in such-and-such a place, working on the investigation, when, in fact, you won't know where the hell I am.'

'So you won't tell me where you're going?'

'I don't *know* where I'm going.'

'You're asking me to put blind trust in you,' Beresford said.

'That's right, I am,' Meadows agreed. 'If we can't trust each other, then this team's nothing. If we can't trust each other, then DCI Wellbeloved's won, and we've all lost.'

'At least tell me your disappearance will be connected with the case,' Beresford pleaded.

'It might well be connected with the case – I don't know yet – but it's definitely connected with the boss,' Meadows said.

'And you won't give me any details?'

'If I did, you'd feel obliged to stop me. You wouldn't like doing it – in fact, I think you'd hate yourself for doing it – but you'd do it anyway.'

'You're being – what's the word – enigmatic.'

'That's right, I am.'

Beresford thought about it. If the request had come from anyone else, he would have turned it down flat, he thought.

But the simple fact was that Kate Meadows was *not* like anyone else – she was a force of nature that, just coincidentally, happened to hold the rank of detective sergeant.

'You've got twenty-four hours with me acting as your cover,' he said. 'After that, you're on your own.'

'You're a real sweetheart, Colin,' Meadows said. She grinned. 'What I meant to say was, thank you very much for being so considerate, Detective Inspector Beresford.'

'You're most welcome, Detective Sergeant Meadows,' Beresford said worriedly.

At noon, the Seeds of Mutual Destruction played the last number of their set, and the RockStately Festival was officially over. Though a hard core of the Seeds fans stayed seated, hoping – against all odds – that there would be yet another encore, the majority of the audience bowed to the inevitable, and headed quickly for the exits.

The most seasoned fans had packed up their tents before the day's music began, and they were the first on the shuttle buses which would take them to Whitebridge railway station. The rest of the campers pulled up tent pegs, released guy ropes, and began to roll up their tents, wondering, as they did so, how such a big tent had ever fitted into such a small tent bag.

By a quarter past one, there was not a single tent left standing, and the roads in all directions were jammed with traffic.

It had not been Woodstock, the fans agreed, but then – if you stripped away all the hype – maybe even *Woodstock* hadn't been Woodstock, and, all-in-all, it had certainly been a festival to remember.

It had taken Paniatowski almost her entire reserve of moral strength to come back to Stamford Hall, but she had done it, and now she stood on the roof, binoculars held up to her eyes, watching the Devil's Disciples pull out.

Three of them were her rapists, she thought, and three more – maybe the same three – had beaten the crap out of the countess. And perhaps, when she had finished reviewing the surveillance tapes, she would discover that one of them was also a murderer.

If one of them *was* the killer, she realized now she had had time to think about it, then her attempts to cover up her rape were probably doomed to failure, because once she had arrested *one* of the Devil's Disciples, any number of other dirty little secrets about others would come floating to the top of the slime pit which was their existence, and the rape was likely to be amongst them.

So in solving the case, she would be dooming herself.

And for what!

To solve the murder of a gutter press journalist who was probably guilty of damaging any number of lives with the stories he had tracked down and published.

So wouldn't it be better, after all, to ignore any evidence which pointed to one of the Devil's Disciples – to let that one Disciple get away with the killing, just as she was prepared to let the other three get away with raping her?

The Devil's Disciples had ridden in single file down the narrow country lanes, but once they had hit a main road they switched to two abreast.

'The animals went in two-by-two,' the woman in the side road, who was watching their progress, thought whimsically.

She was sitting astride a 1000cc Yamaha that had been kept in mothballs since she'd left the Midlands, but which had started like a dream the first time she'd kicked it up. It would, she reckoned, easily keep pace with any of the bikes the Devil's Disciples were riding, but her aim was not to race them, but to follow them and find out where they camped for the night.

'And once I know that,' she told herself, 'the fun can really begin.'

PART THREE

Aftermath

9th–10th August

FIFTEEN

9th August – afternoon

If only Charlie Woodend was still around, Paniatowski thought miserably, as she wandered
through the ornamental gardens of Stamford
Hall, trying to decide whether or not to return to
the surveillance control room.

If he'd been there, he'd have found some way
to foil George Baxter's plan to destroy her. If
he'd been there, he would have offered his wise
guidance on the dilemma she was struggling
with at that very moment.

And suddenly – *almost* unbidden – her old
mentor was inside her head, talking to her.

'*On the one hand, Monika,*' this imaginary
Woodend said, '*we've got a woman who's
triumphed over all her disadvantages and has
done some real good in the world. That's right,
isn't it?*'

'*I suppose so,*' the equally imaginary Monika
Paniatowski answered dubiously.

'*On the other hand, we've got a grubby little
journalist who's spent his whole working life
trying to drag other people down into the same
gutter he inhabits. Am I correct?*'

'*I don't know, Charlie,*' the imaginary Paniatowski answered, glad that he was there to take all the decisions.

'And what I'm expected to do,' this wise and wonderful Woodend continued, *'is to destroy the former just to get some – probably unmerited – justice for the latter. Well, I won't do it – I'm going to bury the case.'*

Would he *actually* have said that? Would he have let her off the hook so easily?

Probably not.

It didn't really matter anyway, did it? Because Charlie *wasn't* around and she *was* – so any decision that was made was going to have to be made by her.

But somewhere at the back of her mind, the decision had already been taken, she realized – because if she didn't do all she possibly could to solve this murder, she wasn't the woman she thought she was.

And if she wasn't the woman she thought she was, then what was the point of her remaining a chief inspector?

'Well, if it is the Devil's Disciples who are responsible – and I solve the case I wasn't even assigned to – that will at least be one in the eye for George Bloody Baxter,' she said aloud.

Which was some consolation, when you thought about it – though, to be honest, not a hell of a lot!

Something seemed to have changed in the surveillance control room since the last time she had visited it, Paniatowski thought, but she couldn't quite put her finger on what that something was.

And then it hit her with the force of a house brick!

Where there had previously been a stack of video tapes, there was only an empty work surface.

She checked the cupboards under the monitors, and they were completely empty, too. She opened all the video machines, and discovered there were no tapes in them, either.

The tapes had all been removed – and there was only one person who could have done that.

She rushed down the stairs, then around the side of the Hall to where her car was parked. She gunned the engine, and sent loose chippings flying in all directions as she pulled away. She had no idea why Edward Bell had taken the tapes, but her instinct told her it was important to find out as soon as possible.

Edward Bell's wife came running out of the Lodge the moment Paniatowski had brought her MGA to a screeching halt in front of it.

'Thank God you're here, Monika,' Rosie Bell gasped. 'I don't know what to do! I don't know how to handle him!'

'Calm down, Rosie,' Paniatowski said, getting out of the car and placing her hands firmly on Rosie Bell's shoulders. 'You need to take a few deep breaths and calm down. Do you understand?'

Rosie nodded, and did as she'd been instructed.

'Now tell me what the problem is,' Paniatowski said.

'When ... when Edward came home at lunch-time, he had a big sack with him. I asked him what was in it, and he told me to mind my own business.' Rosie's upper lip quivered. 'He's never talked to me like that before in all the time we've been married. He's always been so considerate.'

'He's been under a lot of strain recently,' Paniatowski said. 'What happened next?'

'He said he didn't want any lunch. He went straight into his study, and he took the sack with him.'

Yes, he would have taken it with him, Paniatowski thought – because that sack contained the surveillance video tapes.

'Go on,' she said.

'He keeps a bottle of whisky in the study. It's a very special bottle of old malt that the earl gave him. He has one small glass of it every Christmas. Otherwise he never touches it. I think the bottle was about three-quarters full before he went in there, but I've just been in myself, and it's sitting on his desk – completely empty.'

'Is he in his study now?'

'No, I'd never have gone in if he'd still been there. I'd have been too frightened to.'

'So where *is* he?'

'I ... I don't know.'

'Haven't you any idea at all?'

'When he left the house again, he had the sack with him, and he was heading towards the orchard.'

The orchard!

'Then that's where I'll start looking,' Pania-towski said.

'I don't think you should go alone,' Rosie cautioned. 'I think you should take some other bobbies with you.'

'And why would I need to do that?'

Rosie hesitated, as if she was not sure who she needed to protect or how to go about protecting them.

'I just think it might be better,' she said evasively.

'What makes us different from the beasts of the field is that we know when we've done wrong, and – if we're any kind of men at all – we're willing and ready to take the consequences,' Edward Bell had said, only a couple of days earlier. *'I'd like to think that if I'd been George Baxter, I'd have picked up a shotgun, gone into the orchard, and blown my own bloody head off.'*

'It wasn't just the sack he was carrying, was it?' Paniatowski asked. 'He took his shotgun as well.'

'Yes,' Rosie admitted tearfully. 'Yes, he ... he did. That's why I think you should...'

But she was talking to empty air, because Paniatowski was already sprinting towards the orchard.

Bell was in the centre of the orchard, holding a shotgun in his hands, with the barrel pressed tightly against his chin. The missing surveillance tapes were piled up in an untidy mound beside him.

Paniatowski sniffed the air. She could smell

sweet and calming apple blossom, but overlying it was the stink of petrol.

'Don't come any closer, Chief Inspector!' Bell shouted, when he saw her walking towards him.

She brought herself to an immediate halt. 'Is this all right?'

'You're fine where you are – but no further.'

'What's this about, Edward?' Paniatowski asked.

'I have failed my master,' Bell said. 'I know that means nothing to you – you have no master – but it cuts me to the quick.'

He was very drunk, Paniatowski realized.

'Even if you have failed the earl – and I don't believe for a moment that you have – I'm sure he'll forgive you,' she said.

'There can be no forgiveness – because I can't forgive myself,' Bell said. 'He wanted to create something beautiful with the RockStately Festival – and I destroyed it.'

'That's a foolish thing to say.'

'Is it? Then let me ask you this – when people look back on the festival, what is it they'll remember? Will it be peace and love? Or will it be murder?'

'Why don't you put the gun down on the ground, Edward?' Paniatowski suggested.

'You think *I* killed Terry Lewis, don't you?' Bell demanded. 'You think that's why the surveillance tapes are here.'

'No, of course I don't think you killed him,' Paniatowski replied.

And she didn't. It would have taken a brilliant actor to seem as innocent as Bell had, and, for all his education, he was nothing but a plain and simple man.

'I *didn't* kill him – but he's dead *because* of me,' Bell said.

'I don't think that's true,' Paniatowski said quietly.

'Then you're a fool – and you know *nothing*.'

'Put down the gun, Edward,' Paniatowski urged. 'Think of your wife and children. They love you.'

'They love me now – but will they still love me when they find out what I've done?'

'Of course they will,' Paniatowski said. 'Love doesn't end just because you've made a mistake.'

And she was thinking – but what mistake *has* he made?

Because if she knew that – if she could work it out in the next few moments – she might just be able to persuade him to put down the shotgun.

'To think it should end like this,' Bell said bitterly. 'The shame of it! The humiliation! What kind of man am I if I can throw away three hundred years of faithful service as if it was nothing?'

She could see his finger tightening on the trigger of the shotgun.

'Please, Edward!' she begged.

Bell reached into his pocket, took out a lighter, and flicked it open. In the shade of the apple trees, the flame burned much more brightly than it would have done if exposed to full sunlight.

Bell gazed at the flame for a moment – as if he had never seen such a wondrous thing before –

then seemed to lose interest and threw the lighter, almost carelessly, on to the pile of surveillance tapes. He waited for the first few tapes to start burning, then squeezed the trigger of his gun.

His jaw disintegrated, and a fountain of blood and brains spurted out of the top of his head. He staggered backwards – a corpse doing an impression of a man who was still alive – then crumpled to the ground.

There was nothing she could do for him now, but she might still be able to save a few of the tapes, Paniatowski thought, rushing towards the small bonfire.

If she had taken time to consider what to do next, she might have looked around for something she could smother the flames with. But there was no time for considering – not with the fire taking hold so quickly – and she reached into the conflagration, avoiding the flames as best she could, and pulled three of the tapes from it. She grabbed another three – and then two more – before accepting that that was all she was going to be able to save.

She looked down at her hands – at the black plastic which had melted on to them – and realized just how much pain she was in.

SIXTEEN

9th August – evening

The woods that Badger had chosen for the Devil's Disciples' overnight camp had a country road running along their northern boundary and a small river at their southern end.

The trees in the woods were mainly silver birches, though there were a few elms and oaks, transported there as seeds by winds which had suddenly lost interest in them. The ground cover consisted mainly of snowdrops in the early spring and bluebells towards the end of it. Squirrels inhabited some of the trees, and a variety of birds built their nests in others. It was, in the opinion of most of the people who picnicked there in the summer months, nature at its best.

The Devil's Disciple orthodoxy despised nature in all its forms, and Badger had selected this particular site because the trees provided defensive cover, and the river meant that there was one side, at least, from which an attack was unlikely to come.

Not that an attack of any kind *was* very likely. The gang which claimed this particular part of Staffordshire as its home patch was called the Razors, but its reputation did not live up to its fearsome name, and if it had any sense, it would pretend not to notice that the Devil's Disciples were crossing its territory. Even so, a good commander does not take unnecessary risks, and Badger – who considered himself to be just that – had taken the precaution of posting a couple of sentries.

From in front of his tent, he surveyed the rest of the camp. The other Devil's Disciples' tents had been spread around – for defensive reasons again – but, as usual, a large fire had been built in the centre of the camp as darkness fell, and in its flickering light Badger could see gang members playing cards, drinking or getting high.

The only thing that was missing was women, he decided, and half-wished they'd stopped in Stafford and picked some up.

Getting women was easy for the Devil's Disciples.

Some of them came to the camp more than willing, some had to be cajoled or even lied to. It didn't matter *how* they got there, because once they *were* there, the Disciples would put them to work, making them perform acts that even a hardened prostitute might have baulked at.

They were trash, these bitches – even the ones who sobbed their hearts out as they were forced through their paces – and once they had satisfied every need, they could, like any other trash, be discarded without a second's thought.

Badger wondered if it was too late to send a couple of the lads out scouting for girls – and then realized he wouldn't have to, because a slim woman in a very large purple wig and a very short skirt was walking across the camp towards him, apparently oblivious to the rest of the gang.

She'd become aware of them soon enough, he thought, for though the other Devil's Disciples were letting her pass unobstructed, they were following directly in her wake, so that by the time she reached him, she would have the whole gang behind her – and there would be no escape until she had done exactly what each and every one of them wanted her to do.

Meadows could sense the growing tension and excitement just behind her, but it didn't bother her at all. She was used to getting that sort of reaction from all kinds of men, and anyway, she had a big – and really rather unpleasant – surprise in store for them.

She came to a halt in front of Badger, who was still sitting on the ground – taking his time, savouring the moment.

'I'm Zelda,' she said.

Badger licked his lips. 'And you've come here for a good time, have you?' he asked.

Meadows smiled. 'No,' she said. 'As a matter of fact, I've come here for information.'

'Not much in the tit line, but you've got nice legs,' Badger told her. 'Take off your kit and show us the goods.'

He saw himself as a hard man, Meadows thought, and the Devil's Disciples standing behind her thought they were hard, too.

They were wrong.

They might be brave, they might be ruthless, they might be willing to withstand any amount of pain – but that still didn't make them hard.

They had probably never even met any really hard men – men with iron in their souls – but they were about to.

The quiet tension was suddenly shattered by the roar of powerful engines, and a score of new motor bikes drove through the trees and rapidly formed a semicircle around the Devil's Disciples who were themselves forming a semicircle around Meadows.

'Rules numbers one and two of running a successful gang – never concentrate all your forces in one area, and always keep one eye on your boundaries,' Meadows said.

The new arrivals were all mounted on Harley Davidsons, a fact which would have drawn gasps of admiration and envy from the Devil's Disciples, had not all their eyes been focused instead on the sawn-off shotguns that the riders were holding in their hands.

'What the bloody hell is this?' Badger asked, trying to keep the quiver out of his voice.

'This,' said Meadows, 'is my friends, the Pagans.'

'Jesus!' Badger gasped.

Meadows smiled again. 'I take it from your reaction that their reputation precedes them,' she said.

The leader of the Pagans, Doc, got off his bike and walked towards Meadows and Badger.

'Back off,' he ordered the Devil's Disciples who were behind Meadows, and both his words and his shotgun said he meant it.

Looked at from treetop level, the scene might be reminiscent of a small intimate theatre, Meadows thought, with herself, Badger and Doc at centre stage, the Devil's Disciples in the stalls, and the Pagans in the circle.

On the ground, it didn't seem like that at all – on the ground, it felt like an overcrowded rat trap.

She knew she was the focus of attention, and that everyone else was waiting for her to speak.

If Monika Paniatowski had been in this situation, she would have seized the opportunity to find out what part the Devil's Disciples had played in Terry Lewis' murder, Meadows told herself – except that with that attitude, she would never have *had* the opportunity to find out, because the Pagans would have sussed her as a cop long ago, and she would already be dead.

She wasn't about to make that kind of mistake herself. She would ignore the information that DS Meadows might have wanted, and would find out only what Zelda needed to know.

'Last night, three of your gang raped a woman in the grounds of Stamford Hall,' she said. 'That woman is my sister, so what I want to do now is to have a word with those three heroes. All right?'

'I've no idea what you're talking about,' Badger snarled.

Meadows sighed. 'You know – and I know – that none of these tossers here could rape a woman without bragging about it to anybody who'd listen,' she said. 'I want those names.'

Badger said nothing.

'The nicely-nicely approach isn't working out, Doc,' Meadows said to the big Pagan, 'so I suppose we'll just have to show them how serious we are.'

Doc turned to face the Devil's Disciples, who had moved some way back but were now effectively penned in by the motorbike-mounted, shotgun-wielding Pagans. He lowered his own weapon, and seemed to be aiming it at the ground. Then he pulled the trigger, and the right foot of one of the Devil's Disciples closest to him exploded in a cascade of leather and blood.

The wounded man screamed and fell to the ground, as the other Devil's Disciples instinctively backed away to give him space.

Doc reached into his pocket, pulled out a roll of bandage, and threw it down beside the fallen Disciple.

'If you want to stop him bleeding to death, you should wrap that tightly round the wound,' he said indifferently.

Two of the other Devil's Disciples knelt down beside their wounded comrade, and while one of them cut through the remains of his boot, the other first stuck a rag in his mouth and then held him down.

Meadows waited until the bandage had been wound around the damaged foot, then said, 'That's what happens to people who *don't* cross us – so you can imagine what *could* happen to the people who *do*.'

'I...' Badger gasped.

'I want those three names from you,' Meadows snapped, 'and I want them now!'

'I can't tell you,' Badger said. He was slowly getting over the initial shock, and his voice was starting to sound firmer now. 'We're a band of brothers, bound by blood, and we don't betray each other. So kill me if you want to – but you'll get nothing out of me.'

He meant it, Meadows thought. If he gave her names now, he was finished, and within the twisted code which governed his existence, death was preferable to dishonour. And his death, in many ways, would be the crowning achievement of his life. It would bring with it a kind of immortality, and he would die happy, knowing that he was already on the way to becoming a legend.

She scanned the faces of the other Devil's Disciples, and found the same kind of resolve there – so it was just as well, wasn't it, that she had a fall-back plan which involved a fate *worse* than death?

'Phase two, Doc,' she said to the massive Pagan.

Doc nodded. 'Get your clothes off, scumbags. Do it now, or somebody else will lose a foot.'

None of the Devil's Disciples moved.

'You,' Doc said, pointing his shotgun at one of the younger Disciples, 'what's your name?'

'Cobra!' the boy said defiantly.

'Cobra!' Doc repeated, with derision. 'Cobra! All right, *Cobra*, I'd really appreciate it if you'd show the rest of your mates how it's done.'

Slowly and reluctantly, Cobra lifted his tee-shirt over his head.

'Have you got the idea now?' Doc asked the other Devil's Disciples. 'What we're going to have now is a race to get naked – and the last one over the line gets kneecapped.'

The Devil's Disciples began to strip, doing their best to give the impression they were in no hurry, but all the while watching the others to make sure no one was getting too far ahead of them.

There was a rumbling sound in the distance, and then, through the trees, the Devil's Disciples could see a bus pulling up.

'Don't worry, that's ours,' Meadows said. 'Pagan Transportation, at your service.'

'What do you need a bus for?'

'We need it because we're going to take you into town.'

'What ... why would you...?' Badger asked – and though he had no idea what was coming next, he was already frightened of it.

Meadows smiled. 'Didn't I mention the next part of the plan to you?' she asked innocently.

'No.'

'Well, when you're all bollock naked, we're going to paint your arses yellow, whisk you into Stafford, and chain you to lamp posts all around town.'

Hands stopped undoing belt buckles, fingers ceased to pull down zips. The Devil's Disciples had frozen.

'The race is still on – and the prize is still the same for last man over the finishing line,' Doc reminded them.

A dramatic, heroic death was one thing, but to be chained to a lamp post – to be laughed at and humiliated by the very people who should live in fear of you – was quite another, the looks on the

Devil's Disciples' faces said.

And it would happen – because you couldn't prevent it happening when your foot had disintegrated or your kneecap had been blown away.

'Give her the names,' Chainsaw said.

And all around him, other Devil's Disciples started to shout out the same thing – 'Give her the names ... give her the names.'

'*You* give her the names!' Badger challenged him.

And when Chainsaw did just that – croaking the words in the voice of a Judas who had been pulled down from the tree only half-hanged – there was an almost general feeling of relief.

Though, it had to be admitted, that relief was not shared by Slash, Knuckles and Wolfman.

Spike had been on the road ever since he'd ridden away from Stamford Hall the previous day. He had been driving at high speeds – at dangerous speeds – for most of that time. By rights, he should have crashed – and died – at least half a dozen times. Yet it hadn't happened. That same cruel god who had loved his ancestors for their arrogance – and who hated him for his lack of it – had looked down on him and decided it would be a good joke to let him carry on living.

He had no idea where he had been, and only the vaguest memories of catching a few hours uneasy sleep under a tree. He hadn't eaten at all, but the great emptiness in the pit of his stomach had nothing to do with hunger.

He saw the police station up ahead of him – its illuminated sign a beacon in the dark night of his soul – and he knew immediately what he had to do.

When he got off his bike, he did not put it on its stand, but instead simply let it fall to the ground, because he had no use for it any more.

As he walked towards the main entrance of the police station, the voices of the past were playing in his head.

'You're not half the man your father was,' said his housemaster, as he wielded his cane with a gleeful ferocity, before slashing it across Spike's backside. *'Not a quarter of the man!'*

'Your father would have horsewhipped any man who didn't show him sufficient respect,' his mother had said. *'But you let other people walk all over you. What kind of man does that make you?'*

No kind of man at all, Mother, he thought.

But the worst of his tormentors had been his father himself.

'I find it almost impossible to believe that, coming from such good stock, you have turned out as you have. Is that my fault, do you think?'

No, Father, the fault is mine, and mine alone.

He had thought he had finally found his home – his own place in the universe – with the Devil's Disciples, and in order to sustain that illusion he had excused or explained away anything the Disciples had done which he really knew – deep within himself – was wrong.

But there were some things which even his desperate desire for that illusion could not sustain. He had admired Badger because he needed to – but how could he still admire a man who sold death in a syringe?

He entered the police station, and walked up to the desk.

The desk sergeant, who had been happily reading his evening newspaper, looked up.

'Yes?' he said, in a bored, disinterested voice.

'I want to report a crime,' Spike said.

The sergeant sighed, and pulled out a form from under the desk.

'Name?' he asked, his pen poised over the form.

'Spike.'

The sergeant sighed again. 'Not your nickname, lad, your proper bloody name.'

'The Honourable Sebastian de Courtney,' Spike said.

The sergeant put his pen down on the counter.

'Are you taking the piss?' he demanded.

'No,' Spike said, handing the sergeant his driving license.

The sergeant examined the license, then looked up at Spike again with an entirely new expression on his face.

'Well, bugger me!' he said.

The same woods, a different clearing.

Eight people – four Pagans armed with sawn-off shotguns; three half-naked Devil's Disciples with their hands tied behind their backs; and one sadomasochistic police officer who was playing the role of Zelda, her alter ego, for all that she was worth.

It was Doc who dominated the scene, just as he dominated the scene wherever he was, Meadows thought. Despite the way he was dressed – in tattered jeans and greasy jacket – there was something almost godlike about him.

Back in the old days, he would have killed her if he'd ever found out she was an undercover police woman, and even now – when she was no longer in a position to harm the Pagans – her membership of the force would have been enough to justify her death.

But he hadn't known then, and he still didn't know, and when she had appeared out of the blue – just as she had disappeared *into* the blue, three years earlier – it had been the woman he had once ridden with that he saw. And when she had begged a favour, he had granted her request in a heartbeat.

'Listen, we want to pay you for the fun we had with your sister,' Knuckles said.

'That's exactly why we're here in these woods – to even up the score,' Meadows replied.

'No, I don't mean pay like that,' Knuckles babbled. 'I mean, we'll pay with money. We've got six thousand quid between us. You can have it all.'

'Six thousand pounds is a lot of money. Where did it come from?' Meadows asked curiously, as, despite what she'd promised herself, the detective sergeant in her temporarily nudged Zelda to one side.

'We've ... we've been saving it up,' Knuckles said.

Meadows turned to Doc. 'Do you think he's

telling the truth?'

Doc shook his massive head. 'Not a chance.'

'Where did the money come from?' Meadows repeated.

'We dealt some heroin at that rock festival.'

'And where did you get the heroin from?'

'That feller fixed it for us.'

'He must think I'm bleeding psychic or something,' Meadows said to Doc. She turned back to Knuckles. 'Which feller, Bonehead?'

'The bald feller – the one that hired us as security.'

A few of the pieces of the puzzle were finally starting to click into place, Meadows thought.

'The bald feller!' she repeated, disbelievingly. 'Is that the best you can do?'

'It's true, he...'

'So what else can you tell me about him, apart from the fact that he was bald? Did he have duck feathers sprouting out of his arse?'

'No, he...'

'You're making him up, aren't you?'

'I'm not. I swear I'm not,' Knuckles said. 'I think ... I think I heard Badger call him Elton.'

'So you got the six thousand pounds from selling the heroin that this feller Elton got for you?'

'Yeah, that's what I'm saying.'

'Doc?' Meadows asked.

'Even in a crap outfit like the Devil's Disciples, it'll be the boss that keeps all the money,' Doc said.

'Last chance,' Meadows told Knuckles. 'Where did you get the bloody money from?'

'We got it for beating up that posh tart at the Hall.'

That posh tart?

The countess?

'Who *paid* you to beat her up?' she demanded.

Knuckles told her – and as incredible as it seemed – she thought she believed him.

'I don't want your money, and neither does the ... does my sister,' Meadows said. 'What we're looking for is revenge. Now we could blow a kneecap off each of you, or...'

She paused, and turned towards Doc, and when the Devil's Disciples did the same, they could see the thin scalpel in his hand, glinting in the moonlight.

'No,' Knuckles screamed, sinking to his knees. 'Please, not that. Blow off a kneecap. I don't care. But not that!'

On either side of him, his two companions had followed suit, and were blubbering like babies.

The detective sergeant had all she needed – or at least, all she was likely to get from this man – and she made her graceful exit, leaving the front of Meadows' brain free for Zelda to run wild.

'Hmm, kneecapping you does have its appeal,' she conceded, 'but given the nature of your crime, I think the other option would be much more appropriate.'

SEVENTEEN

10th August

It wasn't until she was walking up the main steps of Whitebridge Police Headquarters that Meadows remembered she still had the 'souvenirs' of the previous evening's work.

Doc had presented them to her – or rather to Zelda – with a great show of ceremony, and she had felt she had no choice but to accept them in the spirit in which they'd been offered.

Actually, Zelda had not at all minded taking them as trophies of war. But Zelda was a creature of the night, and on this bright summer morning, DS Meadows felt rather uncomfortable about having six rapidly withering human testicles in her possession.

She wondered what she should do with them, and, for a second, considered feeding them to her neighbour's cat. But even for Zelda, that idea was a little *too* black, she quickly decided.

She found DI Beresford sitting at his desk and gazing blankly at a space on the wall.

'You look really rough, Meadows,' he said, when he noticed her standing there.

'I didn't get much sleep last night,' she admitted, 'but I may just have come up with a lead.'

Beresford's eyes suddenly came alive.

'Let's hear it,' he said.

'I've established a link between Harry Elton and the Devil's Disciples,' Meadows told him.

'What kind of link?'

'The Devil's Disciples were selling heroin at the festival. Elton was the middleman in the deal.'

'That's a link, all right,' Beresford agreed. 'And since there's also a link between Elton and Lewis...'

'Well, exactly!'

'...we have both a motive for murder and a comparatively small pool of suspects. Where did you get this information?'

'Ah, that's the problem,' Meadows said. 'I can't tell you that.'

'Why not?'

'Because you won't like the answer at all – and because you might even feel obliged to act on the information in a way that I, personally, won't find particularly pleasant.'

'You haven't gone and done anything illegal, have you, Kate?' Beresford asked.

'I certainly haven't done anything I'm ashamed of,' Meadows replied enigmatically.

'That's not what I asked.'

'I know.'

Meadows wouldn't be pushed any further on the matter, however much pressure he applied, Beresford decided. And when you were banging your head against a brick wall – as he clearly was – it was always advisable to stop before you did any permanent damage.

'Are you sure that this information of yours about Elton is accurate?' he asked.

Meadows pictured Knuckles, his hands tied behind his back – hoping against hope that if the truth wouldn't set him free, it might at least save him from a very painful experience.

'It's accurate,' she said.

Beresford sat processing what he had learned for a moment, then shook his head despondently.

'It doesn't matter how good the information is,' he said. 'Without confirmation, I can't really use it.'

The phone on his desk rang, and he picked it up.

'Yes ... yes ... I see ... thank you for telling me.'

When he put the phone down on its cradle again, there was a broad grin on his face.

'That was the Halifax police,' he told Meadows. 'One of the Devil's Disciples – who just happens to be the earl's brother – surrendered himself to them last night, and hasn't stopped singing since. There's your confirmation,' he stood up and walked towards the door, 'and I'm off to Manchester.'

'There is one more thing, sir,' Meadows said.

'And what's that?' asked Beresford, impatiently.

'I think it is more than likely that Terry Lewis was actually murdered by the Devil's Disciples, but when I was doing my "research" last night, I did come across another possibility.'

'What sort of possibility?'

Meadows hesitated.

'It's one I'd prefer to talk over with the boss,

first, if you don't mind,' she said finally.

'I don't mind at all,' said Beresford, who was itching to be gone.

George Baxter's campaign to humiliate Paniatowski into resigning was an ongoing, progressive one, and it was more than likely that, at some time in the near future, he would take her office off her, and assign her, instead, something that was little better than a broom cupboard. But that hadn't happened yet, and it was in her office that Meadows found her.

'You're looking rough,' she said to her sergeant.

'You're the second person to say that to me in less than ten minutes, boss,' Meadows replied. Then she looked down at Paniatowski's heavily bandaged hands, and added, with some concern, 'You're not looking too clever yourself.'

Paniatowski grinned weakly.

'It's not just an old wives' tale that if you don't want to get burned, you shouldn't put your hands in the fire,' she said, 'but I didn't really have a great deal of choice in the matter – the surveillance tapes were burning up, and I had to do something.'

'Where are the tapes now?'

'The lab's working on them. It's trying to salvage what it can, and I'm just sitting on my hands, though not literally, of course,' she grinned again, 'and waiting for the results.'

'I've got something I need to tell you, boss – but I'd rather it was off the record,' Meadows said.

'Off the record?' Paniatowski repeated.

'Off the record,' Meadows confirmed.

'All right,' Paniatowski agreed – wondering just what she was letting herself in for.

Meadows sketched out what Knuckles had told her, steering clear of any reference to sawn-off shotguns, scalpels or castration.

'I need to go to Stamford Hall,' Paniatowski announced, when Meadows had finished. 'I'd like you to rustle me up a driver – unless that's another of the perks that our dear chief constable has decided I can live without.'

'I'll drive you, boss.'

'Can you be spared?'

'DCI Wellbeloved's skulking in his cave, and DI Beresford has gone off – all gung-ho – to Manchester,' Meadows said. 'There's nobody to notice whether I'm even here or not.'

When Harry Elton looked up and saw who had just entered the office, his irritation was evident.

'Not again!' he said. 'Not a-bloody-gain. I'm off the hook for anything that happened in Whitebridge, Inspector Beresford – and you should know that, because you were there when your boss *let* me off the hook.'

'It's quite true, that's exactly what DCI Wellbeloved did,' Beresford told DI James. 'But you see, Harry,' he continued, turning his gaze on Elton again, 'since then, we've received some new information.'

'Like what?'

'Like this whole sorry affair started when the earl hired you to find his long-lost brother,

Sebastian, and you tracked the lad down to a bunch of scumbags who call themselves the Devil's Disciples. Incidentally, that was a rather good piece of detective work.'

'Thank you,' Elton said, reaching into his drawer for a Crunchie.

'Was it the earl's idea that the Devil's Disciples should run the security at the RockStately Festival, or was it yours?' Beresford asked.

'It might have been mine, and it might have been his. I honestly don't remember now,' Elton said, biting into the chocolate bar.

'It was yours,' Beresford said confidently. 'You might have sold it to him as his own idea, but you'd already worked out that it would be a great opportunity to peddle a lot of heroin.'

'Is Harry a heroin dealer now?' James asked.

'No, but he knows a man who is, and he realized that whoever acted as middleman between the Devil's Disciples and Mr X could earn himself a very nice little commission,' Beresford said.

'Mr X?' James said.

'That's what we're forced to call the heroin dealer for the moment, because we don't yet know his real name. But we *will* know it soon, because Harry will tell us, won't you, Harry?'

'In your dreams!' Elton said.

'You're surely not going to pretend that you *don't* know the name of the man you were dealing with, are you?'

'What I'm telling you is that I don't know anything about any drugs,' Elton said carefully.

'We got quite a different story from Spike – or

the Honourable Sebastian de Courtney, as we now know him to be. When he surrendered himself to the Halifax police last night, he said you were right there in the thick of it.'

'He's wrong.'

'Fair enough,' Beresford said easily. 'So let's move on. It was then that you came up with yet another idea – and this one was a real cracker. Why not, you asked yourself, contact Terry Lewis and get him to run an exposé on the whole business? I'm right about that, aren't I? That must have been what he was doing there at Stamford Hall, because it's the only thing that makes sense.'

'I'm not at all convinced about this,' said DI James, playing his assigned part as the slow-thinking sidekick to absolute perfection. 'I mean, if it's true, it was a bit of a risk, wasn't it?'

'Yes, it was,' Beresford agreed. 'But if our Harry could pull it off, the rewards would be amazing. The story had everything, you see – eccentric English earl, a rock concert, a motor bike gang and drugs. He wouldn't have got *that* much money from acting as middleman for Mr X – a grand or two at most – but the Sunday papers would have paid a fortune for the story.'

'Are you sure about that?' James asked.

'I am – but you don't have to take just my word for it. Terry Lewis – who knew all about the newspaper business – was convinced it was huge, too. That's why he was willing to hand over five thousand pounds to Harry as a down payment on his commission – because that was nothing in comparison to what they'd eventually end up being paid.'

'Of course, now we know what was really going on, we also know why Harry looked so frightened when you told him that Lewis had been murdered, don't we?' James suggested.

'Exactly,' Beresford agreed. 'His first thought was that Mr X had killed Lewis – and that he was next. But when I told him that Lewis had been stripped down to his underwear and dumped in the town centre, he stopped being worried – because that didn't sound like something Mr X would do at all.'

'Are you making this up as you go along, Mr Beresford?' Elton asked, with a quiet sneer.

'The Devil's Disciples, on the other hand, could have done both things – and probably did,' Beresford said.

'What both things?' Elton asked.

'What *two* things, Harry,' Beresford corrected him. 'They could have killed Lewis because he was doing a story on him, and they could have taken his hippy clothes off him because they didn't want the police connecting him with the RockStately Festival while they still had a lot of heroin to shift.'

Of course, that still didn't explain why they'd dumped the body in Whitebridge instead of just burying it, he thought, but he certainly wasn't about to start discussing the contradictions in his theory with Elton.

'Anyway, with Lewis dead, there will be no big payment from the newspapers, but Harry's still got the five grand that Lewis gave him, so he's reasonably happy,' he said to DI James.

'But then Sebastian de Courtney turns up at Halifax police station,' James said.

'But then Sebastian de Courtney turns up,' Beresford agreed. 'That changes everything, and also explains our presence here in your place of business, doesn't it, Harry?'

'Does it?' Elton asked.

Beresford looked mildly annoyed.

'I hate it when people I'm trying to browbeat into a confession don't pay attention,' he said. 'It does absolutely nothing at all for my self esteem.'

'Maybe Harry just missed the point,' James said sympathetically. 'After all, he's not very bright, or he wouldn't be in the business he *is* in. So perhaps if you go over it again – much more slowly this time – he'll finally get the picture.'

'You're right,' Beresford said. 'Everybody deserves a second chance. So listen very carefully this time, Harry. We have a chain in operation here. At one end of the chain, we have the Devil's Disciples. The Staffordshire Police are currently rounding them up, but it's not as easy as it once might have been because – for some unexplained reason – the gang suddenly split up last night, with all the members going their separate ways.'

But the police *will* find them, he thought, and when they do, I'll interrogate each and every one of them – and I'll keep on interrogating them until they tell me which one killed Terry Lewis.

In the meantime, however, he had other fish to fry, and one of them – a bald, fat, sweating fish – was just across the desk from him.

'So we have the Devil's Disciples at one end of the chain,' he continued. 'Then we have the other end of the chain – the dealer – but the problem is, we only know him as Mr X. And that – as I explained to you earlier – is why we're here in what's the *middle* of the chain, because we'd like you to tell us who Mr X is.'

'I haven't got a clue who he is, since this has nothing to do with me,' Elton replied.

'I told you he wouldn't talk,' James said to Beresford.

'Fair enough,' Beresford said. 'There is, as we discussed earlier another way to get to Mr X – though that way will be rather painful for Harry.'

He turned, and walked towards the door.

'See you around, Harry – though I doubt if you'll see me,' James said, following him.

Beresford had turned the handle and was stepping into the corridor when Elton said, 'Hang on, what are you talking about?'

'Talking about?' Beresford asked quizzically.

'All this, "it will be rather painful for Harry" and "See you around, though I doubt you'll see me".'

'Oh that!' Beresford said. 'We think Mr X is either based in Liverpool or Manchester, so we're going to spread the word in both places about the deal you made with Lewis. I imagine Mr X will be a little miffed when he learns what a double-dealing arsehole you really are.'

'Then all we have to do is keep you under observation, so that when Mr X sends somebody to kill you, we can arrest him,' James said.

'We'll arrest him *after* he's killed you, of

course,' Beresford added. 'We'll have much more leverage that way than we would have if we stopped him doing the job he was sent to do.'

'We'll offer the hit man a deal in return for leading us to Mr X, and – hey presto – job done,' James concluded.

'You can't do that,' Elton croaked.

'Can't do what?' Beresford wondered. 'State the plain simple truth – that you were working with Lewis – and then sit back and watch what happens? My conscience will be clear.'

'Mine too,' James said.

Elton licked his lips. 'Listen, I want to make a deal.'

'Very sensible of you, Harry,' Beresford said.

The dowager countess was in her sitting room, surrounded by antique furniture and oil paintings of earls and countesses long dead. Though it was the middle of the warmest summer for fifty years, there was a blazing log fire in the hearth, and the heat it was pumping out mingled uneasily with the countess's heavy perfume, filling the air with a sticky-sweet smell which was almost making Paniatowski retch.

The dowager countess herself was sitting in a chair that was so grand it was almost a throne. She was wearing a silk dress which hung slackly on her, and the row of large pearls around her scrawny neck seemed so heavy that it was a miracle she could keep her head upright. She was heavily made-up, but that was not, Paniatowski decided, because she desired to be thought young – she seemed to have little interest in other people's opinions – but rather to disguise from herself, as much as possible, the fact that she was old.

The countess looked up at the chief inspector. She could not have failed to notice Paniatowski's bandaged hands, but she did not comment on them. Nor did she invite her visitor to sit down.

'I wish you to know from the outset that I have only agreed to speak to you because my son insisted on it,' she said.

Her voice was thick with a contempt which could have been directed either at the police officer standing before her, or for the earl who had mandated this meeting – and possibly was meant for both of them.

'And you always do what your son tells you to, do you, my lady?' Paniatowski asked.

'What choice do I have in the matter?' the dowager countess replied, and now, merging with the contempt, there was a hint of self-pity. 'My son is the earl. He owns Stamford Hall, and though I was once mistress of it myself, I am now nothing more than a guest who he tolerates only because he does not have the backbone to throw me out on to the street.'

'If you dislike him so much, why don't you leave?' Paniatowski wondered. 'Don't you have any money of your own?'

'You will cease to be impertinent immediately, or – whatever my son says – I will refuse to speak to you.'

'I'm so sorry – it must be very hard for a woman like you, used to the finer things in life, to admit she's poor.'

'I am *not* poor,' the countess said fiercely. 'With the money my husband left me, I could buy the finest house in Whitebridge.'

'Then why don't you?' Paniatowski challenged.

'Because I am not like you,' the countess said – and her contempt was definitely back in control again. 'If you were to be given a five- or six-bedroom house, you'd think you were in heaven. But I could see through the veneer, and the shoddy modernism which would captivate a stockbroker – or a senior police officer – holds no charm for me.'

'You despise anyone who is not an aristocrat like yourself, don't you?' Paniatowski asked.

'No, I do not despise the common men with hoary hands who built this Hall. Nor do I despise their successors, who have cared for it over the centuries,' the countess replied. 'I have a powerful bond with them.'

'A powerful bond,' Paniatowski repeated. 'How powerful? Did you ever invite any of these successors round for afternoon tea?'

'Of course not,' the dowager countess said dismissively. 'They would be extremely uncomfortable taking tea with one of their superiors – and quite rightly so. But that does not mean that they cannot share in this great enterprise with me. They learned their trade from their fathers, who had learned it from *their* fathers. That trade became their religion – their reason for being on this earth – and this Hall was their cathedral.'

'And you're their priestess?' Paniatowski suggested.

'No, I am just the little old lady in the front pew who wants no more than to sit there and worship,' the dowager countess said, with surprising humility.

'And that little old lady was outraged when your son opened the grounds of the Hall to the rock fans?' Paniatowski suggested.

'My husband was too lenient with both our sons,' the dowager countess said. 'He beat them – as he beat me – when they had done wrong, but he did not beat them hard enough or long enough. If he had, my eldest son might perhaps value the wonderful gift he has been given more than he does.'

'Why did you go off into the woods the other night, my lady?' Paniatowski asked.

'What makes you think that I *did* go off into the woods?' the dowager countess countered.

'You were picked up on the security cameras,' Paniatowski lied.

'But I thought...'

'You thought what?'

'Nothing.'

There is a broad strip of land in the centre of the woods which does not appear on either of the screens, the dowager countess had said, in an accusatory voice, to Edward Bell. *'Why is that?'*

'You thought, having seen the monitors in the control room for yourself, that you'd taken a route which avoided the security cameras,' Paniatowski said. 'Well, you were wrong.'

But she hadn't been wrong. She had charted her course between the cameras exactly right, and, but for the report from Meadows – which

312

had been made strictly off the record – Paniatowski would never have known anything about the other woman's expedition into Backend Woods.

For the first time in the entire interview, the dowager countess was starting to look a little rattled.

'I did go to the woods,' she admitted. 'I felt the sudden need for some exercise.'

'You don't find it easy to walk, even on flat land, and to get to the woods, you'd have to cross some pretty rough ground. It would have been a difficult journey for you, so whatever reason you had for undertaking it, it must have been a compelling one.'

'I am the dowager countess,' the old woman said. 'Nothing – and no one – compels me to do *anything.*'

'Did you go into the woods to talk to your son?' Paniatowski suggested, giving the countess the opportunity to lie.

'My son?' the dowager countess repeated. 'Why would Gervaise have been in the woods?'

'It's your other son that I'm talking about – Sebastian.'

'Was he there?'

'Didn't you know? Didn't the earl tell you?'

'The earl tells me nothing. And even if I had known Sebastian was there, why would I have wanted to talk to him?' The dowager countess paused for a moment, as if the mere mention of her younger son had reignited unpleasant memories. 'I'm tired of playing games,' she continued. 'Why don't you tell me what you know – or at least, what you *think* you know?'

'I know that you paid three of the Devil's Disciples six thousand pounds to beat up your daughter-in-law – but I *think* that was only part of the deal, and that, to earn that money, they also had to kill Terry Lewis.'

The countess looked genuinely puzzled.

'Who is Terry Lewis?' she asked.

'He's the journalist who was murdered.'

'And why should I want him dead?'

'Because he was about to run a story which would have put the earl in a very bad light, and might even have meant he ended up in prison.'

The countess shrugged. 'Why would I care about that?'

'Aren't you the least concerned about the family name?'

The countess's lip curled in disdain. 'We are members of the old aristocracy of England, not here-today, gone-tomorrow television personalities,' she said. 'We don't care what other people think about us, because their opinion is totally unimportant.' She paused again. 'Tell me, is there some kind of date on this film the cameras took of me?'

'Yes,' Paniatowski said.

Or, at least, there would have been a date if the dowager countess had actually been filmed.

'Then you will see from the date that I did not go to the woods until *after* the reporter was killed,' the old woman said.

She sounded so sure of herself that she had to be telling the truth, Paniatowski thought – which meant that the six thousand pounds had been

314

payment for just the *one* job.

'Why did you pay the Devil's Disciples to beat your daughter-in-law up?' she asked.

'You will never be able to prove that I did pay them to do that,' the dowager countess told her.

'You're quite right, I won't be able to prove it,' Paniatowski agreed. 'So you're under no obligation to tell me your motive, and if you're ashamed of what you did, I can quite understand why you wouldn't want to talk—'

'My son is intent on destroying all Stamford Hall stands for,' the old lady said. 'Last weekend it was the barbaric music that he allowed to invade – who knows what he might plan next.'

'And you blame his wife for that?'

'No, I don't blame her at all. Katerina is a typical bourgeois *hausfrau*. She has no plans of her own – all she cares about is what Gervaise wants. She is, in other words, quite sickeningly in love with him.'

'And you disapprove of love?'

'Love is a much-overrated emotion at the best of times, and when it gets in the way of duty, it becomes quite intolerable.'

'What I don't see is what you hoped to gain by having Katerina beaten up,' Paniatowski said.

'Gervaise had a nervous breakdown while he was serving in the army – his father, naturally, was disgusted by it – and is constantly teetering on the brink of a second one.'

'I don't see the connection between his nervous breakdown and his wife being attacked.'

'Then you are an even bigger fool than I took you to be. Katerina being hurt was just the sort of

315

thing that was likely to push him over the edge.'

'And if he had another breakdown, you would be able to seize control of Stamford Hall?'

'Exactly. Before they were married, Katerina insisted on a prenuptial contract which gave her virtually nothing, and certainly no say in how the Hall was run – and as for my younger son, Sebastian, I knew I could snap him as easily as I might snap a twig.'

'What I don't see is why you had Katerina beaten up, instead of Gervaise,' Paniatowski said.

'For such an apparently frail man, Gervaise has a great capacity for withstanding pain,' the dowager countess said. 'A beating might have done no more than strengthen his resolve. Besides, what kind of monster do you think I am? He is my *son*!'

What kind of monster indeed, Paniatowski asked herself.

'I wish I could see you go to gaol for what you've done, but we both know that will never happen,' she said.

'Will you tell my son about it?' the dowager countess asked.

'Would you prefer me not to?' Paniatowski replied.

A look of indecision crossed the dowager countess's face.

She doesn't want me to tell him, but to ask me not to would be too close to begging for her taste, Paniatowski thought.

'You may tell Gervaise precisely what you wish to tell him,' the dowager countess said finally.

'You sound as if you think I was asking your permission,' Paniatowski said. 'I wasn't. I don't *need* your permission.'

'In fact, having thought about it, it might be to my advantage to have him know the truth,' the dowager countess said.

'In what way?'

'He will want to hate me for it, but – because he is so *very, very good* – he will not allow himself to do so. Instead, he will come up with all sorts of reasons to excuse me – I am old, I am in pain, et cetera, et cetera. That will put a great strain on him, and perhaps he will have the nervous breakdown which would so benefit the Hall without me having to lift another finger to cause it.'

'You really *are* a complete monster, you know,' Paniatowski said.

'I am the curator of history and beauty – and that is the noblest calling in the world,' the dowager countess said calmly.

EIGHTEEN

The civilian lab technician's name was Ron Attwood. He had a receding hairline and a top pocket crammed with ballpoint pens. It was widely rumoured around police headquarters that he had a large photograph of Monika Paniatowski on his bedside table, and while the rumour was possibly untrue, there was no doubt that when he was in contact with the chief inspector, he flirted with her in a way which only a true techie would ever imagine might eventually be successful.

He was flirting with her now, as he laid the video tapes on the desk in her office.

'I've done my best with them, but it hasn't been easy,' he said. 'These things were never designed to be fireproof.' He glanced down at Paniatowski's bandages. 'They're a bit like hands in that way.'

Paniatowski grinned. 'The only reason you're pushing your luck, Ron, is that you know that if I slapped you across the face, it would hurt me much more than you.'

'Absolutely,' the technician agreed. 'You have to grab your opportunities while you can.' He put his own hand up to his mouth, in mock horror. 'Oh, sorry, DCI Paniatowski, you can't grab *anything*, can you?'

'Whoever said that our technicians were subhuman was flattering them,' Paniatowski told Meadows. 'So what can I expect from these tapes, Ron?'

'Well, you can expect them to suddenly jump where I've had to splice them, and you can expect several sections to be murky at best, for scientific reasons you couldn't possibly understand.'

'When there's the inevitable backlash against technology, and the villagers turn up at police headquarters armed with pitchforks and flaming torches, and wanting to burn you as a witch, I want you to know I'll be standing there right by your side,' Paniatowski said.

'That's very kind of you, Chief Inspector – and not a little unexpected,' the technician said.

'Think nothing of it,' Paniatowski replied. 'And when you hear me testify to them that I've seen you sacrificing virgins at midnight, I don't want you to take it personally.' She gestured to Meadows that she would appreciate it if the sergeant would put a cigarette in her mouth and then light it. 'Seriously, Ron, you've done a great job, and I really appreciate it.'

'It's always a pleasure to work for you, DCI Paniatowski – though, for the life of me, I couldn't say why,' the technician told her.

Once he'd gone, Meadows slipped the first tape into the machine and pressed the play button.

'What are we looking for?' she asked.

'We're looking for something which would

319

have convinced Edward Bell that the tapes needed to be destroyed immediately, and – possibly – convinced him to take his own life.'

'And do you have any idea what that might be?'

'No, if I'm honest, I don't have a clue.'

The first tape was from the camera that had covered the area around the entertainment enclosure. It was this camera which had captured Terry Lewis cutting through the wire and entering the park. It was possible that this camera would also have filmed Lewis leaving by the same route, but when it didn't, Paniatowski was not greatly surprised.

The second tape covered the area around the smaller of the two lakes. There was no sign of human activity there until ten o'clock, when the butler walked down to the lake and sprinkled breadcrumbs on the water.

'That'll be the bread left over from dinner,' Meadows said. 'Waste not, want not. My butler...'

'What was that?' Paniatowski asked.

'Nothing.'

'You said, "my butler".'

'Did I? I suppose what I was going to say was my butler would find something more useful to do with his time – if I had a butler, that is.'

But she hadn't been going to say that at all, Paniatowski thought.

The third tape covered the South Gate, which was neither the main entrance to Stamford Hall nor the access to the camp site. In fact, Paniatowski remembered Bell telling her that it was hardly ever used.

'This is a waste of time, boss,' Meadows said, after they had fast-forwarded through the first couple of hours. 'Shall I take it out of the machine and put the next one in?'

'You might as well,' Paniatowski agreed.

But just as Meadows was about to eject the tape, a car appeared on the screen, heading towards the gate.

'Leave it!' Paniatowski said to Meadows. 'I want to see this.'

The car stopped at the gate, waited while it automatically swung open, and then drove into the night.

'I know who killed Terry Lewis,' Paniatowski said.

And she should have realized it much earlier, she thought – because she'd known all the relevant facts even *before* Lewis had been murdered.

'I heard you'd burnt your hands,' the countess said, with concern in her voice. 'Are they *very* painful?'

'Not any more,' Paniatowski replied. 'I'm on the mend. And you seem to be, too.'

It was true. The countess's leg was still firmly held by the pulley, but some of the bruising had started to fade, and she looked considerably better and happier than she had two days earlier.

'The doctor says I can go home in a few days,' the countess said. 'It will be a while before I can walk again, but with a wheelchair, I can at least get around and see people. And I do *like* seeing people, you know?'

'From what the nurse has been telling me, you've seen a fair amount of people while you've been here in hospital,' Paniatowski said.

The countess smiled. 'Yes, I have had quite a lot of visitors – especially the tenant farmers and their families. They really seem to like me.'

'I'm surprised that *you're* surprised by that.'

'Well, you know, when you're the countess, you're never really sure whether they're being nice to you for yourself or because the earl is your husband. Yet when they came to visit me, I got the feeling it was because they really wanted to see me – that they're genuinely fond of me.' The countess paused for a moment. 'But you're a busy woman, and you're not here to talk about my revelation that I can be quite likeable, are you?'

'No, I'm not,' Paniatowski agreed. 'The reason I'm here is to tie up a few loose ends.'

'Where would you like to start?'

'Could you tell me about your brother-in-law?'

'Sebastian is fifteen years younger than Gervaise, and Gervaise has always seen it as his duty to protect his little brother.'

'Who from?'

'From their father, initially. My late father-in-law was, by all accounts, a brutal unyielding man. Gervaise tried to shield Sebastian from the kind of punishment he'd had to endure himself, but he was away a great deal – first at boarding school and then in the army – and you can only do so much from a distance. I think what upset Gervaise most was that his father had learned nothing from the experience of bringing up his first child, and made all the same mistakes with Sebastian. I think that if Sebastian had had a better childhood than he'd had himself, Gervaise would have considered all his own suffering to have been worth it.'

'You make your husband sound like a saint,' Paniatowski said, with a smile.

'There are very few saints – but I think Gervaise comes closer to that state than anyone else I have ever met,' the countess said seriously.

'Why does your mother-in-law seem to hate both her sons?'

'I think it is because neither of them came up to their father's expectations – and he blamed her for that.'

'Seriously?'

'Gervaise told me that she once went down on her knees to her husband, and begged to know why it was that he didn't love her. All he would say was, "How can I love a woman who could bring such wretches into the world?" I think she believed she really *had* failed him. And that's why, now he's gone, she wants to keep the Hall just as it was in his day – as a shrine to him! In many ways, she's trying to fill the role of the good son – the son she could never produce herself.'

'When did Sebastian leave home?'

'He left home many times – but he always came back in a few months, because he couldn't really handle the world outside the Hall. But the last time he was there, his mother was particularly vicious to him, and when he left, he swore he'd never come back again. That was three years ago. We kept expecting him to turn up, but he never did.'

'So your husband hired a private detective to find him?'

'Yes.'

'And it was because he was a member of the Devil's Disciples that the gang were hired to provide security for the festival?'

'Gervaise knew he wouldn't come back of his own free will, but he thought that if Sebastian was *forced* to come back, because his gang would be here, he might start to realize how much he missed his home.'

'I think I understand now why you wouldn't admit it was the Devil's Disciples who beat you up,' Paniatowski said.

'Please, you mustn't say it was them!' the countess urged.

'I *know* it was them,' Paniatowski said firmly. 'I even know who paid them to do it.'

'Was it my mother-in-law?'

'Yes.'

'I suspected as much.'

'The reason that you didn't want it known was because it was your husband's decision to bring the Devil's Disciples here – and he would have felt guilty.'

'You're quite right,' the countess admitted. 'He has endured enough guilt in his life, without my adding to it.'

'On Friday night, your car was filmed leaving by the South Gate at around midnight,' Paniatowski said. 'Who was driving it?'

A sad smile came to the countess's face. 'I

could say I have no idea, couldn't I?'

'Yes, you could.'

'Or I could say that Edward Bell asked to borrow it – and he can't contradict me, because he's dead.'

'That's true.'

'But Edward was an honourable man, as far as circumstances allowed him to be – and I will not have him thought of as a murderer, now that he's gone.'

'I didn't say anything about murder,' Paniatowski said.

'No,' the countess agreed, 'you didn't.' She paused. 'You know who was behind the wheel, don't you?'

'Yes, I do.'

'And because you know who was driving, you know where to look for the forensic evidence which will prove it?'

'However careful people are to wash away the traces, they always leave *something* behind.'

'So there is no point in lying.'

'None at all – but just to make things perfectly clear, who *was* driving your car that night?'

'I was.'

'And why were you going out so late in the evening?'

'I had to get rid of Terry Lewis' body.'

'Did you kill him?'

'Yes.'

'And *why* did you kill him?'

'Because he left me no choice.'

Cutting his way through the fence without being

noticed had been nerve-racking, but once he has succeeded in that, and left the festival behind him, Terry Lewis starts to relax.

If he can get this story – and if he markets it right – it could earn him anywhere up to one hundred thousand pounds, and even after Harry Elton has taken his cut, he'll still have a great wad of cash left over for himself.

The park is much larger than he'd thought it would be. You could drop the whole estate on which he lives into this park, and it would hardly be noticed. And unexpectedly, he finds himself resenting the man who owns Stamford Hall.

Why should the earl have so much money?

Why should he be able to put on this rock concert – almost as a hobby – when a poor bloody journalist like Terry Lewis has to struggle to meet his mortgage payments?

It is new to him – this envy. Perhaps it is a result of all he has gone through in the previous few months. He certainly doesn't remember experiencing anything like it when he was drawing a regular salary. But it doesn't matter what has caused the feeling. The simple fact is that it is bloody-well there!

As he approaches the woods, he starts to tense up again. He is spying on a motorcycle gang dealing in heroin, he reminds himself. If they catch him at it, there is no telling what they might do.

He will take the whole thing cautiously. He knows the gang is camped at the right-hand edge of the woods, so he will enter from the left. He will move through the woods slowly, and if he has any doubts, he will not move again until the doubts have gone away.

He doesn't need to get too close to them, because he has a telephoto lens on his camera.

He doesn't have to even hear their conversations, because he knows they are selling drugs, and he can make those conversations up. After all, it isn't as if a motorcycle gang is going to sue him for slander, is it?

The couple are so well hidden in the trees that, if the woman hadn't moaned when she did, he might well have walked right up to them before he even realized they were there.

But the woman does moan, and he stops in his tracks.

There are more moans, and some grunts. They seem to be having a better time than he's had in bed since he lost his job. No, that's not quite true, he admits bitterly, as a feeling of inadequacy sweeps over him – they seem to having a better time than he's ever had in bed.

He knows he should not want to watch them, but he does. He slowly circles around so he's got a better view.

It's training for spying on the Devil's Disciples, he tells himself. That's all it is – training.

The woman is on top, bouncing up and down with a vigour which almost takes his breath away.

And then he realizes that he recognizes her – that in researching for this article, he must have seen at least a dozen photographs of her!

He carefully takes out his camera and aims it. The click it makes when he presses the button seems as loud as a gunshot to his ears, but the couple are so engrossed in what they are doing that it is doubtful that firing a cannon would disturb them.

He takes a second picture, and then a third.

He knows now that whatever he might have told himself over the previous few days, he would probably never have been brave enough to go close enough to the Devil's Disciples camp to get his story. But what he would – or would not – have done doesn't matter any more, because, without even looking for it, he has stumbled over a story which is just as good.

He thinks about confronting the lovers immediately, but the man is big and solid, and might turn nasty. Besides, the man doesn't matter. He is nothing. It is the woman who is the prize.

They are still ploughing away at each other. They are like randy goats, he thinks in disgust – and wishes he could be like them.

Finally, they finish. They get dressed without saying a word to each other, then the man goes off in one direction, and the woman in another.

He gives the woman a good start, and then runs after her. She has almost reached the Hall when he catches her up.

'Countess!' he gasps.

She turns around, and he can see the fear which is already in her eyes. This is going to be easy.

'Who are you?' she asks.

'I'm a newspaper reporter,' he tells her, 'and I've just got one hell of a story to report.'

She glances around, worried that someone

might have seen them, then she points to the stable block, and says, 'In there.'

There are three magnificent horses in the stable. He does not know what breed they are – how could he? – but they only serve to fuel his rage to even higher levels of intensity.

How much would a single one of these horses cost, he asks himself.

And answering his own question, he thinks, thousands and thousands of pounds.

'What do you want?' the countess asks him.

'As I said, I've got a fantastic story – the countess and her lover. I could sell it to one of the Sunday papers for a fortune, or...' He pauses for dramatic effect. '...I could sell it to you.'

'How much do you want?'

Shoot for the moon, he thinks.

'One hundred thousand pounds,' he says.

She gasps. 'I have a little money of my own, but nothing like that amount,' she says.

'That's the price,' he says firmly. 'Get it from your husband – he can afford it.'

'Yes, he has the money,' she admits. 'But how could I get it from him without telling him what I want it for?'

'That's really not my problem,' Lewis tells her.

'Please,' she says, as the tears stream down her face, 'be reasonable. I can give you five thousand pounds now, and more next month. You would get your hundred thousand pounds in the end.'

'How long a period of time are we talking about, here?'

'I don't know.'

'One year? Two years?'

'Much longer than that.'

'I'm not prepared to wait. And I don't see why I need to. Your husband won't want this story spread across the front pages of the newspapers any more than you do.'

'You don't understand,' she says, and she is really sobbing now. 'I don't want him to know about it. I wouldn't care if the whole of the rest of the world knew – if everyone pointed at me and ridiculed me wherever I went – as long as Gervaise didn't find out.'

He has planted the seed of fear, and the woman's tears will make it grow, without any help from him.

'I'll give you a week,' he says.

He turns his back on her, and starts to walk towards the stable door.

He never even sees the blow coming.

'I love my husband,' the countess said. 'I really do love him.'

'I believe you,' Paniatowski tells her.

'But I am still a fairly young woman, and I have needs in bed that Gervaise is unable to meet. It ... it sounds so weak, so selfish, to talk about something which is, after all, only physical, but the lack of fulfilment was making me ill – it was destroying my mind.'

'Go on,' Paniatowski said.

'I chose Edward Bell. I did not love him. I don't think, in all honesty, that I even really found him attractive. But I knew he would be discreet – and that he would fulfil my needs.'

'How did he feel about you? Did he ever tell you?'

'No, we never discussed it. Physically, we were very compatible, but I doubt he was emotionally involved. He was my husband's servant, and he would have done anything for him. If Gervaise had been unable to walk, Bell would have carried him halfway around the world without complaint. If he couldn't satisfy his wife, then Bell would take that strain off him, too. He loved his own wife. I'm sure of that. And in sleeping with me, he was not betraying her – he was merely doing what had to be done.'

'Did you tell him you'd killed Lewis?'

'No, he must have found out the same way you did – from the surveillance tapes.'

Yes, that made sense, Paniatowski thought. Bell could never have carried off the innocent act if he'd actually known what had happened.

'He burned the surveillance tapes to protect you from being charged with murder,' she said aloud. 'Don't you think that argues that he *did* feel something for you all along?'

The countess laughed. 'Of course not! He wasn't worried about me at all. His only concern was the effect that my being arrested would have on Gervaise.'

There was no more that needed to be said, Paniatowski thought.

She stood up.

'I'll be back later with some other officers to take your statement, and after I've taken it, you'll be arrested and charged.'

'Do I have to say *why* I killed him?' the

countess asked.

'What do you mean?'

'Couldn't you just say that I killed him because I was so outraged that a man like him had dared to invade the estate?'

Anyone else making the suggestion would have done so with an eye to pleading diminished responsibility, Paniatowski thought. But the countess wasn't doing that – her sole aim was to prevent her husband learning of her affair.

'I could play it for all it was worth,' the countess continued. 'The grand lady looking down on the filthy peasant – the jury would hate me.'

'I'm sorry—' Paniatowski began.

'The judge, too,' the countess interrupted her. 'He'd be bound to give me a much longer sentence than he'd hand down if I told the truth.'

'I'm not interested in you getting the longest possible sentence,' Paniatowski told her.

In fact, if it was up to me, you wouldn't be in prison for long at all, she thought.

'Justice would be served whatever story I told, wouldn't it?' the countess pleaded.

'I'm sorry,' Paniatowski said. 'I'm *really* sorry. But I can't do it.'

'No, I don't suppose you can,' the countess agreed sadly. She sighed. 'Poor Gervaise! He was born under a bad sign – and so was I.'

Paniatowski was almost at the door when the countess said, 'Can I ask you one more question?'

'Of course.'

'How could you be so sure it was me driving the car?'

'One of the great unanswered questions in this investigation was why the killer risked dumping the body in Whitebridge, when it would have been considerably safer to bury it somewhere,' Paniatowski said. 'And a second was why – having stripped him of his clothes so we wouldn't know *where* he'd died – the killer left Lewis' wallet where it was bound to be found. There was only one answer which could successfully resolve both questions – and that was that the killer had done it so the body would be identified as soon as possible.'

'Yes, I see that,' the countess said.

'But why would the killer *want* us to identify it – when that was bound to help us?' Paniatowski continued. 'Again, there could only be one answer. The killer – which, in this case, was you, and could only have been you – wanted Lewis's wife to know, as soon as possible, that he was dead. You didn't want her to be like you were in Prague, wondering for months if he was still alive, while knowing, deep inside, that he wasn't. You wanted to give her certainty – so that she could start to come to terms with her grief.'

'It would have been inhuman to have done anything else,' the countess said.

Epilogue

30th September, 1976

The doctor sat at one side of the desk – the medical reports in front of him – and Paniatowski sat at the other.

The doctor's name was Brydon. He was in his mid-forties, and Dr Shastri had recommended him as being both discreet and sympathetic. Paniatowski liked him as a man, but hated her reasons for having to visit him, and had resolved that once this matter had been cleared up, she would never see him again.

The doctor picked up the report.

'The good news is that there are no apparent internal injuries and you do not seem to have contracted any sexually transmitted diseases,' he said.

'That *is* good news,' Paniatowski agreed.

'However,' the doctor continued, 'there is the other complication.'

'What other complication?'

The doctor frowned. 'You do realize that you are pregnant, don't you? You must have noticed you've missed your period.'

'I ... I can't be pregnant,' Paniatowski gasped. 'I was tested, years ago, and the doctors told me

I could never have children.'

'Medical science can never say never,' the doctor told her. 'The human body is capable of surprising the most skilled practitioner – and let me assure you, you *are* pregnant.'

Paniatowski closed her eyes and was back in the woods – her head aching and her vagina on fire.

She could sense the presence of the three Devil's Disciples. She could feel their breath on her face. And she could hear their voices.

'You're just like all the other slags that we've screwed.'

'If I was you, bitch, I'd just put it down to experience.'

'And let's be honest, you must have enjoyed being shagged by three real men for a change.'

'I would recommend an abortion under any circumstances, given your age, but under *these* circumstances, I don't think there's any question about it,' the doctor said.

'I can't have an abortion,' Paniatowski told him.

'I think you need to consider the risks,' the doctor advised. 'And even if the birth goes without a hitch, how you will feel about the child once it's born, given the nature of its conception?'

'I can't have an abortion,' Paniatowski repeated.

'Are you saying that on religious grounds?'

'Yes.'

The doctor looked down at her folder again.

'There's no indication here that you have any

335

religious affiliation,' he said. 'I'd have handled the matter quite differently if there had been, but, you see, I didn't *know* you were a Catholic.'

'No, neither did I,' Paniatowski said.

CPSIA information can be obtained at www.ICGtesting.com
Printed in the USA
BVOW08*1346270715

409640BV00002B/6/P